Warm Aloha for Wai-nani: A Voice from Old Hawai'i

"Wai-nani refuses to be bound by the shackles of society and follows her heart—finding a destiny beyond her wildest dreams. Follow her—no join her—on this incredible journey."

— Joyce Anthony-author of *Storm*

"I was fascinated with the way Linda Ballou had taken us into the intimate and unknown world of the Hawaiian people through the eyes of an unforgettable heroine. Wai-nani is fierce, passionate, and deeply connected to the land and ocean—and to her complex and multi-faceted warrior husband."

— Toby Neal-author Lei Crime Series, Maui Hawaii

"Wai-nani is like no other book I have ever read. Linda Ballou is a master of language, pulling the reader in and evoking emotions hidden deep within. Her imagery will tickle your senses, allowing you to feel the story more than merely reading."

— Nancy Harless- Woman Kind Connection

"Linda Ballou's first novel is a masterpiece that tells the dramatic and heart-warming love story of Wai-nani. By weaving the ancient legends of Old Hawaii into this compelling story, Ballou captivates the reader with her beautiful descriptions and very real characters that come alive in your imagination."

— Bonnie Neely, Editor of Real Travel Adventures

"Delicious reading. What pulls me in the most is the story being told through all the senses."

— Muriel Lindsay, Author of *Chronicles of the Savannah River Dolphins*

"Written like pure poetry, you will become entranced with the story of Wai-nani and amazed by the beauty of the history of the Hawaiian woman. I could not put the book down."

— Reviewed by Danelle Drake for Reader Views

"Linda Ballou takes you to a different place where suddenly life is more vital. Her characters are painted with such intense feeling, it makes the reading an obsession!"

— Carol Wood, editor

"How I love a book like Wai-nani. One I learn something from! One that stays with me long after I turn the last page."

— Carolyn Howard-Johnson, award-winning author of *This Is the Place*

"Your writing skill is both comprehensive and impeccable. Wai-nani will please readers with your ability to create believable people, places and events."

— Kumu Lomi Dane Silva-Hawaiian Healing Center, Hilo, Hawaii

"Wai-nani was a joy to read! The interaction with the bottlenose dolphins is realistic for those of us who have developed an extraordinarily intimate relationship with them."

— With ALOHA, Roberta Goodman - WildDolphinSwimsHawaii.com

"Reading Wai-nani was a captivating experience! What a moving, colorful, rich in Hawaiian history and culture story! I felt a part of the land, the events and the people. Ms. Ballou enabled a story of the past to touch my senses in the present."

— Tiki DeGenaro, General Manager,
Kalani Oceanside Retreat-The Big Island

"Linda has caught the beauty, mystery, and heart of the Hawaiian culture. I found this book both educational, and inspirational; a seductive journey through time and to a place of great majesty and history. A must read for all those who enjoy romance and history."

— Yolanda Renee, author of *Murder, Madness, and Love*.
Top Amazon Reviewer

"A true and brilliant watercolor of imagination and reality! For those who know and love the islands, it brings forward a visual feast of the past— For those who have yet to experience the rare beauty and history of Hawaii, a remarkable yet educational trip of truth touched by beauty and fantasy."

— Connie Harper Nelson

Map by Steve Strickland

Wai-nani

A Voice from Old Hawai'i

LINDA BALLOU

ISBN: 978-1-7379253-3-0
Library of Congress Control Number: 2008926768
Edited by Barbara Milbourn
Interior design by www.formating4U.com

Cover image by Alexandra Corza
Map art by Steve Strickland

Previously published 2014 in United States of America

Wind Dancer Press 2021

Dedication

The red flower at the top of the ohi'a tree
Sprinkling bright joy smells sweet.
Where is the blossom?
There surfing
Standing on the curling wave
There swimming
Cresting with pearl-gray Eku
There dancing,
Beneath the sway of palms
Bending low to the ground
With the breath of the sea
In the night-beam sad smile of Hina
There singing
With the shining shells of Waipio
There walking,
Beside Makaha,
Sharing his burdens-giving him wisdom.

In the name of Wai-nani
With Great Aloha

— Linda Ballou

Acknowledgments

Wai-nani bears out the basic Hawaiian precept "No job is hard if it is done all together."

A special thank you to Steve Strickland who graciously contributed the map of ancient Hawai'i in the opening pages to help readers get their bearings. This story is rife with Hawaiian words with punctuation alien to modern technology. I am indebted to Judi Fennell at www.formatting4U.com for her efforts to lend as much authenticity to the finished product as possible. Without the practiced eye and caring attitude of my editor, Barbara Milbourn, Wai-nani would likely still be a spectral figure in my imagination trying to break free. I am especially grateful to Carolyn Howard-Johnson for providing me with a road map for navigating the perilous publishing journey. A word of appre-ciation goes to Denise Cassino, for her "Web Wizardry" that has given me a life in cyberspace. My deepest gratitude to my partner, Steve, who has supported me in every challenge I have taken on. The generous help of capable allies has allowed me to live up to my dream of bringing my beautiful Wai-nani to life.

Mahalo Nui to all those who have given their warm aloha to me and Wai-nani.

Preface

Contradictory accounts of the time of Kamehameha the Great and his favorite wife, Ka'ahumanu, make it difficult for a modern interpretation of their tumultuous affair to be accurate. *Wai-nani: A Voice from Old Hawai'i,* inspired by the lives of these two legendary icons in Hawaiian history, is not a documentary. It is a creative effort that uses techniques including dialogue exchanges, time compression, and composite characters to achieve a dramatic arc. It is not my intention to set the record straight. I leave that to scholars like Lucia Jensen, author of *Women of Hawai'i* who generously provided me insights into the psyche of the ancient Hawaiians and their living descendants. My quest is to enliven a dynamic part of the dim past in a way that modern readers will find engaging. *Wai-nani* is a poetic rendering of the ancients with tales of heroes and heroines doing supernatural deeds of mythological proportions.

Since the 1970's there has been an aggressive effort on the part of Hawaiians to understand their own past. The vigorous attempt of living descendants to unravel and restore their culture after European contact has overturned traditional accounts written by scholars. The people of old Hawai'i were connected to nature, played freely, loved passionately and communed with gods that dwelled in every tree, rock and flower. Service to the land and the sea and sharing the bounty that came from them is the centerpiece of the Hawaiian culture.

Still, the penalties for breaking the laws of the land were harsh. A man or woman who donned the garment of a high-ranking chief was promptly put to death. Wai-nani would have been burned in a ground oven in the first chapter if I adhered strictly to all of the taboos of her time. Inbreeding was the order of the day among the ali'i (royals) but not the common people. The highest caste was achieved when one woman married two men, and the children from these separate unions married and had offspring. The result was an athletic race of handsome giants with men that towered over women who often reached six feet. Infanticide was commonplace when these practices delivered a less-than-perfect specimen, or if the child was of mixed blood that might confuse or interfere with the royal lineage.

There were four major gods in the Hawaiian cosmology. First was Kane, creator of man, symbol of life and the god of living waters. A favored legend is that he formed the three worlds: the upper heaven of the gods, the lower heaven above earth, and the earth itself as a garden for mankind. Kane was dark with curly hair and thick lips. His counterpart Kanaloa, the ocean god that created the tides by inhaling and exhaling, was tall and fair. Ku, the god of war and chiefs, was also god of the forests, canoe-making and fishing. Ku took many forms, but is best known as the snatcher of lands. Lono, the god of fertility, clouds and weather, was also a healing god.

The kahuna, or elders, were the protectors and communicators of the wisdoms of time and the gods. The gods ruled over all from the distant ocean land of Kahiki. Like the Greek and Roman pantheon, the Hawaiian deities interacted with living humans, transformed themselves through sorcery into plants, animals or birds, had power of the elements and were subject to human emotions. Beneath the big four were thousands of lesser gods to be feared, cajoled, worshipped and called upon in times of trouble. In addition, each individual had an 'aumakua—a protecting spirit of a dead relative looking over them.

While Kamehameha lived, he held the tottering 2,000-year-old kapu system in place by the sheer force of his will. Even so, his last edict "to save the men for the king" ended human sacrifice. Within six months after his death, the priests that meted out harsh penalties upon the common people were divested of their power. Ka'ahumanu was instrumental in bringing about this change. With the overthrow of idolatry and destruction of the kapu system, most of the wooden gods were burned. A few that were concealed by their caretakers are presently on display in the Bishop Museum in Honolulu. The Christian missionaries arrived in 1820—one year after the death of Kamehameha the Great—in a religious vacuum that allowed perversions of the Hawaiian culture by 19th century westerners to take hold.

While she was alive Ka'ahumanu was revered as Mother of the People, but she is remembered by many Hawaiian historians as "the flaw that brought down the chiefdom." Her legendary promiscuity with high-ranking chiefs was considered by the powerful kahuna of her day to be a threat to Kamehameha's prophesied rise to power. She has been accused of aiding the priests in an attempt to pray the Hawaiians' greatest ruler to death. In her later years, she took the teachings of the missionaries to heart and helped spread the "good news" to her people. Now, two hundred years later, you may be the judge. Was Ka'ahumanu a forerunner to the modern woman and a daring liberator, or was she a traitor to her times?

1
Dolphin Dance

The red apple of the ohi'a tree tasted sweet in my mouth as I watched the drifting plumes of Pele, Goddess of the Volcano, cast shadows upon the shimmering sea. Frothy surf reached my ankles then receded, leaving tiny bubbles of foam upon a blank tablet of sand. The crescent sail of an outrigger flared upon the horizon. The ancestors who lived in the long-long ago sailed here in canoes like this, bringing pigs, dogs, bananas, breadfruit and the gods with them. Just beyond the arcing swells, I spied my dolphin friend, Eku. His playmate Laka's dorsal fin cut through the clear water in the opposite direction of his as they dallied away the day in their dance of secret yearnings.

My hair felt hot and heavy on my shoulders. I longed to feel it floating free in the sparkling sea. I untied the knot of my pa'u and let it fall to the ground. Splashing through the shallows, I dove under a cresting wave. Once on the other side of the breakers, stretching arms and legs to maximum stroke, I swam to Eku. The crystalline water soothed and cooled me as it swirled through my mind in gentle rivers.

Halfway to Eku, I called out to him in his squeaky tongue. He would have to come quickly to protect me from Laka, his jealous lover. I had named her after the Goddess of Dance because of her graceful, swift movements. Once, long ago, she rammed me hard in the belly with her rubbery beak. Eku had to stop her before I drowned. I always noticed when Laka was near.

I swam fast to get to Eku. His dorsal fin sliced the water as he came toward me, then his sleek body rose out of the water as he picked up speed. Laka was close behind. When Eku reached me, he circled about then rolled over on his back so that I could rub his tender belly. He loved this greeting and giggled when I massaged his underside. There was much squeaking and head bobbing from Laka as she circled about us, but she did not come near. I reached around Eku's body, draping myself around his mottled frame. His skin trembled at my touch. We rolled to and fro in the heave of the deep blue swells.

I grabbed hold of Eku's ragged fin, aligning myself on his right side. Laka took her regular position on his left. He let out a long, low whistle signaling us forward. We churned through the clear water, creating a wake in our path. I kept my head above water where I saw bubbles and brilliant blue sky, while he maintained a stable level so that I could breathe. Laka stayed with us, knowing exactly which direction he would turn, how slow and how fast he would go, without a sound from Eku.

I feared nothing, not even Mano the shark, when I was with Eku. His round soft eyes and constant smile spoke of kindness. His strong body moved with grace at exhilarating speeds. I felt at rest and safe with him. I wondered if I would ever meet a man with Eku's strength, tenderness and loyalty. Could I feel this joy with a man? As we skimmed across the blue mountains of water, these thoughts trailed out behind me.

When I returned to my family's houses that night, my mother was tapping her mallet on a carved wooden block used to stain a design onto kapa. This was the work of maka'ainana, but she loved to create her own designs and scent the cloth for her many dresses with the perfumes of fragrant plants. The smell of the fish wrapped in luau leaves steaming in the ground oven reminded me that I was hungry.

"Oh Wai-nani, my wandering wahine, has come home in time to eat, but not in time to help her mother," she said without lifting her head from her labors. Her dress, tied at her shoulder, was stained with the colors of a lavender sunset. She wore a lei po'o of braided coconut fibers to hold in place a thick shock of black hair laced with silver streaks. Once renowned for her beauty, my mother was no longer lithe and athletic, but her glittering orange-almond eyes held many secrets, and she remained my father's favorite wife.

"I'm sorry." Inwardly I grumbled as I watched our servant fill the kou bowls full of rich purple poi to be delivered to my father, my brother and the other young warriors of our village in the men's eating house.

"Why is it forbidden for me to eat with my brother? We swim, wrestle, and fish together but when the evening sun sets, I am no longer welcome in the company of the boys of our village."

"Men face great dangers; they carry war sticks to keep peace, snare birds and fish so you may eat. You don't want to do these things," she said, impatient with my protests.

"This is not a good answer," I said.

"You are the blossom from the topmost branch with beauty unsurpassed. It is time you put away childish pleasures and follow the royal path."

She held out a slim hand and beckoned me to come to her. I settled down beside her.

As she combed tangles from my hair that smelled of salt from the sea, and massaged pungent ginger oil into it, she tried again to answer my question.

"Many things that come to us from the ancients we don't question. In the beginning, Wakea, the God of Light and the Heavens, married Papa, the Goddess of Earth. From this great love came a daughter, the Heavenly One Who Made the Stars. She was so beautiful that Wakea could not resist the sweet smell of her skin and the dance of the sun in her eyes. He schemed night and day to have his daughter without Papa knowing and becoming jealous. His kahuna smashed the head of a black pig and read the entrails to find the solution."

As she talked story and stroked my hair to a lustrous shine, her aloha for me softened my questioning heart.

"'Build eating houses separate for men and women. Tell Papa that this is the will of the gods. This way you will always know where she is and can know your daughter's great charm without discovery,' the kahuna advised.

"Wakea thought well of this plan. He made it kapu for men and women to eat together and set aside tabu nights of separate sleeping. He lay down with his dazzling daughter of the Heavens. From their coupling came the birth of the islands of Molakai and Lanai."

"Do you believe this story?" I asked.

I felt a sharp tug on my scalp. "It is the way of our people," she said, putting an end to our talk.

I left her and went into the velvet night to ask the winking stars my question. But, no answer came. I crept into the shadows cast by the walls of the men's hale, peered through the thatching and eavesdropped on their talk. Their bowls of poi were empty, and they sat talking of the day and drinking 'awa. Much of the drink from the bitter root was shared as they laughed and challenged one another to sport. The day had been spent wrestling. Soon it would be time for the festival of makahiki, and their contests would begin in earnest. They had to be fit to win these mock battles. Death or injury could easily come to the warrior who was not swift and daring.

"Will you be in the wave-sliding contest tomorrow?" my younger brother, Mimo, asked Kali, as he swilled another cup of 'awa. "Today was a sorry day for you in wrestling, but no one can beat you on the olo board."

"That's true. No one can beat me in the water. I am the most powerful of all the swimmers on Maui."

"So you say," said my brother. "I place a wager on Maka. We will see who is the richer at the end of the day." He took the shark tooth necklace from his chest and held it up so his friend Maka could see the strength of his bet. I left the hale saddened that I was not allowed to meet my brother's challenge. I knew I could wave-slide as well as any of them, if not better.

The next day found Maka and Kali floating belly down on boards that weighed as much as me and were twice my height. They rested behind the curl of cresting waves that came in sets of seven and waited patiently in the midday sun for the right wave. A crowd gathered on the shore. Mimo stood among the villagers, waiting for the match to begin.

I whistled to Eku, signaling him to come to me in the quiet cove out of sight of the others. Soon, he and Laka arrived. He let me place a vine noose about his nose while I tried to stand on his slippery back. I couldn't keep my balance in even a small wave surge. I slid from side to side and grabbed hold of his dorsal fin for balance. Puzzled at my antics, Laka squealed in high-pitched cries as I kept trying to stand up on Eku's back. Eku called to her in an eerie, shrill voice. She came up to his side, close enough for me to place one foot on her back and one on his. I rose from a crouched position and steadied myself with my rope. It worked! Soon, we were riding the white-backed waves together!

Eku, Laka and I came around the long finger of the rock jetty and got into position with the other wave-sliders. Maka saw me out of the corner of his eye, but too late to stop me. A great wall of water forming behind us lifted, heaved forward, and broke over the top of us. I caught the movement with Eku, who found the perfect balancing place to take us to the base of the foaming green giant shot through with sunshine. As we slid across the wave, I rose and stood in the tube of luminous water. With one foot planted on Eku, the other on Laka, I rode the great white bearded one and felt the power of the sea churning beneath me. Dazzling light shafts penetrated the wall of the wave, creating a continuous rainbow. I became a sea goddess riding the comet as it streaks through the starry sky—free of all manner of human weakness—free of all kapus, graceful, filled with divine mana.

When my ride ended, I could see that Maka and Kali had both fallen from their boards. I was the winner. I gave Eku a vigorous rub on his white belly and kissed Laka's beak. Even she seemed to smile as I parted from them. I strode to the shore through the surf, eager to share my glorious adventure. The crowd murmured at my approach. My brother frowned when he realized that I was wearing his malo. It is kapu, punishable by death, to wear another warrior's malo. The small congregation went silent. He glowered at me with burning eyes and snatched the loincloth from my body.

My budding breasts stand rigid and high, and my slim hips ride on sturdy, solid legs. Still, I felt burning humiliation in my nakedness. My father stomped across the beach wearing his shoulder cape of yellow feathers. His mood was as dark as Pele's heart. His face was turgid, purple with rage. His hand trembled on his spear as he drove it into the sand at my feet.

"Wai-nani, what is this? Do you think you are a warrior?"

"No, Father," I replied, meeting his fierce eyes, framed in the tattoos that curled to his forehead. "But you do not love Wai-nani as you would a son." I cast my eyes down afraid of his rage.

I was just a keiki when I witnessed him put to death a servant girl who had come too close, letting her shadow fall upon his royal presence. A seasoned warrior, he could pull an arm out of its socket or crush the rib cage of an enemy with his skilled hands, but something that day kept him from bashing me unmercifully or ordering my tongue removed for insolence. Instead, he turned to the villagers who had witnessed my miraculous surfing feats. Although they were in awe of my grace in the water their fear of my father kept them silent. They fell back when he shouted,

"There will be a contest. I will place my necklace at the highest point of Nihow," he said, pointing to the isle on the horizon. He took off his choker woven from human hair with an ivory pendant made from the whale's tooth, and held it high for all to see. "The warrior who swims to the island and returns the necklace to me will have my daughter as his wife and become a chief."

He turned back to me. "You will have a husband and children and honor the ways of all wahine before you."

I was thunderstruck. I didn't feel a woman's love for any of the young warriors of Hana. Although I was terrified of my father's violent nature, I looked into his murky black eyes.

"My father is a cruel chief who has lost his mana!" I said, this time holding his gaze. He stared blankly back for a few tense moments then he struck me solidly in the face with the back of his hand. The taste of blood trickling from my torn lip told me this was not a dream. The sky spun, lights whirled in the black around my head and my ringing ears were deaf to all around me. His next words sounded far away.

"The contest will begin with the new sun." Any tenderness he once possessed for his first daughter retreated behind stony eyes.

Whirling about, I ran back into the surf. My tears tasted of blood and the sea. I dove under a pounding wave and paddled frantically out beyond the breakers. Calling out in a high-pitched whistle, I clicked my tongue furiously, trying to bring Eku to me. I made the sounds of a stick rubbing against a gourd, but the squawk of sea birds was my only reply.

The sun rose the next day, casting a crimson flare across the sky. Jagged purples kissed the horizon. Black plumes from the distant volcano rose high above white clouds. Twelve young men stood on the beach awaiting the signal from my father. In the middle of the line was Maka, my old friend who had taught me to cast nets, spear fish and throw stones from a sling. We had spent many hours diving in the cave pool where the octopus hides under the rocks. His stout, sturdy legs were bowed from birth. He smiled at me with gentle brown eyes, exposing strong white teeth. He was a fair and generous man, but I couldn't imagine myself with him in the marriage bed.

The twins Makoa and Keha standing beside him were identical except for the jagged scar that went across Keha's belly. Mano the shark had made him warrior when he was still a child. Makoa's dark eyes were filled with deviltry. Given to pranks, he had once taken my pa'u while I sunned myself beside the rock pool. No passion passed from me to either of them. Boasting Kali strutted before the group and came up to me. He put his hand to his chest and said, "When the sun turns red, Wai-nani will share my mat."

I feared his dark eyes with heavy brows that knit together, forming one line across his bold features. He had bullied and bested the others at wrestling and sport all the seasons I could remember. I recoiled at the thought of this braggart for my husband. Even though his six-foot-six-inch frame, supported by flat, firm muscles alive under his brown skin spoke of royal blood, he was fouled fruit to me.

My father arrived wearing his finest yellow feather cape and the crested helmet of an ali'i chief. He planted his spear and spoke to the warriors before him.

"There will be no wrestling, no bone breaking and no gouging. The swiftest, most agile swimmer will have my daughter, Wai-nani, for his wife."

When he finished speaking he clasped his spear, lifted it high over his head, then dropped the tip into the sand, signaling the race to begin. My brother was among the warriors who dove into the calm sea, rippling the prism of morning sun upon the water with broad strokes. My marriage to him would produce an ali'i ruler of the highest blood caste. As I watched them swim into the horizon, I glimpsed a fin arching like a quarter moon. Untying the knot of my pa'u, I let the drape of cloth drop to my ankles. Casting a last glance over my shoulder to my father, I ran into the sea and dove under a foaming wave. My hair swirled like seaweed about my face as I kicked with strong legs, stroking hard to reach Eku.

He heard my shrill whistle and came dashing to me. Excited, he circled me swiftly once then came closer so that I could rub his tender underbelly. I did, then clasped him in a rolling embrace. I reveled in his affection and acceptance. The familiar tingling I felt whenever he was near brightened my spirits. He took me on a plunging ride, lifting me completely out of the water as I clung to his dorsal fin. We flew so fast I felt the chains of my father's edict falling from my mind. Racing from the embrace of a man I could not love, I left behind children destined to be conceived in hate and cast my fate like a fisherman's net upon the sea.

I saw Pele, Goddess of Fire, resting on the clouds with her shining lava-black hair falling down on round shoulders. She wore a white flower spiked with red on her left ear, and a blood-red kikepa tied at her shoulder. Drifting in the cloud cradle that circles the smoking cone of the volcano above her billowy bed, she dozed with her feet crossed at the ankles and her hands lying peacefully on her belly. Her full lips were parted in a wistful smile. The lids of her eyes, laced with long black lashes, were closed. I held onto Eku's muscled neck as his great strength lifted us out of the deep with cool spray flying. I could feel the pull of Pele and prayed I would find shelter at her tumultuous breast.

2
The Pull of Pele

The warmth of the sun was gone, but still I clung to Eku's muscled neck. My heart soared as we surged through the black water following the gleaming path of the full moon. I gazed into his benevolent eye, wishing I could transform myself into a great sea creature that could match his strength. After many hours in the ocean, it seemed that water flowed through my mind. The trickling sound of its constant motion gently washed away my fears.

Finally, releasing my grip, I slid free from the security of his mighty force. My powerful, froglike kick propelled me through the deep. I fell into a seamless stroke, my breath matching the pulse of moana, the sea. Feeling one with the rhythms and movements of the midnight blue water, I swam with Eku and Laka. Sensing their signals, I turned when they turned, slowed and speeded up with them. I don't know how long we traveled or how far. Lifted by the buoyant water, never struggling against its great strength, I flowed with the will of the sea.

By the time I reached the rugged coastline of the island that is Pele's home, my arms were aching. The brilliant sun overhead burned my eyes as I strained to see what lay in the black, barren landscape with many hard edges. The cone of the volcano poking through a cloudless blue sky wore a skirt of lavender-gray mist that obscured the lush green life clinging to its steep slope. A plume of white billowed above the sea where a living flow of hot lava met the ocean. Vast rivers of black, crystallized rock cascaded down the sides of the willful goddess's resting spot. What had beckoned from afar was, in fact, a ragged, treacherous shore.

I feared I was destined to die in the arms of Kanaloa, god of the vibrant sea. Hungry and weak, I whistled to Eku, wondering why I had left my water-rich Hana home for the barren shore before me. I feared the powerful spirits of the ancients that dwell in this place and was afraid to be alone. Eku did not come to me. He sped out to sea when I swam dangerously close to the rocky sea wall. I felt a wave surge mounting, but I didn't have the strength to fight its sucking pull. I'd come this long way to be dashed against the porous edges of the lava that rimmed this unwelcome land. My death would be a fitting punishment for having disobeyed my father's commands.

I spied a tiny opening in the rock wall and a strip of black sand. Stroking wildly to reach the opening, I caught a great wave that lifted then hurled me to the sea floor. Caught in the churning rage of the ocean, I held my breath until the world went black. When I awoke, I lay naked on the shore. I crawled to the shelter of a sea cave in the cliff, where I slipped into a dreamless sleep.

I awoke to the sound of birds chirping as the sun crested on the clamshell pink horizon. I rose to look for a ti leaf to cover myself. My new home was made of braided lava fields. Tall tufts of gold bunch grass clung to the sides of the black rock, softening the lava to a shimmering white glow. The wind whipped the weed into undulating waves. I discovered a path through the curling rope patterns in the lava worn smooth by the feet of ancient travelers. Stacks of rocks marked the way. I walked two days and two nights on this trail, leaning into a cold wind that never rested. I ate the tiny grasshoppers that bounced off my legs, some tiny red berries and the tall white grass. Feeling lightheaded from hunger, I turned to the higher ground of the volcano's side, where giant fern fronds lined the way and green moss covered the rocks where streams trickled from old rains.

I came upon a clearing where I saw a man with golden skin bowed in the sun. He stood knee deep in water pulling grass weeds from the base of his taro plants. I crouched low behind a fern, watching the man with the muscled body of an ali'i warrior doing the work of the common people. I spied the pitched roof of his hale at the edge of his taro field. Neat and orderly, the camp appeared to have been his home for at least one season. There was no one else in sight.

As I thought about how I would meet the man, a short-legged dog with a stiff strut came out of the hut. The dog picked up my scent, and though confused, it was convinced there was a stranger near. He circled madly as though chasing his own tail. The man stood up and sniffed the air with the alertness of a wild creature. He laid down his digging stick, picked up his spear, and stood stock still. Trembling, I held my breath and hid under a fern frond, pulling it over my body, curling like a snail under the broad leaf. The frantic dog ran back and forth at the edge of the clearing just feet away from my hiding place, insisting someone or something was near. The man came up behind the dog.

"What is it, dog?"

He must have heard the pounding of my heart, for he stared intently in my direction with wondrous dark eyes. He licked full, moist lips beaded with sweat. His forehead slanted up like that of an ali'i chief. Elegant elongated limbs rippling with muscles beneath almond skin spoke of his royal heritage. The dog came straight to my hiding spot, routing me out. When I rose, I could not find my voice but met the eyes of the seven-foot giant towering above me, blocking the sun.

"Who are you, and why are you here?"

"I am Wai-nani, born of royal parents. I fled my village in Hana, clinging to the breast of Eku, my dolphin, to the land of Pele. That is all that I know," I sputtered. "Who are you? Where am I?" I dared to ask.

He leaned on his spear and looked up to Pele's resting spot as he considered what to do with the girl-woman before him. Finally, he spoke. "I am Makaha. You are in my thinking place."

His eyes softened to shining pools of tenderness as they traveled down my body. Heat rose from the pit of my belly to the cleft of my breasts. I felt a rash spreading on my chest. Mercifully, his gaze stopped at my feet, which were torn and bleeding. He knelt down, lifted my ankle and surveyed the mud-caked sores on the soles of my feet. Putting my foot down, he took my hand. I felt the calluses in his palm when he intertwined long brown fingers with my own. Silently, he led me back to his hale.

Makaha filled a koa bowl full of rich, thick poi and handed it to me.

"Rest," he said, then left me alone. Believing no harm would come to me, I fell into a deep, dream-filled sleep. I saw myself drifting on the ocean floor, awash with the undercurrents. A shoal of brilliant yellow tang fish circled around me. Breathing easily through gills in my sides, cushioned in the silence of the deep, I let my fears float free to the surface of the sun-shot sea.

I awoke to the sound of Makaha pounding 'awapuhi in a mortar in the lava. After mashing the ginger to a gooey paste, he knelt down beside me. Sitting on his ankles, he lifted my feet onto his thigh and spread the paste thinly on the ragged soles, blowing lightly to seal the soothing, moist medicine. Then he gently stroked my calf and thigh muscles, which were aching and sore from my journey. The palms of his hands, large as pulu leaves, were warm on my skin. When he finished, I returned to the sleep of a child nestled to her mother's breast.

The next morning he was gone from his camp. He had risen with the song of the mamo bird and walked for an hour to his meditation temple. His heiau stood on a wind-blown platform, high on a plateau that overlooked the desert of K'au and the blue-green sea crashing on the shore far below. Resting under the shadow of Pele's home, the pulsing womb of all creation, it was, he said, a place of great mana. He sat there for hours with his eyes rolled upwards, chanting a mele, then returned to work in his fields.

He had cleared the plot for his taro patch of all lava rocks, using them to form a boundary to keep pigs out. He dug a pit to create a pond to collect water from the thunderous rains. Removing a section of the rock wall allowed the water to tumble into small channels and to flow through his field when the rains were gone.

A task that would take ten men working side-by-side many seasons to complete had taken him but one. I was amazed to see turbulent waters bent to his will, gently nourishing his fields.

"Why do you do the work of the maka'ainana?" I asked, as he bowed his back over his taro patch in the midday sun, pulling tall grass that threatened to choke his plants.

"I do the work of Kane. In a vision he told me to carve streams into the ground like veins in the leaf."

"But you are ali'i."

"It steadies me to serve the land," he replied.

I left him to his task. As days passed, I thought it strange he was not interested in taking me for his pleasure. I wondered if he preferred the touch of a boy. I determined to make myself useful to him in other ways. Each day I carried the fish net and spear he gave me down the rock path to the sea. I spread the net over the tide pools and popped my hands to bring the translucent ones into my trap. Many times I called to Eku and stared at the horizon hoping to see his fin slicing through the dazzling blue. Not once did I see him during the many hours I waded in the tide pools. When no fish came to me, I took sticks and beat the waters, walking the 'ama 'ama and aholeahoe into my net.

Memories of sweet lobster lured me to the crevices in the coral reef where they hid in the shadows. When I reached into dark holes, I feared I would meet the mottled face of the eel. If he clamped his fangs into my wrist, I would have to cut off his head to release his grip. The lobster called me still deeper into the clear waters of the coral reef. I dove into the cool waters and found him with my spear.

Makaha steamed the lobster in his imu. We ate our meals separately, in silence. He ate his meal in his hale, and I remained by the fire. He allowed me to share his hale for sleeping, but his head was full of his own thoughts, and he spoke little to me. While I pounded the pandanus leaf into kapa cloth, I watched him mend his fish net and listened to him hum a soft oli to himself. I missed the laughing children of my village, my brother and the other young warriors, even my mother's scolding for being lazy.

We slept back-to-back on our mats, curled like mollusks in our separate shells. One night a fierce storm brought hail and violent winds that threatened to rip the grass roof from over our heads. When I awoke, Makaha was standing at the door of his hale watching the deluge of water test his handiwork. "I have caught the power of the storm," he said, smiling broadly for the first time.

Once the storm passed the moon traveled quickly through dark clouds, casting bright light that brought the taro field alive with luminous veins. Standing side by side, admiring the cold face of the moon, listening to the drip of the water down after the downpour, we shared the wet world.

"The bearded surf will be bold today," he said. "Do you want to wave-slide with me?"

He possessed the perfect swimmer's body, with broad powerful shoulders, narrow hips, long muscled legs and broad flat feet to shoot him swiftly through the water. The humiliation I had felt when punished for besting the young men in my village rose to my cheeks. I felt hot and hesitated for a moment before answering, afraid that if I outshined this warrior he would turn into a cruel host. Knowing I could not enter the water without becoming half-fish, half-human, I worried about the outcome of the day but was unable to refuse the chance to swim with him.

"Yes. I am at home in the sea."

Pink dawn found Makaha poised on a lava rock ledge, back flattened, arms straight behind him with palms up, and eyes riveted on the horizon. He dove gracefully into the water without creating a splash. He melted into the sea, propelling himself past the coral reef where the great walls of water came in powerful sets of seven. I slipped into the surf and followed him. As we neared the foaming mountains of water that could hurl the mightiest swimmer a hundred feet, crushing him to a breathless pulp on the coral bottom then sucking him down with the undertow, my thoughts went to Mano. The shark, sleepless in the shadows, never stops searching for his next meal.

We reached the breaking place of the monsters and bobbed

there six feet apart. I saw the calm expression on his face as he ducked under the immense curls of green cresting over our heads. He took note of the time between waves before attempting to ride one of the giants. Seeking the balancing place, like Eku, he waited for his moment. Trusting his timing, when he turned and began stroking to catch the movement of a wall of water that kept rising until it was out of my sight, I followed. At the end of a seventy-foot ride, I fell and was driven down by heavy water in the over topple. The world went black as I tumbled with my feet at my ears. Makaha quit his ride, came back to me and pulled me up to the surface with his dolphin-like strength. I felt light in his arms, like a child. After that, we faced the great waves together over and over again. Two specks in the billowing sea, floating freely as in a dance, we rode or ducked the waves as one.

Now each morning while Makaha was pulling mana through his fingertips deep into his belly by making supplications to Kane, I was secretly stripping the bark of the mulberry and pounding it to kapa for my wedding skirt. In this time we shared he seemed not to know that I was a woman. Determined to make Makaha look at me with love in his eyes, I climbed high into the mountains to get the yellow flowers of the 'ilima for garlands to decorate my ankles and wrists. I made a crown of ferns and a lei of crimson lehua blossoms and silver leaves to adorn my breasts. I practiced my wedding hula on the black sand, letting the sifting energy of the surf enter my body. My fingers, massaged into the delicate, tapered tips of a chiefess, would speak to him of the love in my heart. I prayed to Laka, Goddess of Dance that I would sway with bent knees, arms to the sky, full of grace and win his heart.

I am the seed of a too-powerful love. Before I was born, my mother, Ha'aheo, the favorite wife of Pano the Moi of Maui, enjoyed her own lavish court. Pano allowed her many lovers but grew jealous when she took a younger man she favored over him. Pano threatened to tear her tongue out, but she would not relinquish my father. When her belly swelled with me, Pano, the most fierce and feared of chiefs, ordered my mother and father killed. My parents fled his court in Wailuku, making the treacherous journey up the side of Haleakala Crater. They found a secret path through the impenetrable forest on the side of the "House of the Sun" and hid in a lava tube. I was born in the depths of a cave where my infant cries could not be heard above the crashing waves below, and my mother was safe from Pano's anger.

I prayed to the gods for my mother's power to fire the hearts of men and called upon her spirit to help bind Makaha's soul to my own. I swept the floor of his hale and placed fragrant flowers in a koa bowl beside his lau hala mat. I heated mountain ginger oil and spread it on my arms and legs as well as on my belly and breasts, taking special care at the plump mounds yet to be caressed by a man. Finally, I massaged my hair with oil until it glistened blue-black in the sun.

When Makaha returned from his field, I rose to meet him, entreating him to join me. He seemed hesitant but took my hand, letting me lead him to the mat. He allowed me to wash his splendid body with a cool cloth, closing his eyes as I let it linger on his forehead. Gently rubbing his temples with my fingertips, I gave him lomilomi massage, the loving touch, to open his heart. Stretching his golden arm above his head, I rotated it in the joint, applying oil and stroking the muscles that lined his side. As I massaged the entire length of his handsome body, he looked at me with steady eyes.

"Wai-nani, are you sure?"

"You are the one," I said, as I continued to oil and manipulate his limbs, gently lifting his thigh and rotating his leg in its socket. Our hearts met as I touched every inch of his lean, muscular frame. I was mesmerized by the texture of his skin that smelled so sweet and pure. His ule grew strong in his malo. I knew that when this night ended my life would belong to him.

When I finished the massage, he rose and took my hand. We stood facing one another in moonlight so bright our bodies cast shadows in the night. His skin shimmered in the yellow light of the kukui torch. He seated himself by the fire and began to thump rhythmically on a drum between his knees, singing a gentle oli. I did the hula my mother taught me in anticipation of this night and pulled the power of Pele into my fingertips to ignite his passion. The goddess pressed my hips forward and back, gently swaying them in a circle. As Makaha increased his tempo, I bent my knees and flexed my ankles, letting the pulsing energy rock my hips. I prayed he found me beautiful.

He dropped his drum to the ground and jumped up, opening his knees wide then in, then wide, then in, encircling me with his body. His black hair flying, muscles tense and alive, Makaha's steady gaze met mine. He came to me, enclosing me in his dark beauty. I drank of him, taking him into my center. He exhausted his great strength in me, leaving his seed behind.

For the rest of the full moon we took turns rekindling love's fire. Discovering each other's secret delights, we dove ever deeper into blue waves of desire. I consumed his strength, basking in his musky odor. He lay compliant, one leg draped over my middle, murmuring, "You are a sweet, never-fading flower."

We lived in love for the rest of the growing season. I gathered the gifts of the sea while he hiked up the volcano wall deep into the forests to find the nene goose and breadfruit. Our days were spent as two birds bringing straw to their nest. We wanted for nothing. Each morning and night we reunited our bodies and spirits, finding perfect peace in each other's arms. I was not ready when Ka'eo arrived, placing his terrible truth on our doorstep.

3
Message in the Sky

Wai-nani, this is Ka'eo," Makaha said, draping his arm around the shoulders of the mahogany man wearing a crown of coarse black hair streaked with white. "He raised me as his own and taught me all that I know.

"Ka'eo, this is Wai-nani, a gift from Kanaloa. She came to me from the sea."

Ka'eo smiled easily out of soft brown eyes buried in deep grooves etched on his face. "Now I understand why Makaha has stayed away from our village so long," he said, hunching over the walking stick he clutched with gnarled fingers.

"Come sit. You have journeyed long," I said, ducking inside our hale to get our guest coconut milk and poi. I joined them by the fire that cast shadows on Makaha's face and made him look fierce and stern, like my father. He gave me a reproachful glance, reminding me that it is kapu for a woman to sit with men when they eat or drink. Blood pulsed into my head. I choked back my anger, not wanting to explode in front of this kind kanaka. Instead, I would wait until he was gone to tell Makaha how I railed against the ancient custom of separate eating. While unwitnessed, we had shared all things.

I left the men to talk their talk and slipped silently onto the mat I shared with my husband. Sadness lay heavy in my heart as I slid off to a fitful sleep. I saw my lower body wrapped in tight, scaly skin. My legs were trapped. Unable to propel myself through the water, I sank like a gourd weighted with a stone to the sea bottom. I settled there, anchored like a coral polyp. Next morning I awoke to an empty mat. Ka'eo was sitting by the blackened fire pit staring into it as though it might give him an answer to some burdensome question.

"Where is Makaha?" I asked, stretching the stiffness out of my body.

"Gone," Ka'eo said, looking up at me tenderly.

"Gone where? I don't understand." My voice was trembling and I became lightheaded. A strange premonition stalked me. I felt something terrible moving toward me.

"I came to tell him that his uncle, Lako, Moi of Hawai'i, has called him back to Kealakekua. He is making war on Pano. Makaha is his best warrior. He must be with the other young warriors to teach them the art of war and test his own strength. I'm sorry to bring you this sadness, Wai-nani."

Crumbling to the ground, landing on my knees, I let my body round into the curl of a new seed in the womb. Digging my fingers into the red soil, I clung to it so that I would not dissolve into the nothingness that threatened to spirit me away. I melted into the pain that surged over me in heavy, crushing waves more powerful than anything I'd felt in the sea. A pressure in the pit of my stomach rose into my throat, overtaking me. I lifted my head to the silver sky, stretched my neck back and gave way to a howl that washed over me like an ocean swell. The ancient growl coming from my throat ripped through my body.

Makaha had gone without the courage to say goodbye, leaving me with an aching sadness. I lay down on my side, pulled my knees to my chest and rocked, hugging myself. Shuddering, I let tears flow. Ka'eo touched my shoulder tenderly with his hand.

"This old man's arms are here for you," he said, lifting me into his lap. I huddled into his great chest and listened to his heartbeat until my own heart grew calm.

"How could he go without a word, no matter what his duty?" I murmured.

"He told me to remain and tell you the story of the warrior to whom you are bound."

"His past has no meaning to me," I said.

"His past is his future. I alone know Makaha's truth. Even he does not know his truth. Until now I would have taken it with me to my burial cave."

"Why are you telling me this?"

"He has made me your servant. I will teach you, just as I taught Makaha. You will know the heart, soul, secrets and dreams of the one you dare to call husband."

As I listened to Ka'eo, I knew no truth could change the pain of Makaha's betrayal. Nothing he said would close the raw wound that was my heart. Pele, a wicked goddess, who shrivels her lovers with her fire, is hateful to mortals. Twice she tricked me into believing her powers to be kind. First she lured me to this bleak land from the sparkling waterfalls of my Hana home. Then she gave me perfect love with a warrior who cast me aside, to drift in her dark, barren womb. Ka'eo held me until the sun sank into the gray clouds that cling to the heaving breast of Pele and rocked me, whispering, "There, there … There, there."

Ka'eo let go a long sigh as he stared into the fire casting a glow on his withered face. A sparkling canopy of stars pricked the black sky. The warmth of his loving gaze filled my heart with calm. His aloha encircled us and eased the quaking in my belly. Reaching back into the years, he began his tale a year before Makaha's birth. I closed my eyes while he talked the story of my husband's past.

"The sky was filled with fleecy white clouds the day we set sail for Maui," he began. "Malana, the young chiefess to become Makaha's mother, sat under the shade of the platform in the waist of her double-hulled canoe. A dozen warriors dipped paddles into the placid waters in unison. The rhythmical sound of their paddles gliding through water, marked by the beat of a sharkskin drum, was all that was heard for many hours. Malana's gaze remained riveted upon Haleakala Crater coming closer with each stroke of the warriors' paddles. Pano had summoned Niolo, her husband, to his court. Not wanting to offend the fearsome Moi of Maui, Niolo, who was bent over his staff and blink-eyed, sent his splendid, sacred bride in his stead.

"She was no older than you, Wai-nani, when old Niolo thrust the spear in front of the wedding house claiming her as his possession. Like you, she was tall with long limbs that swayed like the leaf of the palm in a sweet breeze when she walked. She had flashing, haughty eyes and at thirteen was in full bloom of her womanhood. Graced with slender regal form and delicate features, there was no fault about her. I was to be her manservant, a gift from Niolo, to assure her safe journey.

"Our passage was peaceful. Dolphins played in our wake, surfing the blue swells that lifted our canoe and thrust us forward. Upon the shores of Maui we were greeted by a dozen warriors with a manele for Malana. Poi and coconut milk were provided as refreshment after our long crossing. I followed the procession on foot along a jungle trail stained with pink fruit fallen from heavily laden trees. Tiny gnats breeding in them flew into my eyes and nose as we marched up Wailuku Pass to Pano's village.

"Many hales were clustered about Pano's 'House in the Heavens' nestled in a lush valley with a staggered cascade at its head. As a child, I had heard of the lavishness and splendor of his court. Women pounded kapa cloth in the shade while children ran shrieking through the village. Fishermen spread their nets in the sun, picking them clean. The smell of pig roasting in a steaming imu scented the air.

"Our progress stopped in front of a great house large enough to store six double- hulled canoes. Two stout warriors stood guard at the entrance. They lifted the cloth door, inviting us to enter. Once inside, I dropped to my knees and touched my nose to the ground before the great Pano. Kapu, strictly enforced at his court, meant a man's shadow cast upon his royal figure ensured a swift and certain death. A retainer was always sent ahead announcing the arrival of the great Moi of Maui, signaling all to bow in his presence. He lay on a lau hala mat, resting his head in his hand on bent elbow. His fly-brush bearer gently waved the plumed staff over his languid body. The sides of his fierce face and flat belly were covered with tattoos. They traced his cheekbones and curled around his eyes to his forehead. Even the lids of his black eyes, as deep as a starless night, were darkened with patterns designed to bring him greater mana.The shape of Mano covered his right thigh. The gaping jaws of the shark spread around the knot where gut once bound him to his mother.

"He surveyed Malana and waved her to come closer to him. She obeyed, moving toward him on hands and knees, placing her forehead on the mat before him. His eyes traveled licentiously over the hills and valleys of her voluptuous form.

"'How is it with the Chief of Kailua?' he asked with a sly smile.

"'Niolo is resting as is fitting for a gentle, good chief,' she replied, still kneeling and speaking to the floor, not daring to look directly at Pano unless he bade her to. His cruelty was as legend as the lavishness of the court he held. He shifted to a seated position, clapped his hands twice and signaled Malana to sit beside him. She moved quickly to obey. A dozen retainers scurried to get drums and to stir the hula dancers. It was to be a night of story telling, feasting, music and games.

"Servants set to roasting dozens of dogs and pigs in the steaming imus to succulent perfection while we ate breadfruit, poi and fish. A line of twenty hula dancers made their entrance with drums beating, hips dropping low to the ground. I jumped into the line unnoticed. When the dancers exhausted themselves, Malana rose, her young blood pulsing for a man with the strength to satiate her magnificent body. She turned to face Pano, looking only on him as she performed an ancient hula designed by Laka to melt the hearts of men. Pano clapped his hand three times, signaling all to leave, save the young chiefess."

"But what of my mother? She was the favorite wife of Pano. Where was she when you arrived?"

"Ha'aheo was not there. She kept her own court on Maui in Lahaina, saying that the sour disposition of Pano stole the sunshine from her life. Your mother's court was famous for dancing, music, laughter and gaiety while Pano was solitary and sullen. He was known to sneak through his own village at night, listening in the dark for traitors.

"His interest in Malana was fleeting, and soon we were making our way back to Hawai'i. 'Please don't tell Niolo,' she begged me. I alone knew of this formidable coupling, and have kept this secret in my heart for fear of the confusion this truth could bring to Makaha. If he knew Pano was his father, he would not be able to carry out his destiny to do battle against him."

"Pano, enemy to my Hana home, is Makaha's father?" I stammered.

"Malana had lain with old Niolo for more than a year but remained childless. Within a month from her return from Maui her belly began to swell. She convinced the ancient chief that it was their joyous reunion that had planted the seed growing in her generous, fertile womb. She feared that Niolo would have the child bashed against rocks if he thought anything else were the truth.

"As Malana's belly grew, so did Niolo's suspicions. He went to his priest and asked him to read the entrails of a pig. The priest whispered into the Niolo's ear of a prophecy. He told of a chief to be born on a starless night when a streaking red glow crosses the heavens. 'This ali'i will rise to rule over Niolo's realm. His cloud will rest on the mountains of all the islands,' he prophesied, planting the seeds of hatred and fear in the old man's heart. The priest, covered with white fish scale skin from drinking 'awa, knelt over the wet innards of the pig and said he saw the future clearly.

"'This chief is growing in the womb of Malana,' he hissed. 'You must nip off the bud of the poison gourd.'

"Niolo's fears mounted with each passing day as he watched Malana's belly grow.

"When the time of Makaha's birth came near, Malana called me to her side. Fearing old Niolo would drag the child from her arms still wet and steaming, she begged me to help her.

"'Get a wet nurse. Hide her in a cave and take my baby to her the moment he is born. Don't let me see his sweet face. Don't let me hold him in my arms. You must promise.'

"Though I was the servant to Niolo, I could not deny her young beauty. Outside the birthing hut, I stared at star clusters overhead. The priest was wrong. There was nothing unnatural about this night. I listened to the groans of Malana as she struggled to bring the new chief into the world. Her pain became more intense, her screams more tormented. The midwife called for my help. It is kapu for a man to enter the birthing hut, but once again I couldn't refuse Malana.

"Breathless and panting, she lay on her mat unable to press the child forward. Together the midwife and I got her to her feet. I held her upright as the woman massaged her belly, forcing the child down the birth tunnel. It still did not drop into the hole lined with pandanus leaves readied for the baby. The midwife told me to reach inside and take the head of the unborn ali'i and to pull gently until it dislodged from the womb. I feared crushing the tiny skull with my great, clumsy hands, but in moments Makaha's slippery body dropped into my waiting arms. Holding him up by the ankles, letting the blood rush through his body, I waited for the squall that marked the birth of a great chief. He greeted the world with a mighty howl from a scowling, purple face. I wiped the royal blood from his squirming body.

"'Please...' she whispered, looking at me with sorrowful eyes, reaching her arms up to her son.

"'Just for a moment,' I said. Breaking my promise, I let the child suckle his mother's breast so that her memory would forever be stained on his mind. She wailed when I pulled him from her arms, but I held fast to my charge. Wrapping Makaha in kapa cloth, I placed him in the pack prepared to carry him on my chest. I took the precious child away from Malana, ignoring her pitiful tears.

"Though I had an hour on Niolo's men, I soon heard them clamoring up the trail, close behind us. Knowing I couldn't defend us against a dozen warriors, I stopped for a moment to steady my breath and looked up to the stars to get my bearings. A fiery ball followed by streaming tail feathers of a great white bird raced across the sky. The heavens were streaked with a bright red glow, the fiery confirmation of the birth of the chief that was to rule over all of the islands.

"Fated to bring my tiny ruler to his destiny, blessed by the gods, given the strength of a hundred warriors, I ran swiftly to where his wet nurse lay waiting in a dry lava tube. I crawled into the cave through a dark tunnel, shrouded in giant fern frond. This would be our home until it was safe to journey to Waipio Valley. The clouds opened, giving way to a relentless storm that washed all traces of our tracks, blinding the men who stalked us for the next three days."

Ka'eo stopped his story to gaze upward into the heavens swathed in stars as though looking for another divine sign. He did not reveal the message if he received one, but instead transfixed adoring dark eyes into mine.

"You are so much like her," he continued. "It is no wonder he couldn't say goodbye to you. Makaha is destined to follow a fate stronger than his own mortal heart. I have long wanted to shed the secret of his birth. It is a heavy burden that bends these old shoulders low to the ground."

He stared sadly into the fire before going on.

"For five seasons, I sheltered him in the depths of the Waipio Valley. The valley is bounded on three sides by soaring cliffs too steep to climb. The fourth side of Waipio faces the sea with a curved sandy beach. Gushing waterfalls tumble down sheer pali deep into the heart of the canyon. My father, and his father's father, lived in this place where the steep walls breathe with green life. Throbbing insects, the chirp of the honeycreeper, and the drone of the dragonfly fill the air where trails of the ancients trace the foot of the cliffs.

"Few questions are asked in the valley. There is a quiet acceptance there for the stranger. For a thousand years great chiefs have gone there to restore themselves with the most high mana and harmony found in Waipio. Although the people must have wondered about the mother of the child I was raising, they never questioned his right to be there. We lived peacefully in the patchwork of taro gardens and fishponds, breathing in the rich moist air. He suckled at the breast of his wet nurse for one season. I massaged his plump arms and legs each day so that he would have the long, lithe limbs of a warrior. Before his skull hardened, I shaped his head to a fine point, pressing the heel of my hand on his forehead to give him the regal lines of an ali'i chief. Each evening I held him in my lap and sang meles to him and taught him the legends of the ancestors. I knew one day he would ask me about the truth of his own birth, but I never knew what I would say."

"Why have you not told him?"

"The time has not been right."

"Am I really like Malana?"

"Yes, you have her grace, with no fault about you," he said, stroking my hair with a gentle hand.

4
Hard Path

Ka'eo continued his story, freeing his own heart of the terrible knowledge he had been unable to reveal to Makaha.

"I taught him to walk erect, swinging his arms gracefully with each stride, so he could run miles without effort. Many happy hours were spent on long walks to the soft private parts of the canyons where we climbed slippery rocks up the sides of triple-tiered waterfalls. Sitting at the second pool of the highest fall in the Waipio, Makaha stared intently into the depths of the dark cool waters. Solemn, seldom laughing, he was not shy, but thoughtful. He loved to hear the stories of the ancestors.

"I told him of Maui, half-god, half-human, born prematurely in a season of drought to Hina, who lives in the moon. Unable to murder the feeble infant as ordered by his father Ku, Hina spirited her son to a sea-cave, building a tiny raft for him out of coconut husks. She strapped him to it then left him to sail to his own fate on the sea. Kanaloa, God of the Island under the Ocean, saw the squalling child and took pity on him. Kanaloa raised Maui and gave him godly powers. When the sea god felt it was time for the young man with mischeivous ways to go back to his human realm, he gave him the gift of living waters to protect him in his journey. Maui carried the calabash of life restoring water on his shoulder. A few droplets of this divine water will bring a dying warrior back to life.

"'Did Maui's mother try to find him?' Makaha would ask me each time I told him this tale.

"'Yes.' I always answered in the same way. 'But, she could not go to him in the land beneath the sea.'

"Makaha sensed that his mother was alive and searching for him. He wanted to know her. I wanted to tell him of his royal parents but did not want his young happiness to end. Too soon, he would walk on the hard path of a warrior and know many harsh truths.

"After the birth of her second son, Niolo mellowed toward his still-beautiful bride. Rumors that the Moi of Maui had planted his treacherous seed in his favorite wife faded with time. He forgot about the prophecy of the ancient priest and the threat of a warrior-chief who would one day steal his realm. Malana convinced the old man that it would be a sorrow to him if he did not know his first son before his bones were bleached and hidden in a sacred cave. Niolo finally agreed to let her bring Makaha into his court.

"Malana traversed the sheer wall of the valley with her progress in search of her son. She had only to mention my name to the first person she met and they brought her to me. Makaha stared sternly into the soft almond eyes of his mother, casting his gaze down to his toes when she reached out to him on bent knees with both arms open. Tears flowed from her sweet, sad eyes as she clutched him to her breast. He tolerated her caress but stood motionless, his heart still to her touch.

"I agreed to return with her to Kailua. Court gossips buzzed when the young chief returned to sit by the side of Niolo.

"'The bud of the poison gourd blossoms,' whispered the dour priest.

"Old Niolo was proud of his athletic son who excelled in every sport. Makaha knew how to swim before he knew how to walk. His grace and courage in the water were unsurpassed. He swam for hours each day, outdoing all the other boys at wave sliding and body surfing. He out-maneuvered the young warriors when wrestling, evading bone breaking clenches with liquid movements. Great lung-power and stamina from swimming daily made him the fastest on land and in the sea. The other boys taught him how to kill with fists, clubs, stone blades and the slingshots. In return, he taught them the lessons of moana.

"Niolo's priests taught him astronomy, history, the migrations and omens of fish and birds, along with the punishments for breaking kapu. He learned the meles that would bring him mana, building a reserve of spiritual strength. He wanted to be the most powerful of warriors. The priests took him to the heiau, the temple, to woo strength and blessing from the gods. They filled his mind with the legends of Niolo's genealogy and taught him the ways of the ancient mariners who navigated the world. He was excited to receive the knowledge he would one day need to be a ruler of men.

"Sullen as a child, he became caught in the net of his own mind as he neared manhood. Wandering for days on his own, he traveled to the great throat of Kilauea, down the fern-walled crater to the lava lake floor. Treading across the valley, as cold as the moon, he stopped to breathe the vapors of steam vents until his muscles glistened from their heat. Unafraid of Pele's moods, he dared her to unfurl her hideous power upon him. He walked across her belly untouched by the vile fumes that rise just before she belches black bile into the sky.

"His mother fretted his return, but he barely acknowledged her caring for him. Strangely, it was Niolo he turned to if he had a question I could not answer. When the old man's health began to fail, Makaha saw the loss of the chief's mana as the work of evil ana'ana priests. He suspected the priest of poisoning and praying Niolo to death.

"'I will avenge you, Father,' Makaha vowed, kneeling at the withered chief's mat.

"'Go to the house of my brother Lako. You will be safe there,' Niolo whispered before leaving to join our ancestors.

"Badly confused by the good chief's death, Makaha wandered in the desert of K'au, searching for the truth of his own heart for over a year. The prophecy of his birth weighed heavily upon him. He built his temple overlooking the sea in search of the strength to fulfill his destiny. In time he did go to Lako, and became his best warrior. You have found him in the thinking place he returns to each season. That is the spirit you have bound yourself to, Wai-nani."

When Ka'eo finished, the moon was high in the sky. Hina's cruel smile chilled my heart. Safe from the anger of Ku, who chased her up the rainbow, I envied her hiding place above human suffering. Exhausted, I hugged my knees, resting my chin on their smooth surface. Now, Makaha's truth was to remain with me. I rocked until the flames of the fire consumed the wood. The cold wind whipped the sparks that lashed out at the black night. I wanted to vomit, to spit out the burden of understanding. I needed to be consoled, to be held in my proud lover's strong arms. I wanted to have him with me to laugh away my tears as he kissed me with tender lips, sending quivers of pleasure through my body. Memories were all that kept me from floating like a vapor to the lifeless realm between the stars, vanishing forever from the gaze of mortal women—sisters to my misery.

Ka'eo tended to my needs for one full turn of the moon. Weighted by my sorrow, I hid from the sun in the hale. Heaviness settled upon me. I had no desire to witness the splendor of the rising or setting of the sun. I cared no more for the lilting song of the mamo bird outside the dark cool cave of grief in which I dwelled. My appetite for life, even for food, was gone. I closed my eyes to the world and looked inside the deep, blue darkness of my mind.

Ka'eo lifted my head into his lap and rocked me like a lost child he had found after many years of separation. He softly sang to me and told me stories, just as he had for Makaha when he was a keiki. I too loved the stories about Maui raised in Po, the murky land beneath the sea.

"Maui had no sympathy for silly human emotions," Ka'eo said in his rich, soothing voice. "He enjoyed playing endless tricks upon the Island people," Ka'eo continued. "He didn't want to come back to his home in Hana, but Kanaloa forced him to plunge back into the world. Maui was a careless boy, letting the gift of living water splash from his calabash as he traveled. He lost many drops when he changed himself into the shape of the mamo bird with glowing yellow feathers beneath his wings to win the favor of a beautiful girl by a stream. He lost more drops when he battled with Kaoeow, a giant that he defeated by turning himself into an owl so he could pluck the great warrior's eyes out. He lost so many drops of the water that when he reached Hana, he barely had enough of the precious liquid left to revive his father from the dead."

I drifted to sleep listening to Ka'eo's stories, curled into his lap like a seashell. I laid my head on his broad chest with my ear to his heartbeat and remembered falling asleep in my father's arms as a child. I dreamt of my water-rich Hana home where shimmering waterfalls tumble down moss-covered boulders into seven pools. When my mother broke with Pano, she and my father fled from his men through the crater of Haleakala. The warriors could not track them across the floor of the volcano, and my parents were able to escape to the remote village in Hana where my father ruled with a firm hand. Many times Pano sent his men to kill my father, but they were exhausted by the journey and easily trapped by the net of our warriors waiting for them.

My thoughts drifted as though caught in a great sea current as I floated in and out of the past. Ten seasons ago, I was swept out to sea by a fast moving tide. After swimming for two hours, I rolled over on my back to conserve strength. I could hear the breakers pounding the jagged seawall. The currents were moving me ever closer to the dip before the swell of the great walls of water. I feared the bearded monsters would crush me down to the bottom of the sea floor and drag me through the coral polyps, shredding the flesh from my bones.

Eku appeared with a fierce blast of water through his blowhole. He formed a figure eight as he swam around me, creating swirls of water that lifted and massaged me gently. Although terrified by what this sea creature might do to me, I could see no anger in his human-like eye. I feared my fate alone more than I feared him. He alternated between brushing against my skin with his body and shooting off to see if I would follow him in his water dance.

When he came close, staring at me with immense wonderment, I felt a tingling, prickling sensation that buoyed me and made me feel light. He clicked and whistled, trying to talk to the frail, gawky human who had entered his domain. I surrendered to the shimmering moment, closed my eyes, content that this would be the way I would enter Po, the underwater world of the dead. He came closer still, nudging me with his long, rubbery snout, rolling me over in the surf. I did nothing to prevent him from bumping me again. He sidled up to me, allowing me to cling to his dorsal fin. Sensing my weakness, he let me rest the weight of my body on his own. Then, he gently swam me back to the cove where I had entered the sea. I clung to him as he glided through the churning waves. Once he had deposited me in the shallows, he seemed pleased with himself. Circling once, he sped off like a bird in flight, jumping six feet out of the water as he made his way back to the deep. Now, even he had left me to drift alone in the deep sea of my thoughts.

After a turn of the moon, my body strength returned but I wore a costume of skin and bone encasing the emptiness in my heart. After two moons, Ka'eo asked me to return with him to Kealakekua.

"The life of the village will fill your days," he said. "You will soon forget the time you and Makaha shared together."

"I don't want to forget," I said, knowing that I would never release the memories that bound me to Makaha.

"You are free to go," I said, hoping that he would leave me to my sorrow.

He picked up a twig, knelt to the ground and drew a map in the sand.

"If you change your mind, it is a five-day journey for a fit warrior to Kealakekua Bay."

He told me if I followed the lava trail I had traveled to reach the thinking place of Makaha back to where I had entered the desert of K'au, I would find stone markers that would lead me safely to the realm of Lako.

"You will be welcome in his court," Ka'eo said. "You don't need to fear the nights, for all the people you will meet on the journey are ruled by the strong hand of Makaha's uncle. But don't go to the mountain villages hidden in lush ferns near the top of the volcano. The people there worship the fire goddess. Those who dare to enter her realm often never return."

5
The Wisdom of Water

I watched Ka'eo bend into the wind, leaning on his walking stick, until his body became a small dot on the yellow horizon. Many days passed after he was gone before my hunger willed me to the water's edge. Flinging my net across the tide pools, I popped my hands under the water pushing small fishes into my trap. I ate the young anae raw, pulling their firm flesh from the bone with my teeth. I ate the crabs that hide in the crevices of the rocks whole, careful to spit out their carcass before swallowing. I sat for many hours staring hard at the purple horizon, counting the time between wave sets rolling ceaselessly to the shore.

Tiring of this pastime, I moved to the warm, black sand. Stretching my full length, etching my body pattern onto the sand, I let my body go heavy. With my knees bent like the legs of the crab and my palms facing the clear blue sky, I felt the burning warmth of the sun. Closing my eyes, staring intently into the blue-black center of my mind, I slipped into the void of my aloneness. The foaming waves rushed over my thighs as I watched the dance of a pulsing red light in my forehead.

Like the aura that circles the sun, the center of my mind first spread then receded with the breath of the sea. From the top of my head a cone of heaven's light descended down my body. It felt like a rivulet spreading its rich nourishing load into a streambed after the dry season. The tingling force entering my body made me feel light, airy and open in my heart. Thinking harder on the deep purple coursing through my mind in pulsating waves, I saw a circle of strangers standing over me. I recognized the globelike brown eye of Eku. He came closer as he bent over me, examining me with an amused, playful twinkle in his generous eye.

He held the shape of a man in my dream, placing his hand slowly but firmly on my chest. Soothing energy filled the empty spaces in my heart with a warm and subtle, tingling sensation that dissolved the hard edges of hurt. There were six beings standing around me with the sun's aura wrapped around their cone-shaped heads. They leaned in blocking the light, forming a body casement over me, protecting me, guiding me lovingly back to life. The tears flowed. When I awoke, the ghosts of the ancient allies were gone, and my heart was clear.

Sitting up slowly, I searched the azure sea for the quarter moon crescent of Eku's arc. I had not seen him since he had delivered me to the land of K'au. Why he had deserted me, I could not be sure. I hadn't entered the sea since Makaha and I stood on the long backs of the waves. I had locked that moment in my heart, holding it still in time, as I watched the surf crash on the shore.

Rising, I strode forward through tiny bubbles of surf too weak to break. I waded through the wave surge to my waist and dove under the curl of a foaming roller. Immersed in the cool, soothing water, my senses emerged from their deep sleep. The brisk sea smelled and tasted of lovemaking. Water filled the corridors of my mind, washing away all thought. I stroked boldly forward, back arched, chin forward, hairline at the water surface. Lifting bent elbow to the sky, I watched my arm arc out of the water. Scooping the water into my cupped palm, I used it to propel forward with steady, even kicks.

I thought only of these movements for many miles. Each stroke took me further from my pain and closer to freedom. As my hand sliced through the water, I followed it with my vision, looking into the sun on the exhale and listening to the bubbles of my breath as they rose to the surface. Repeating this motion, with no thought of where I was going, or why, I slid through the clear clean water with the energy of a dolphin.

My thoughts went to my village. I remembered the day my brother ripped his malo from my hips, leaving me naked and humiliated before the village, instead of honoring me for my bold wave sliding with Eku. I saw myself striking him fiercely with each stroke of the arm that pulled me forward. Flailing at him unmercifully, my forward movement stopped as I churned the water with brutal force until spent. I floated adrift from my body for many hours, face up, searching the blue sky scudded with white clouds for answers. At the end of my swim I caught a wave, riding it to the shore. When I rose from the sea, with salt sticking to my skin, I saw myself as a sleek water creature emerging to walk on dry land.

For many weeks, I went to the sea each day. Black storm clouds overhead threatened to burst at any moment, but they couldn't keep me from the joy that awaited me in the water. The ocean became my lover, gliding wet hands over the length of my body, caressing every hidden part of me, suckling my toes. Each time I immersed myself, my mind dislodged from the trap of my brooding. I floated above myself, watching each stroke, each fluttering kick bringing me closer to the heartbeat of moana. My arms became strong, sinewy and bronzed. Back muscled, buttocks firm, legs strong, I sliced through the water like Eku.

Fishes floating close to the surface looked as though I could catch them in my hand. The sun rippled through the clear water in moving prisms to the white sandy sea floor. Floating over a forest of fern-green reefs, I watched the moving clouds of fish dance through the coral heads. Some days I caught a ride on sea turtles that wafted in the water like birds flying in the sky. I swam for a long time every day for two moons. It was all I cared to do.

One day while swimming a steady and strenuous stroke through turquoise water, I saw a female face floating up towards me. She had soft round black eyes like kukui nuts, high cheekbones and full lips. Her hair swirled around her body like a cloak of seaweed, hiding her nakedness. She must have escaped from Po: the island beneath the weight of the sea, the inverted black world where there is no air, only swirling dark mist in which fishes and birds drift. She reached her hand out to me. Our arms rippled in the watery dimension, confusing the distance between us. I struggled to reach her fingertips. I was just about to touch her when I was lifted from the water.

Startled, I kicked violently to be free of the sea monster that threw me spinning into the air. Splashing back down, I turned to face my enemy. If it was Mano, my fate was sealed. I would soon join my sea sister in Po. Now, I knew why she was here. She came to greet me and lead me to the chamber below where I would not need food or air. A huge mass moved swiftly toward me at terrific speed. I didn't recognize the sea creature until it breached a full ten feet out of the water. It was Eku! He giggled and skipped backwards on his tail.

Happy tears welled at the sight of my old friend. In his excitement he rushed back, swimming around me in tight circles until I was dizzy. He came up to me, looked deep into my eyes with his own globelike human eye and smiled. I clasped around his great girth and locked my legs about his middle and held on, rolling and twisting with him in the surf until my arms lost their strength. It was not until I had exhausted myself in his embrace that I saw Laka.

Her fin sliced the water calmly in a great circle around us. She seemed not to be in a hurry to interrupt our reverie and was not jealous of our love. It was a strange romance, I know, but it was love that I felt bubbling forth in all manner of happiness at the sight of my friend. I caressed his underbelly, while the old tingling sensation I received when near him traveled through my body like a swift current. When he tired of this treat, he rolled over and steered me toward Laka.

I approached her cautiously, fearing her great strength. She made no attempt to keep me from coming closer. A small shadow hovering near her shoulder drifted with her. Suddenly, the dark sliver breached, slipped cleanly out of the water and did a complete back flip. Laka quickly herded her offspring back in line. Now, I understood why Eku had left me for so long. It was to protect Laka while she carried and gave birth to their first-born.

The tiny mimic of his mother's movement glided with her through the water as though attached. Not wanting to venture so close that I upset Laka, I peered through the clear green water at the tiny spirit I named Puki.

Carefree days were spent swimming with Eku and his family. Laka dove deeply, leaving Puki at the surface, bringing back small fish to share with him. She taught him how to tear the food with his snout into bite size pieces. He suckled daily now, but she would soon be weaning him. Eku glided around them, protecting them from any possible intrusions. He spoke to them with high-pitched bleats and whistles, creating an eerie sea-song. I yearned to touch Puki but dared not get too close. I dove deep to get treats for Laka. I brought them to her to show her I was a friend. In time, she let me rub Puki's tender underbelly, making him tremble with delight.

I struggled not to be jealous of Eku and Laka's happiness. Even though I had found my strength in the sea, I felt that I was an outsider. Feeding off of the dolphin tribe's contentment, not being with my own family, made me melancholy. I would find my way to Lako's village. The chief is like Mano, not to be tampered with, but my need for Makaha was greater than my fear of the Moi of Hawai'i.

Sitting on a warm rock, I lay back and spread myself open to the sun. I reached down to the dark flower between my legs and began to gently rub tender flesh. I felt the blood pulsing to the place only Makaha had known and gave way to violent need, giving myself pleasures as powerful as a set of seven waves. Basking in the sun's intense life-giving rays, caressed by the delicate kisses of the sweet scented breeze, adrift in the deep purple of my sex, I felt the earth shift beneath me.

At first, I thought it was part of my dream, but the rock beneath me was shaking so furiously it wrenched me back to the day. Dark shadows blocked the sun. I opened my eyes to see black, billowing clouds rising from the fiery mouth of Kilauea. The heavens swirled fitfully, and I felt heat rising from the earth. I trembled as the ground heaved like ocean swells towards me. I stood and balanced my body with bent knees as though wave-sliding to keep from toppling from my rock perch. Fiery clouds surrounded the black volcano cone. White steam billowed from vents threatening to rupture. Red-hot light burst from the mouth of the volcano. Pele spit boulders to the sky, a warning of her mounting rage.

I looked to the sea for escape. A rainbow of yellow and pink, then lavender to indigo arced across the horizon. Certain that Naikopo, Goddess of Death, would soon have my spirit if I didn't leave the land, I embraced the rainbow. Not knowing what awaited me on the other side I dove into water as warm as a boiling pot and swam toward the foot of the fanning colors. Lifted as high as the tallest koa tree, then plummeted into the valleys of the swells so deep the mountains of water blocked the sun, I fought the white-backed waves. Stroking steadily and kicking rhythmically, I struggled not to let terror seize me.

The heavens were awash with black, brooding smoke that sullied the powder- white clouds. A wild, hot wind churned them to pearl gray. Pele's breath was upon me. I felt the building wrath of the sharp-lipped goddess who devours even the rocks and trees. The rainbow was much farther away than it appeared. Tossed and buffeted in the raging swells, I felt my strength waning. Reaching the misty base of my destination, I discovered that what from a distance shimmered with color was built out of gray moody droplets. Before swimming through the arc, I turned to look back upon the fiery mouth of Pele. Red rivers of rock oozed over the lip of the crater, charring everything in their path. Koa trees burst into flames, making torches that lit the path of the glowing lava as it flowed to the sea.

I swam hard until I was safely on the other side of the rainbow in a cooling rain. Droplets hit the calm water, bursting into wet pearls. Perfect circles spread from the center of their striking point. Soon the heavens would open in earnest. Though used to swimming many miles, I feared the full tumult of moana. I swam along the shore looking for a haven for the night. I whistled for Eku, clicking my tongue like a stick on a gourd, but he did not come to me.

I found shelter in a sea arch over a narrow strip of black sand where I made a bed of the rotting leaves of the hau tree clinging to the sheer cliff of black stone. Curling into the shape of a mollusk, I had only the weight of my hair to keep me warm that long, black, night. The steady roar of the surf breaking outside the reef and the gentle wash of the waves on the sand nearby took me to Niolopua, the God of Sleep.

6
Journey to Kealakekua Bay

The warming rays of the morning sun burned my tired eyes open. I heard the clicking of my bones as I uncoiled my body and plunged into the water, bringing tingling life back into my limbs. I tried a popping sound with my tongue to draw Eku. Then I whistled in the high pitch he used to call Laka, but still he did not come. Stroking seamlessly for hours, keeping a cautious eye toward the rugged shore, I continued to call to him. The sea was calm and placid, allowing me to make good progress with minimum effort, but hunger was making me weak.

I caught a glimpse of a shimmering silver body emerging deep in the shadows. I strained to see the nature of the faceless beast flitting in and out of the shafts of light. The creature was following me. I slipped into a sidestroke and let my head rest in the water as I listened to the groans of captured spirits rising from the sea floor. Voices of ancestors adrift in the realm of Po filled my heart with dread. I heard a woman's muffled scream coming from the depths.

I stopped swimming and peered into the water, straining to know the nature of the shadowy monster with which I shared the ocean. A woman with a tangled mass of black hair hiding her face came toward me through the murky submarine world. She extended a bloodied, bruised arm to me. As she came closer, I saw a gaping black hole in the middle of her face, and tears of black pearls flowing from her terror-filled eyes. It was the girl I saw killed by my father's priest, Ikea. He cut off her nose with a sharp stone before he had three warriors club her to death. Her body was given to the dogs of the village. She had been careless and let her shadow fall upon that of my father, an ali'i chief, a descendant of the gods.

Stretching my arm down to her, our fingertips were about to touch when the creature following me shot through the water. Instead of being sucked into the land of Po, I saw the familiar mottled body of Eku. He had heard my poor imitation of his language, recognized my call, and found me in the vast, sparkling space that is the sea. He had teased me, pretending to be Mano. He giggled and circled about me, buoying me with his water massage. Staring deeply with salt-burned eyes I strained to see the girl again, but she was gone. I turned back to Eku and reached out to him.

Never was I happier to see his luminous round eye. I kissed his rubbery, white snout after a loving tryst in the surf. Laka and Puki were close behind him. I rubbed Puki's belly until he could bear it no longer. Even Laka seemed pleased to see me and let me rub her silken skin. Together again, we traveled for many hours with me hanging onto Eku's dorsal fin. I alternated between gliding through the water pulled by his great strength, and stroking vigorously by his side. Swimming parallel to the shore but keeping far enough at sea not to be taken by wave swells that crashed on the feet of braided rock rivers, we made good progress toward a safer shore.

The burning sun settled onto the horizon, leaving a curtain of fiery pink and orange behind. My power sank with the sun. The coast was too treacherous to attempt at night, so I rolled over onto my back, letting my body go slack, drifting with the rise and fall of the sparkling water. I listened to the talk of sea creatures, a clicking, squealing cacophony of dark life. If my legs drifted too far toward the ocean bottom, Eku would gently lift them with his nose, putting me upright so that I wouldn't drown while sleeping. He kept a constant vigil for sea enemies, guarding me through the night.

Laka shared a piece of Puki's fish with me so that hunger would not crowd my thoughts. We followed the luminous path of

Hina grinning down on us from her seat in the full moon. I stroked rhythmically, thinking only of my breathing for many hours. Synchronized with the rising and falling of the swells, kicking from toe to hip, I stretched my arms towards Hina's cold cradle. When once again the golden sun broke open with crimson fury, its shimmering track on the water was broken by a small fishing canoe drifting with a lone fisherman in its bow.

I approached the boat directly. Eku circled, and Laka stayed back with Puki at her shoulder. The fisherman with burnished brown skin and eyebrows orange from the sun nearly fell out of his boat, he was so startled to see a wahine with a dolphin family. He rubbed his eyes to make certain he wasn't dreaming of the scaly creatures that kept him company during the many days he spent alone at sea.

"Will you not offer a hand to a stranger?" I asked.

He extended a rough hand and hoisted me out of the water like a mahi-mahi. I landed hard on the bottom of his canoe.

"Why have the gods brought you to me?" he asked.

"I am Wai-nani, born of royal parents in Hana, on my way to Kealakekua," I told him. "Have you food for me?"

Stunned at my arrival, he stared at my nakedness for long burning seconds, before reaching into his calabash, bringing out poi, breadfruit and salted fish. He watched in silence while I ate all that he had. I felt the weight of the food in my belly, too long empty, and I told him I needed to rest. He pulled in his nets and turned the canoe towards a sandy crescent beach.

The kanaka's thatched hale rested under a cluster of hau trees beside a chattering creek. His wife stood at the shore in a kapa dress tied at the shoulder. One hand on her wide hip, the other on her furrowed forehead to block the sun, she strained to see what her husband was bringing back to her. He usually stayed upon the water until his boat was full of writhing fish. When he returned she would salt and hang the fish on the drying racks in the sun. The canoe struck the soft white sand of the protected cove with a jolt. The fisherman jumped out, pulled it to high dry sand, and tied it to a fallen coconut tree.

A covey of girls streamed out of the hale squealing and giggling at the sight of a stranger. They clustered at their mother's side, the youngest peeking out behind her knee with round, curious eyes. It seems that each season, for the last five, had brought the fisherman and his wife another girl child. The children's heights were layered, like rings inside a tree. Luana, their mother, had a gentle round face with a broad flat nose and fine white teeth that she exposed in a welcoming grin. Her strong brown hands rested on the heads of two of her daughters. The fisherman whispered into his wife's ear. She responded by extending her hand to me and led me to a small hale and a mat where I fell into the sleep of a stone.

When I awoke, the scent of akule roasting on an open fire was drifting through my dreams. Red cowry lures, mother-of-pearl lures, hooks of seashell, dog bone, and human bone were scattered on the walls. Crab and shrimp nets hung from the roof. Basket traps with hooks of pig bristles were stacked in the corner. Nets of one, two and three finger size were draped on the walls. The hale smelled like the seashore on a hot day. I rose and tied the pa'u Luana left beside my mat around my waist and followed the smoke of the fire.

"Now you will have a fine meal, not the lunch of a fisherman, but sweet fishes fit for a goddess," he said with a broad smile, as he knelt over the great fish cooking on hot stones.

"I like to watch it turn gray and crisp it up to a nice brown," he said. "That is the way I like my akule."

Luana and the girls placed koa bowls filled with poi, plates of fish, and breadfruit in a generous display. White hibiscus blooms rested in the middle of the eating mat. I felt the warmth of their maka'ainana home. Remembering the eating kapu of my ali'i class as we all gathered to eat, I feared for the lives of those who had shown me such great aloha. Kili, the fisherman, proudly placed the steaming fish in front of me and signaled me to begin.

"Our gift is humble," he said, as he seated himself cross-legged beside his wife's plump body. "We would have more to offer, but Lako's men were here last week to collect the tax for makahiki festival. We had many dogs and pigs, but now are left with just our breeding animals."

"But we always have the blessings of moana," Luana added, flashing a dazzling smile while pouring coconut milk for me.

"But you are kapu breakers? It is tabu for men and women to eat together. Why aren't you afraid?"

"I would be a lonely man if I did not share my eating mat with my wahine. There are worse things than dying."

"But you will all be burned in an imu if you are found out."

"And who will tell Lako? Will it be you?" Kili smiled wide.

The girls stared at me with fierce interest. It was as though they had never seen another female, beside their mother.

"Don't stare at Kaikilani," Kili said to his daughter as he chewed on a flaky piece of the excellent fish. "She has been wandering a long and lonely time. Just this morning she rose from the shadowy depths of the island underneath the sea where Kanaloa has been hiding her from Lono."

"Who is Lono?" the youngest daughter with a brown freckled nose, missing two front teeth, asked her father.

"He is the most bountiful and generous of gods, but he has been wandering alone ever since Kaikilani hid from him generations ago."

"Why did you hide from him?" the girl asked. Before I could say that I was not the wandering wife of Lono, the goddess Kaikilani, Kili continued.

"Lono was sitting by the second pool of a cascading waterfall when he heard the voices of a couple rising up from the first pool below him. A young man was begging the girl to elope with him. He leaned out over the mossy rocks that looked like shaggy drooling monsters, to see who belonged to the voices. Below the stone precipice he saw his beloved wife in the arms of a young warrior. Without waiting to hear what her answer would be, he dove from the rock ledge, landing in the pool below and dragged the young warrior under the black water. He held him there until there was no more life in him. Kaikilani fled from her angry husband, never to return. Ever since, Lono has been wandering the upper and lower worlds, trying to find her to tell her that he is sorry and to beg her forgiveness," the fisherman said as he stuffed more fish into his mouth.

"For many years Lono was so troubled he would insist on wrestling with any warrior unlucky enough to cross his path," Kili continued. "With his great god strength he sent them quickly to an undeserved death. That is why we have the makahiki festival today, so the young warriors can practice their skills. That is why the tax collectors come to gather food for Lono's return," he explained, leaning back on bent elbow and patting his full belly.

"So what will he do if he finds Kaikilani here?" asked the daughter with wide brown eyes.

"I'm not Kaikilani, I am Wai-nani. Lono will know that," I said.

"But I saw you riding on your sea brother's shoulder," Kili said, unconvinced.

"And I will leave with him in the morning, taking your kindness with me in my heart. Though it flatters me that you think I am a goddess, I am not."

Kili ate the rest of his meal in silence.

"Get me my drum," he finally said to the girl with many questions. She ran into the hale, returning with a coconut shell drum covered in sharkskin. He placed it between his leathery knees. Patting it gently, he raised his rich voice to a gentle oli. His family of females gathered around him. The glow of the fire warmed our full bellies. When he finished, Luana stood beside him lifting her voice of liquid sunshine to the stars. Roused by the beauty of her singing and the gentle thump of Kili's drum, I rose to dance a hula to thank them for a feast meant for a goddess.

7
The Place of Refuge

Next sunup found me sailing through gentle waters resting on Eku's neck. Kili never did accept that I was mortal. Instead, he believed I wanted my identity to remain unknown. He told me that in a day's swim, I would reach the Place of Refuge. Defeated warriors, kapu breakers, outcasts and criminals are given a second chance in this place, if they can touch the sacred ground before their enemies do. He told me I could spend the night there without danger. From there it was one day's journey to the bay of Kealakekua and the court of Lako.

My arms grew weary and hunger gnawed at my belly. Ghostly moans and strange mewing sounds eminated from the sacred temple that harbors strangers from harm. I left Eku to frolic in the depths and swam towards the crackling sound of shrimp that grew louder as I neared the rocky shore. Resting at the mouth of a gentle cove, shaded by a grove of palms trees, the Refuge was protected from the moods of moana by a great rock wall.

A lone woman with a great hump in the middle of her back was bent over the tide pools in the lava ledge outside of the wall. Gray, stringy hair hung to her waist, covering skin withered from the sun. She stared intently into the tide pool as though looking for an omen. I made my way to her.

"Aloha, how is it with you, old mother?" I asked.

She lifted her face to see who called to her. The sun shining brightly behind my head hurt her blue-black eyes that were covered with a white film. Squinting hard, she looked away from the sun and back into the clear pool of water. Ignoring me, she continued with her search. She reached down into the pool until water came to her shoulder and snatched a plump crab from a crevice to place in her calabash.

"Let me help you," I said, getting down on my knees to peer into the tide pool for other morsels. I pulled up two crabs and handed them to her. "Is this the Place of Refuge?" I asked.

Her crinkled face softened into a toothless smile. "Yes. What brings you here?"

"I am Wai-nani, of royal parents, on my way to Kealakekua," I said.

"You can spend the night here under a cover of stars, watching the surf find its home on the shore. You may eat what can be taken from the pools, but you can't go inside the great wall."

A thick stone wall surrounded the village where kapu breakers were spared hideous fates. It was built of lava stones the gods must have lifted and fit into perfectly formed spaces, for no man could have done it alone. A massive wooden image of Ku, God of War, with a scowling face, bulging all-seeing eyes, flared nose holes and a toothless grimace guarded the heiau. An image of Kane, the God of Life Giving Waters, the Restorer of Life, was taller, less angry and had an elongated head covered with swirling designs. An imposing figure of Kanaloa, Ruler of the Sea, also stood beside the sacrifice platform of the temple. Three warriors wearing white malos and holding tall spears stood guard to the entrance of the sacred village.

"I will stay and gather seaweed and crabs and shrimp for you, if you tell me why you are here," I said.

"It is not a long story. I was taken from my country home when my breasts were still full from my second born, to nurse 'Ele 'ele, son of Lako and Ohaha. It was an honor to hold such a special place in court, but I always yearned to hear the laughter of my own children. As years went by, it became known that I have traveled to the other side of death and that I can read the omens. I was often called into the court of Lako to read the 'awa leaves.

"Beneath the glow of a new moon, the future came clear to me in a rush. I saw spirits rising to the heavens from the flames of the wooden images of the gods set on fire by the people of the earth. I told Lako and Koa the priest, of my vision and gave him this prophecy: 'The Islands will be united, the kapus of the gods overthrown. Those of the heavens—the chiefs—will be brought low, and those of the earth—the maka'ainana—will be raised up.'

"Two nights ago, a warrior dragged me from my sleeping mat and told me if I didn't run to this place, I would not live to see another sunrise. Koa feared my vision. He accused me of giving a lock of 'Ele 'ele's hair to the ana'ana priest as bait to be used by the evil priest to pray the young chief to death. Ohaha knows that I am a loyal and that I guarded the private matters of the house of Lako with my life. She knew I would never give the evil kahuna this weapon, so she sent her bodyguard to give me warning."

Leaning back on a ledge of rock, she let her knees fall open while tears spilled from her inflamed eyes down creviced cheeks. Placing my arm around her frail shoulders, I hugged her as she let go of the great hurt inside her.

"Cry, old mother, it is good to cry," I said.

"All those years, I pined for my husband who remarried in my absence. Still, I kept my unhappiness from my eyes and let no one know of my sorrow. Tomorrow morning, I will go to the priest who rules this Place of Refuge," she said. "He is a good chief. He will let me go to my country home at the foot of Mauna Loa where the mists lie heavy on the land. Once again, I will wade through emerald green grasses that drip with dew and smell the breath of white ginger. My grandchildren's eyes will know me, and I will be able to return to the spirit world with peace in my heart."

"It will be so," I said, rocking her to and fro, chanting a mele that would take her back to her country home. While we spent the night under a moonless sky, blessed with a warm wind, I told her of my love for Makaha.

"When Makaha came to his uncle's house there was much clicking of tongues," the old one told me. "Though he had proven himself in the games with the young chiefs, there were whispers about his lineage. Lako took Makaha into his heart and treated him as a son. When a challenge came to the house of Lako from the chief of Hilo, Lako, slack in the flank, was grateful when Makaha offered to fight for him.

"Young Makaha battled the giant warrior with clubs, stone hammers and spears. When they had dropped all their weapons and were down to wrestling, Makaha, though bloodied, slithered out of the clutches of the warrior like an eel. He out-danced his clumsy enemy. After exhausting hours, he picked up the warrior and held him high over his head. He whirled him until the giant was dizzy, then tossed him onto the spear planted at the feet of Lako. The young chief of Hilo died loudly, while Makaha smiled. Lako was so pleased that he rewarded Makaha with lands in Kohala and Kona."

"Makaha is born to rule," I said.

"He is born to die a warrior," the crone replied. "Who has two heads, walks like a man but makes love like a woman?" she asked.

"I can't answer that riddle."

"You will know him by his cunning, cruel eyes. Keep your tongue in place and listen carefully when you reach Kealakekua. There are others in Lako's ohana who believe they are born to rule. Lako is an ambitious chief. His court is filled with heron who watch the harbor like spies."

She turned her palm up, exposing two polished stones that looked like black pearls and offered them to me. "Take these with you. They are the tears of Pele. They will protect you from those who will fear you."

"Thank you, old mother, now rest your tired head on my shoulder." I put my arm around her and held her tightly as we looked up to the great curved sky that wrapped us like a lover for the night.

8
The Secrets of Women

I left the old one to her destiny and swam a half-day to the rocky shore of Kealakekua Bay to meet mine. I rose out of the opalescent water, feathered by a flirtatious breeze, and walked straight and tall to the shore. A small group of villagers gathered at the water's edge and stared at my body. With firm muscled legs and a flat strong belly, I was as sleek as Eku.

"No woman should be so beautiful," I heard a man whisper.

The men mending their nets and the women collecting fishes in the reef stopped their labors. They hung back, murmuring to one another as they stared at the stranger who emerged from the sea. Keiki ran up to me, screaming, leaping, and reaching out to touch me. I took the slender palm of a young wahine with long, fine fingers, held it in my own and walked with her to her mother standing on the shore.

"Can you take me to the house of Ka'eo?" I asked.

"Ka'eo is in Waipio," said a wahine with wide hips and three small ones hugging her legs.

"Where is the hale of Makaha?"

"Makaha is in the mountains with the 'Alapa warriors carving war canoes. Who are you?" she demanded.

"Wai-nani, born of royal parents in Hana. I am the wife of Makaha."

The shocked women looked to the others for guidance. A stubby short man with a pig face approached me.

"How did you come from Hana without a canoe? It is a week's journey in double-hulled outrigger with a good wind at your back."

"I swam."

The crowd gathered on the shore gasped in disbelief. "No human could swim that far," the man said, circling me. He stared blatantly at my behind as though looking for the fish tail that would confirm suspicions of godly interference.

"Take her to the women's hale," the short man with the pig snout snorted with authority. "I will tell Lako of the wahine who swims with the fishes from Hana and says she is the wife of his best warrior."

Kealakekua was a village of long and short grass houses that lay sprawled about the bay with steep precipices of black lava at its back. Clumps of coconut trees and arbors of low-spreading hau trees scattered along the shoreline gave shade from the burning sun.

The pig-faced man took me to the women's hut. I crouched to enter the small doorway. It smelled of human bodies too close together for too long a time. Like an animal den, the scent of the women was deep and fecund. The oversweet smell of fading 'ilima blooms and coconut oil from flickering kukui lamps camouflaged the scent of blood. One woman, lying on her side facing the hut wall with her arm resting on full round hips, did not stir. Another wahine, pounding the skin of young breadfruit shoots for kapa cloth, stopped her labors and peered at me through the shadows. A third, stripping leaves for a hula skirt, squinted into the bright sunlight and covered her dark sunken eyes when I entered.

"I am Wai-nani from Hana," I said, breaking the stillness.

No one spoke for a very long time. They seemed to have no interest in the stranger in their midst. I wondered if I were a ghost being. Had my spirit slipped from the corner of my eye in the night? Was I dreaming that I was present among these wahine who saw no one? A frail, young woman rose from her mat and came toward me. She extended her slim arm and took my hand in her own delicate one.

"I am Huali. Tell us of your journey," she said with a soft, generous smile.

The beating of my heart was stilled by the tenderness of her touch. The others stared blankly from the black shadows of their private chamber, making no sounds of welcome.

"Come sit with me. Let us know your story," she said with a voice that held the lilt of birdsong.

Not yet woman, Huali was narrow of hip with budding mounds for breasts. Her skin was light, as though it had never known sun, and she smelled of ginger. Clasping her polished black hair that fell to her ankles, she lifted it with one hand draping it over her bare shoulder, and settled onto her mat. She pulled me gently down beside her. For many hours I talked story, sharing my journey from Hana with her. The others gathered closer to hear my tale. I saw their dark eyes brighten with excitement when I told them of my surfing adventures with Eku.

"Where is Eku now?" came from the wahine who had feigned sleep when I arrived.

"He is with Laka and Puki in the heart of moana."

"Does he come to you when you call him?"

"Not always. When I swim, I whistle to him in his tongue. He does not always hear me."

"Is Laka not jealous?" she persisted.

"She knows now that I am a friend. Still, I don't tempt her emotions with carelessness."

"What of your father? You have broken his kapu. Will he not kill you when he finds you?" the wahine stripping leaves asked.

"Makaha is my husband. He is a great warrior and will protect me from harm."

"He left you in K'au," came from a wahine with deep furrows in the forehead of her moon-shaped face.

A hush settled over the women waiting for my reply.

"He was called by his chief. He did not have the heart to say good-bye. He will know me as his wife when he returns from the mountains."

The beautiful wahine on the mat resting her chin in the crook of her arm laughed. "A man's love only stays as long as his ule."

The other women giggled.

I took Huali's hand in mine. Her tapered fingers, having been massaged from birth to make them long and slender, were those of a chiefess that never knew work.

"Let's go outside and feel the sea breeze on our skin and the warmth of the sun," I said.

She looked at me with tender, almond eyes laced with long black lashes.

"It is kapu for women to leave this hale while they are impure. You are a stranger being tested. It is not wise," she said.

"I care nothing for such wisdom."

Huali, born of the highest blood caste, was forced to live her life in seclusion. Long hidden from the vitality of daylight, sequestered from the company of others her age, she chafed to run free. I saw excitement mounting in her innocent brown eyes as she contemplated freedom from restraints placed upon her from birth.

"Take me to a rock pool where I may rinse the salt of the sea from my skin," I said.

She trembled nervously, but I could feel her gathering strength from me. She turned to the others. "Speak to no one of this. Keep it locked in your heart with the other secrets of women," she said to the others, who looked upon us with fear in their eyes.

Then she grabbed my hand, lifted the cloth blocking the sun and spirited me out the door. She ran airily and lightly along a trail lined with frilly ferns like a butterfly flitting on the breeze. I followed her through green foliage brushing aside giant fronds shading the path. Plumy palms overhead protected us from the burning rays of the sun filtering through their leaves in streams of light. I heard a rustle in the thicket and chanced to see the moho bird. It cannot fly or swim in the sea, but only lives in the woods' cover because if it went into the ocean its feathers would become heavy and water-soaked. It stared at me with beautiful black eyes.

I felt its helplessness. This bird is easily captured in its nesting home, and its flesh is used as food, but today she would remain free.

Huali ran ahead laughing with her lavish black mane flowing behind her. When she reached the foot of a sheer cliff she did not stop but scrambled up the slick root-strewn trail. I grabbed hold of tree roots embedded in the mud wall and pulled myself up the face of the cliff. She seemed not to notice that her legs were covered with rich red mud from climbing. She leaned out over a ledge in the cliff and looked down upon me, laughing with small, pearl-white teeth.

"Wai-nani, come quickly. We are almost there."

She disappeared into the thick green and was gone like a mamo bird grown cagey from hunters with their bird poles in hand. I could hear the full throat of a torrent of water tumbling down the wall of the mountains. Scrambling to keep up, pulled by the sound of life-giving water, I was breathless when I reached the cleft in the pali where Huali stood waiting for me.

We stood on a broad rock ledge overlooking two great rivers merging into one powerful torrent that cascaded into a mountain pool deep enough for swimming. A three-banded rainbow arced over the fall in the rising mists. A grove of palm and banana trees gave shade to the pool. Maidenhair ferns clung to the sides of the lava bowl along with tufts of golden bunch grass. She glanced over her shoulder to see that I was behind her then plunged headlong into the pool. I gladly followed her into the mountain stream. I shot deep into the water, feeling an icy chill as I went deeper. Blood rushed to my brain. I swam up to the light filtering through the clear water to catch my breath and found Huali at the surface. Laughing, she splashed water in my face and kicked away from me, sending a powerful spray in her wake.

Huali climbed the lava rock ledge beside the torrent and waved me to follow. Though my feet were hard with callus, the porous rock cut into my skin. When I arrived at the top of the ledge, where the life of the fall began, she had vanished down a faint path worn into the black rock. I followed, calling to her to wait. After a breathless romp across the barren ledge, I found her sitting beside a steaming rock pool with her dark hair draped over her shoulders.

"Menehune, the servants of Pele living at the bottom of this pool, keep the fires burning here," she said.

I sprawled beside the lip of the smoldering, boiling pot long enough to catch my breath. Then, I gingerly put a toe in to test the water. It was hot, like the breath of the volcano. Huali laughed and slipped over the lava lip into the pool, sinking down to her shoulders in the scalding broil. Following her lead, I sank into the pool and felt my flesh begin to melt from my bones. Resting my head on the rock ledge, I watched streamers of cloud wisps drift across the sapphire blue dome overhead. The voice of the twin waterfall charging over the ledge into the deep rock pool filled my thoughts. It spoke of old lives made new. It whispered of the ghosts of maidens hiding in the rocks behind the sheer white veil of water from the deep heart of the mountain. Muscles, used up from many days of swimming, slackened while my spirit floated freely in the white mists of the boiling pot.

"You are the only one who knows I come here," she said. "My father hides me from the sun and the eyes of young warriors."

"Why have you trusted me with your secret?

"Because I know you are not afraid."

"But I am afraid. I know that death comes to those who break kapus. I have seen it."

Soon sweat poured over my brow and dripped into my eyes. Huali laughed at the sight of my crab red face. She pulled herself upon the lava rock ledge out of the steaming caldron and ran laughing back to the waterfall and plunged headlong again into the cold pool. She remained submerged for a full minute, frightening me, before she reappeared beaming with exultation. I jumped in. Red blood burst in my brain when my hot flesh hit the icy mountain flow. A tingling flush rushed through my body, stopping at my fingertips. Starbursts of white light, like fireflies in the night, circled around my head. As I swam in the rock pool, I felt the churning underneath the surface from the thunderous water pouring down from the heavens. I swam closer to the torrent and felt myself being sucked under into the churning whirlpool beneath the surface. Fearing the lonely monsters that lurk in the depths of rich water, I kicked hard to be free of their pull.

Once back on land, I sprawled on the warm lava rock to dry. The intense rays of the sun spiraled deep into my belly. My body became heavy, as though melting into the earth. Mana pulsed through my palms, up into my arms to settle deep inside my belly. I chanced to break the spell, opened my eyes and blinked back the bright aura of red sun. Huali had joined me and lay still on the rock with arms spread to the warming rays. She smiled wide. Her beauty dazzled me. Spirits buoyed, we both felt powerful that day.

I spied a clump of perfect bananas overhead ripening in the sun. The heavy purple bloom with dangling fruit nearly drooped to the ground.

"I will get them, Huali, if you will have one with me," I said, pointing to the red bananas of Ku.

"No! You know they are kapu. We will die if we eat them. We will be stoned by the priests."

"I don't believe we will die. Who will tell them?"

Huali looked at me with serious, dark eyes, then looked up at the bananas.

"I am hungry," she said softly.

I shinnied up the trunk of the banana tree and grabbed the clump of bananas. Swinging over the rock ledge, I pulled them free using the weight of my body and landed on the ledge beside Huali. I held the largest banana up to the sun, peeled its firm skin from the ripe flesh and held it up to her. She broke a piece from the crown of the fruit and I took another. We looked deeply into each other's eyes. I extended my piece to her and she put her piece close to my lips.

"If this is to be my last breath, it will be a sweet ending."

"If this is to be my last breath, I will find you in Po," she whispered.

We ate of the banana together, daring time to stand still.

9
The Village of Kealakekua

The glimmer of light on the mountains found me at the shore watching a pod of spinner dolphins play in the opalescent water. In the still morning I heard their breath as they shot puffs of water into the sky from their blowholes. There were so many I couldn't count them all as they plunged in and out of the pearly water in musical unison. Silently, they each knew the steps of their secret dance as they churned the water into a frothy broil. Several babies breached the water doing complete circles in the air. Unable to contain myself any longer, I slipped into the cool to join them in their watery world. Water has a double life of power and humility, but most of all it touches me with companionship. I no longer felt alone and frightened at what would come of the day.

I could see the heiau grounds at the foot of steep cliffs on the north shore of the bay. Ka'eo had told me about the maka'ainana who lived on the south side of the bay. Lako, the Moi of Hawai'i, and the high chiefess Ohaha lived with the other ali'i at the north end. His hale was long with a peaked roof thatched with pili grass. Many smaller hales surrounded his long house. He was much loved, and his power was great. This day, I would meet Lako and learn my fate. Would it be death for disobedience or a life of sweet love from a gushing spring with Makaha?

Stretching my arms out in knifelike strokes that cut through the placid calm, I tried to absorb courage from the all-powerful sea. The coolness and rhythmical breathing of the ocean steadied me. The life of the village faded from my mind, and my thoughts grew still in the billowy cushion of water. The caress of the wet arms of moana made me light in heart, body and mind. When I reached the dolphins, I watched their powerful, silver bodies streaking beneath me. I called to Eku, but he was not there.

After my swim, I waited for Huali in the wahine's hale to come for me. Her time in the women's hut was over, but she was to return to take me to the house of Lako. Makaha was still in the mountains gathering koa wood for war canoes. I was to face the Moi of Hawai'i alone. The sun had crowned the mountaintops when she lifted the flap to the hale, entered and took me by the hand.

"It is time for you to meet my father."

"Your father!" I was stunned.

"Yes. I told him that you are my friend."

I followed Huali's graceful, liquid body down a well-worn path paved with stones through the center of the village. Her lavender and purple p'au, draped over slim hips, swayed like a palm tree in the breeze as she walked. Many eyes were upon us. Children giggled and ran around us in circles. Women stopped their labors and looked upon me with suspicious stares. Men placing wood in the imu for the evening meal looked at the stranger in their midst with wild curiosity. I kept my eyes to the ground, not wanting to offend.

When we passed by the temple grounds I caught the stench of burning hair and flesh floating on the air. I saw the remains of two warriors with fat dripping onto hot embers from the oven where they were to be cooked until they were ashes.

"What kapu was broken?" I asked.

"They were accused of having shared food with me," Huali said without flinching. Someone had told her father of their indiscretion with his daughter. My life was in her hands. If she hinted to Lako that we had shared a kapu banana, I would quickly join the warriors in the ovens as punishment for breaking the sacred laws of the land.

Two retainers stood at the entrance to Lako's court. Once inside the long thatched house with a high-pitched ceiling, I dropped to my knees, and put my forehead to the mat-covered floor. Lako sat in the center of a small gathering of royals. A priest holding a white-feathered kahili staff sat beside the high chief. A retainer fanned Lako with a huge palm to keep the flies at bay. I kept my eyes to the ground. I dared not look into his eyes until he acknowledged me.

"This is Wai-nani, from royal parents in Hana. She has traveled many miles to our village," Huali said.

"Why have you come?" asked Lako, the Moi of Hawai'i.

I dared to meet his gaze. "I am wife to Makaha."

"Only you say this is so."

"Ka'eo knows this truth."

"Ka'eo is in Waipio Valley and will not return on your account."

"Wai-nani is an ali'i chiefess, the daughter of Malu, chief of Hana," Huali said.

"Yes. But, my father does not know I am here."

"Do you not respect your father's wishes?" asked Lako.

"I look for pardon in your wisdom, oh heavenly one," I replied softly.

"A wahine who does not obey her father will not obey me," he said sternly, squinting eyes coated with a ghostly white film. Long yellow nails curled at the end of his knobbed fingers. Lako had ruled the island of Hawai'i for many years, and though not long from the underworld of Po, he was still alert and insightful.

"She could be useful," Ohaha said from a reclining position at her husband's side. Her deep voice rose like a bird escaping its cage. She struggled to lift her bulk to sit upright. Her great breasts heaved with a fearsome ocean swell of sensuality. She stretched her head up as though trying to lift it outside her mountainous flesh. Her deep-set eyes, the color of kukui nuts, were those of a woman who was once a great beauty. The aging chief, with smoke-white eyes, looked to his wife for wisdom.

"Your mother was wife to Pano," she said, scrutinizing my body.

The chief sniggered slyly at this news.

"Yes, my mother, Ha'aheo, was the favorite wife of Pano,"

I nodded. "But when her belly swelled with me, she left his court with my father, and our ohana became the enemy of the Moi of Maui."

"You are right, Ohaha. There may be more than a silly wahine who thinks she is the wife of my best warrior before us." Lako smiled, exposing rotting teeth.

A slender young man with long slim legs coiled by the right side of Lako taunted me with cunning eyes. I felt warm as blood rushed to my cheeks under his scrutiny.

"Pano would enjoy the seed of his favorite wife for dessert," he said with a sneering laugh that made me remember the riddle of the old woman at the Place of Refuge.

"What has two heads, walks like a man, but makes love like a woman?" That which was secret was no long hidden. It was 'Ele 'ele, the girl-boy high chief born to this royal pair.

The priest looked upon me with suspicious eyes. He looked to be drawn a long way under from drinking 'awa. "What if she is a spy of Pano?" he asked.

Fragrant is the soup of the big mullet, for Ohaha, whose body was swimming in the broth of prosperity, spoke for me. "A spy would not be so foolish. She would not come to our shore with no introduction," she said, making the truth seem obvious.

"A spirit traveler would have no such fear," the priest responded, still nervous about my presence. "She should be tested so that we may know for certain whether she is a spirit or human," he persisted.

"Koa is right. Give her the test now, then," Lako said.

Koa brought forth a bowl of water and pointed with a long, thin finger, indicating that I should lean over it so he could look for my reflection. The reflection is the spirit of a living person; a mere spirit casts no reflection. Koa hovered close to my face to see me smiling back at him in the water.

"She is a living person sent by the god Kanaloa, Ruler of the Sea," he proclaimed.

Lako grunted acknowledgment that I had passed the test. "You may live until Makaha returns." Then he dismissed me to the women's long house to ponder my fate and wait for Makaha. If he did not declare me his wife when he returned, I would be a toy for the court, or killed. If he declared his love for me, I would sit at his side as an ali'i chiefess in the house of Lako.

10
Clapping Waves

While awaiting the return of Makaha, I remembered the legend of Ku and his bride from the underworld. In the long ago, the great war god Ku was mortal and lived on the western side of the island of Hawai'i. He chose Hina, the Goddess of the Moon, to be his wife, and she bore two mortal children. Their son, Hiku of the Forest, lived with his mother in the woodlands of North Kona. Here he learned the sounds of the forest, the rushing winds, and the secrets of the cool mists that cling to the mountainsides. Their daughter, Kewalu, dwelt under the care of guardian chiefs and priests by the temple in Kealakekua, and she learned the ways of the sea.

Kewalu played in the tabu surf waters of Kona, riding great waves on her board. Her beauty was legend and her skill in riding the surf exceeded that of anyone the people had ever seen. Multitudes gathered from near and far to watch the grace of this beautiful woman in the sea. Their pleasure was so great that when they clapped their hands, the sound was like the voices of many thunderstorms. Hiku heard the clapping from his mountaintop and came down to the seashore to see the reason for the happiness of the people. Hiku was so struck by the beauty of his sister that he anointed himself with the oil of the kukui nut and joined her in the foaming surf.

I determined to bring Makaha to me just as Kewalu brought Hiku to her. Kealakekua Bay is flat and has sharp jagged lava rock ledges surrounding the harbor. The bright green parrotfish and the black and white striped angel fish and many fishes of rainbow colors live in the reef, but there are no waves. Still young, many of the shores on the island of Hawai'i are lined with the harsh edges of new lava. I swam first up the coast, then down until I found Hookena, a cove where the surf breaks on a bow-shaped beach with soft white sand.

Huali gave me 'Ele 'ele's olo board that stood twice my height. I paddled on it for an hour each day to reach my surfing cove. Each time I paddled out, the ocean delivered me some unexpected gift. On the worst days when the waves were rough chop breaking too soon on the shore, I learned better timing. On the smallest days, when the sea was flat, I waited long moments between rides, rocking in gentle swells watching colorful shoals of fish and the green sea turtle floating beneath my board.

Then there were the perfect days when glassy, head-high waves peeled from my favorite breaking point. I met them at the jade green face, was lifted into the great heave of the swell and rode the waves balanced on my board in the sun-shot curl, beneath the cresting foam, until the wave crashed to its death on the shore. Each wave was unique in its power and form. I imagined myself in a dance with the sea and tried to absorb its rhythm through my feet.

My thoughts went to the journey of each wave. I looked to the limitless horizon and wondered from what place had each wave's life begun. Did it begin at the heart of a storm and like a pebble thrown into a pond, ripple away in many circles? Did the swell gather power from smaller waves, absorbing them, becoming higher and thicker with life? Strong enough to lift the blue whale and toss the fisherman's canoe, a great wave rolls on oblivious to all in the way of its destiny to die on a far shore. I realized that the mystery of moana would never be grasped, that I could only try to live in harmony with the heartbeat of its pulsing power.

One day an unusual swell came without warning as I basked in the sun on my board. I felt the immense power mounting before I saw the smoking back of the bearded giant. Standing in the heart of the wave, my mind finally quieted as I caught a long ride. There was nothing in the universe but the power of the water beneath my feet. I knew then I could not live without the ocean, that I was as much a part of it now as the turquoise parrotfish darting in and out of the green coral reef. When I left the sea, I saw pricks of sparkling light flying about my body, the mana of moana.

Others began to join me at my cove. First Huali came with her retainer. She sat in the shade of a great palm tree hiding from the rays of the sun blazing in the blue dome overhead. Born of the highest blood-rank, she was surrounded at all times by specially selected attendants. She was permitted to walk abroad only during the twilight hour, since it was considered unfitting that the noonday sun should ever shine upon her. It was an act of great courage that she should venture forth in broad daylight to watch me. Her father was a stern chief who enforced the ancient kapus, but Huali was his favorite child from a union with his sister, who died at her birth, and therefore bold in the light of his love. Floating upon the heaving swells of azure blue on my olo board, feeling the breeze tickle the backs of my legs, I pitied her and at the same time was grateful that she was my friend.

Like the rippling water where birds gather, her quiet peaceful nature attracted others. Next the young boys and girls came to test their skills. Thirty or more keiki rocked with me in the lap of moana, waiting patiently for the next set of waves to rise. Soon men and women left their labors in the village to come and watch the wave-sliders each day before the sun settled into its burning bed for the night. I heard them clapping on the shore as I ducked in and out of the waves, tipping my board up the crest and then sliding down the smooth face of each one.

One day, while perched atop my board, scanning the horizon, I spied a familiar ragged fin slicing through the water. I clicked my tongue and whistled in Eku's voice. He lifted his rubbery snout from the water and rested it on my board. I looked deep into his soulful eye, slipped off my board and greeted him in a watery tumble until I felt the old tingling in the pit of my belly. We rolled in great circles for a few seconds until Laka appeared with Puki, now a strong swimmer, at her shoulder. After a warm aloha, Eku let me glide with him through the cresting waves. I clung to his dorsal fin and lost touch with all else but the grace of the moment as we caught wave after wave together.

Children ran into the waves squealing with excitement at the sight of the fish-woman. The old chief Lako came with his chiefess Ohaha. Her retainers carried her to the shore in her manele so that she might watch Eku and me riding the deep blue waters. Thatched covers were built for the royals, and food was provided for their comfort. About thirty children bobbed just beyond where the waves break, waiting for the next set. Once they found their balancing spot, they moved forward onto their boards then dipped back to the rear with bent knees. They rocked, turning their boards into the frothy waves as they rode across the bay.

Each day I looked to see if Makaha had heard their laughter from the mountains and would be drawn to the source of joy. My love for him, like a billow before my eyes, left a constant yearning with the image of his perfection ever before me. A full moon passed before Makaha returned with the other warriors, bringing with them the double-hulled outrigger canoes they carved with care out of koa trees. They brought bundles of breadfruit and bananas from the mountains for the makahiki festival soon to begin. But when they arrived the village was empty.

The people had gathered at my surfing cove and covered the mountainside so thickly there was not a place for a bird to light. Makaha strode through them to stand at the seashore. A rainbow aura arced over his head as he stood with strong legs, arms crossed over his mighty chest. I trembled at the sight of his regal bearing. His muscled body glistened in the sun as he watched me with an intense, inscrutable stare. If he denied knowledge of me, I might have an eye gouged out or even be clubbed to death by Koa the priest for my acts of disobedience. If he embraced me, I would live by his side and know respect from all the Island people.

A hushed silence settled upon the villagers. Even Lako and Ohaha remained still as they awaited Makaha's decision. My heart flew from my breast to his when he plunged into the surf and swam to me with powerful strokes. When he reached me and clasped me in his great arms, my breath began again, and my heart rose and fell with the swells of the sea. I clung to him with strong legs wrapped about his narrow waist. He threw his head back, flashing a dazzling smile, and laughed long and loud.

"Wai-nani will swim with me today."

The crowd cheered in great pandemonium as we body surfed together. He loved the ocean, caressing each wave. He treated it tenderly as if handling a woman. Fanning straight arms out from enormous shoulders, he glided atop the waves as though he were a merman. Like Eku, he swam with the speed of the wind, finding the heart of each wave, becoming a part of it. Eku, who watched from a distance, lifted his silver body out of the water and skipped backwards on his tail. Laka laughed, clicking her tongue like a stick stroked across a gourd. Excited by our love, Puki clapped his jaws and swam frantic circles around us. Then, my dolphin family sped out to sea, leaving me to wave-slide with Makaha.

I gave him my board. We paddled together to the deep belly of a swelling wave. We were lifted and found our balancing place. Once astride the white back of a powerful wave, Makaha put strong hands about my waist and lifted me to his shoulders. I rode upon the comet's fiery tail through the arc of the rainbow embracing us in our joyous reunion. Above the roar of the waves I heard the din of the clapping multitudes. When our ride ended, Makaha took me by the hand and led me to Lako. Ohaha, resting on her side, lifted herself in our honor. Huali gazed upon us with loving wonder. 'Ele 'ele stood in the shadows and looked upon our open love with steaming eyes.

"Lako, you have met Wai-nani," Makaha said with a seldom-seen grin.

"So it is true."

Makaha said, "Yes. She is my wife."

And so, I was accepted into the royal house of Lako and became known as Makaha's bride.

Makaha and I went to the boiling pot by the waterfall where I rinsed his shoulders with a sea sponge. I was prepared to forgive him for leaving me without a word. If unable to do this, I would have made the great journey to Kealakekua Bay and risked my life to enter his village in vain. I hoped he would at least ask me to forgive him. But he saw no wrong in his doing.

"You left me without a word of your going," I ventured.

"Ka'eo was left to care for you. I would have come back to my thinking place."

"But not for me" is what I wanted to say, but I kept my lips silent. He had chosen rightly today at the seashore. There would be no more talk about his rude departure, even though my heart was still as tender as a too-ripe banana. My love was for a mighty warrior with a fate larger than himself. When love is given, love should be returned. Anger is the thing that gives no life.

11
Makahiki

With the return of the warriors it was time to celebrate. Eight moons out of the year the Island people labor long and hard fishing, pounding kapa cloth from mulberry bark, tending their taro terraces, thatching houses, weaving and waging war. Now, for four moons it was time to rest and feast, and for the warriors to strengthen their war skills through sport.

A feast was made ready for Lono, the God of the Clouds, Winds, Seas and Fertility. Lono called the people to enjoy their island-wide harvest. Flags hoisted over the heiau waved gaily in the gentle sea breezes. Koa led a procession carrying the image of Lono, a cross figure bound with pieces of the pala fern, hung with feather leis fluttering in the wind, through the villages. A piece of white kapa cloth was basted to the cross piece, from which hung another length of white cloth. This banner was carried from ahupua'a to ahupua'a by the chief's tax collectors throughout the island, collecting bounty for the festival.

Maka'ainana paid in kapa, pigs, dogs, fowl, malo and pa'u of soft cloth in many wondrous colors. Finely woven mats, fishnets, adzes, bundles of pounded taro and the prized crimson and yellow feathers of the mamo and 'o'o birds used to make the capes of royalty, huge mounds of breadfruit, bananas and sweet potatoes were collected for the high chiefs. Most of the bounty went to Lako's long house and to the priests for ritual; the rest was shared among all who lived in the village.

The tantalizing smell of many pigs roasting in ground ovens

scented the air. Before the sun was high, men stuffed wood and shredded banana tree trunks into the long, deep imus filled with cooking stones. In the early afternoon, red-hot stones were placed inside the cleaned pigs. Bundles of sweet potatoes, bananas, taro, fish and other delicacies wrapped in ti leaves were then placed beside the meat in the imus. Rushes were then laid over the cooking food to seal in the heat. Before sundown the flesh of the pork would be tender and ready to shred. I helped collect delicacies from the sea—opihi, crab and squid—to be blended with taro tops and coconut milk.

While the meal was cooking the people played games. The elders hunched over konane boards while children squealed as they swung on morning glory vines. There were races on walking stilts and contests with spinning tops made of kukui nuts with bamboo splinters for stems. Young boys practiced fencing with blunted spears. Warriors practiced spear throwing and bowling. I loved to watch the papa holua racing. The long, narrow wooden sled was covered with lau hala matting and kapa. Thick cordage was used to bind the hard woods used for runners. A sledding track was made on the slope of a hill on a rock foundation that was surfaced with soil. Any rocks on the run were covered with grass and oiled with kukui nut oil to make the run slippery. I yearned to join the men screaming in mock terror on these rides, but this sport was restricted to male ali'i.

A crowd gathered to watch the boxing and wrestling matches between the 'Alapa warriors. These young men, bred for strength, grace and agility, all of the highest ali'i cast, were Lako's pride. They all stood over six feet tall with rippling muscles gleaming of kukui oil that made them slippery and harder to catch in the death clenches of an enemy. Lako sat beneath a thatched cover for shade on a platform overlooking the contests. Ohaha lay on the mat beside her husband, resting her head in the palm of her hand. Beads of perspiration formed on her brow and nose, and her breathing was labored in the thick afternoon air. I sat beside Makaha, who watched with keen interest the match between a maka'ainana and one of his best warriors.

Mau, a solid, sturdy fisherman, did not have the stature of the ali'i warrior, but he was nimble and out-danced his opponent, who seemed ponderous and slow beside him. Stocky and low to the ground with bunched muscles, Mau circled the warrior looking for his chance to strike. In a swift action he rushed inside the circle, clasped the towering warrior with arms as strong as koa wood and lifted him off the ground. The warrior squirmed to be free, but Mau held him tightly with the relentless grip of the eel. The 'Alapa warrior lifted his knee and landed a powerful blow squarely into Mau's groin. He let out a low groan but still did not release his hold. The warrior flailed like a gaffed mahi-mahi struggling to be free of the hook. Mau let go of his neck, swirled him about in one quick movement, took hold of the warrior's arm and lifted it up behind his back until it reached his head. The crunch of bone was heard as the warrior's shoulder gave way under the force of Mau's hold. When he finally released him, the luckless warrior's arm fell limp to his side. Lako lifted his spear signaling the end of this match. Makaha waved to Mau to come closer.

"You are maka'ainana?"

"Yes, I am a fisherman, a loyal servant to Lako."

Makaha looked to Lako. "I want this man with me in battle," he said.

Lako looked at Mau. "Go home and tell your family that you are to join the ali'i. You will sail to Maui and be a part of the war against Pano."

Mau beamed at the great honor.

Shining ginger and ti leaves along with ferns and gay blossoms decorated the eating mats. The air was filled with the mingled fragrance of flowers and many steaming imus bulging with savory foods. Great sprays of ulu bearing both fruit and large glossy leaves were laid beside mounds of steaming food. Two mats were prepared: one for the men, to be presided over by Lako, and another for the women, with Ohaha at the head. Even during makahiki it was tabu for the Island people to eat together.

Makaha always sat at his uncle's right side and Lako's birth son 'Ele 'ele sat at his left. Since the death of his brother Niolo, Lako had raised Makaha as though he were his own son. He had given his strong, athletic nephew every advantage. The kahuna had tutored him for long hours in the ritual chants handed down from the ancestors. Lako's best warrior was assigned to Makaha to teach him the arts of spear throwing, wrestling, boxing and tactics of war. Makaha thrived under the adoring eyes of his uncle and would do anything to please the aging chief.

'Ele 'ele was slight, like his half-sister Huali, and had slim hips that swayed like a woman when he walked. His face was narrow with high cheek bones and glittering almond-shaped eyes. Of the highest caste, he did no labor. He had been assigned twin warriors at his birth to carry him, so that his feet did not touch the ground. His skin was smooth and his limbs long, elegant and lean. Once 'Ele 'ele took his place beside Lako, the chief stuck two fingers into his poi bowl, lifted the rich purple paste to his lips and smacked them with great delight, signaling the feast to begin. Lako spoke between mouthfuls of shredded pork roasted to succulent perfection.

"My brother told me that you are the lifter of the Naha Stone, Makaha. Is this true?"

"It is so. While a beardless youth, I lifted the boulder resting in Hilo."

"The priests have said that the lifter of the Naha Stone shall rule the Island people," Lako continued, searching for the nature of Makaha's ambitions.

"Prophecies of priests do not always come true in ways that we know," Makaha said.

Lako laughed. "It is said that no warrior can defeat the lifter of the Naha Stone. Who better to lead my men against Pano?"

"Why do they call you the hard-shelled crab?" asked 'Ele 'ele.

"It was the name given to me when I won my first battle," Makaha said.

"The strength of the crab is in the claw—all noise but no action. We have not seen you in a match, Makaha. What if two warriors were to meet you on the playing field? Would this be a fair battle? Could you then be defeated?"

Makaha remained silent and continued to eat his meal in thoughtful contemplation before replying to the challange.

"A match between the twins against Makaha," 'Ele 'ele persisted, addressing his father, "would test the prophecy."

Lako agreed. "Yes, that would be a good match."

"I am not in need of proving, but if you wish this match it will be my honor to defend the great chief Lako. I will meet the twins in the playing field," Makaha said.

That evening when the purple clouds, tinged with pink, slipped into a wine dark sea, the torches were lit for the hula dancers. Dressed in a ti-leaf skirt, draped in leis made from 'ilima flowers and seashells, I stood with the other women holding hands beneath the hau trees waiting to hear the voice of the conch shell. We meditated, silently praying to Laka, born in the clouds, for grace to flow through our movements. I remembered the story of the girl raised with dolphins. She learned to move gracefully by watching the flowers bend in the breeze and the palms that sway in the wind. She learned to sing by listening to the melodies of the streams. The haunting deep throat of the shell rang through the twilight.

Before beginning our dance, we went to our knees touching forehead to the ground before the image of Lono and asked for his blessing. Ohaha sat on a hollow platform with legs splayed around the hollow gourd used to make music for the dancers. Two more large women, with bulging arms and gray hair bound in long braids down their backs, sat by her side. They pounded their gourds rhythmically on the wooden floor and tapped them with their hands to create a steady solid beat. Ohaha sang out in eerie, sonorous tones telling the story of the birth of her royal children.

She pulled her great body forward, straddling a hole in the platform readied for the mock birthing. She moved her upper body in circles from the waist and made supplications to the gods with arms extended to the heavens. Groaning in guttural sounds that came from deep in her belly, she remembered the pain. She breathed into the agony and did not struggle against it. Exhausted from the reenactment, she let out a high-pitched yell when the remembered child dropped from her womb into the waiting basket. Then she folded over, resting upon the gourd held between her legs.

This marked the time for a line of wahine dancers to enter. With knees bent, hips swaying, we slid into formation. Many rows of dancers doing the same steps in unison gained power from one another's mana, as we lifted fingertips to the darkening skies. The click of the shells strapped to our ankles added to the music made by the steady repetitions of the palms upon the gourds. A warrior beat solidly on a drum made from the skin of Mano the shark. We danced until the bright moon overhead cast shadows. I felt energy rising from my toes to the top of my head and felt it shoot to the heavens.

When the dance ended, I was moved to song. My voice carried through the still air like liquid sunshine. I spoke of my love for Makaha whose cloud would rest on the mountains of all the Islands. I bragged about his tenderness to me. Sleeping in my lover's arms, I felt like Pele floating in the mist around Mauna Kea. I felt tremendous power as my supplication to Makaha from deep in my heart rose to the sparkling stars glittering in a velvet sky.

Where are you?
Budding kukui flower.
I tasted a delicious morsel
So sweet in the throat.
Persistent is this one thought
That you and I be close together
Here is the rope, looped
To snare your heartbeats
My budding kukui flower.

At the end of my song Makaha came to me. He took my hands in his, tenderly kissing them before the multitude. They were to know of our great love. Then he led me away from the rest. I followed him through the forest filled with night sounds, the hoot of the owl and the rush of the wind stirring the palms, to a bluff overlooking the sea. The moon cast a bright path across the dark water breaking on black sand in an undulating line of quick-silver. He took me in his arms, enfolding my body with his own.

"Wai-nani, my sweet, never-fading flower," he whispered. He cupped my breasts in his strong hands and sucked on them like a greedy child. He loved me many times in many ways. Above me his face, framed in a wild tangled mane, was lit by the halo of the moon. He looked down upon me with dancing eyes. Behind him I saw the jealous gaze of Hina, Goddess of the Moon, looking down upon our coupling. Once married to Ku, she knew of the pleasure I was receiving and the joy of two bodies binding on the powerful current of love.

12
The Keeper of Ku

Slate clouds curled on the horizon on the day of the match between the twins Keku and Puahia and Makaha. The sun, struggling to be free of its wet blanket, sent silver shafts of light down on the still waters in Kealakekua Bay. Heavy rains the night before had made the grass slick and the ground slippery red mud. Still the villagers came to see the final contest of makahiki between the mighty warriors. Bets were placed by ali'i and commoner alike to be held by Koa. The priest carried the mask of Ku the war god and snatcher of lands, a bright yellow featherhead with sunken eyes and a royal red helmet, atop his spear. He planted it next to Lako, sitting upon his platform overlooking the wrestling field with Ohaha and 'Ele 'ele on either side. I sat next to Huali in the cover provided for her by her retainer.

The twins were to wield short ihe spears. To even the contest Makaha was given a poluolu, the long spear with a blade point formed by trimming down the round shaft of hard wood in cutting edges. The butt end was thicker and used for pounding the enemy. The twins' short spears were about half the length of the poluolu with barbed heads at the tops of the shafts. My belly churned with bile at the thought of Makaha's innards being dragged from his body on the barbs of a spear that found its mark. They each had a pahoa dagger at their waist. Makaha's dagger was capped with shark teeth while the twins carried long curved blades.

The warriors faced one another in silence, awaiting Lako's signal for the match to begin. When Lako drove his spear into the wet earth, Makaha and the twins tensed into the warrior's stance with knees bent, staring intently into one another's eyes, and began to move in a circle. The twins, of regal descent, were magnificent with long bones wrapped in tense muscle beneath lava-black skin. The blaze of fire in Makaha's eyes frightened me.

Each warrior looked for a vulnerable moment in which to thrust a spear. The twins struck first, moving in together trying to confuse Makaha. Makaha blocked their attack with a single swipe that caught both of the twins' weapons. The twins thrust their spears in unison, like fish brothers feeling their way in the sea without words. Makaha evaded their thrusts, catching them both with the solid blows of his long spear. The knock of wood upon wood sounded like the beat of the war dance.

Many long minutes they circled one another, neither losing nor gaining ground. Suddenly, Makaha charged the twins, flailing his spear in a circle that caught them off guard. Keku tripped and went to the ground, and his brother stepped in front of him to protect him from Makaha's death strike. The crowd let go a communal gasp. Keku recovered and jumped back in time to fend off Makaha's thrust of the spear that missed his flat belly by an inch. Makaha's spear stuck in the ground, leaving him vulnerable. Puahia lunged toward Makaha with jagged barbs strong enough to gaff a swordfish. Makaha sidestepped the plunge and took the spear in his powerful hand, yanking it from the grip of Puahia, who was dazed and stunned by his action. The crowd cheered wildly. Lako smiled wide at his best warrior's feat, and 'Ele 'ele looked sour as his cousin displayed godlike powers.

Puahia pulled his dagger from its sheath, signaling the next round of the match. Keku and Puahia circled Makaha like Mano waiting for a weak moment. Makaha held his spear overhead, taunting them with an unprotected belly. An ugly sneer curled his lip, and his eyes were fired like Pele's cauldron. He looked now as though the taste of blood was all that would sate his rage. It shocked me to see cruelty in the eyes of Makaha, who had shown me only tenderness.

Keku and Puahia separated, jumping one behind Makaha and one in front of him. Makaha slipped the butt end of his shaft into his palm and lifted it savagely under the chin of Keku while the spear tip kept his brother at bay. Keku's head snapped back, and blood sprayed from his mouth in pink foam. Knocked senseless with the blow, he went to his knees. His brother was left to defend himself against Makaha, who turned to face his enemy. Blood lust fired, he was eager to send the tip of his spear to Puahia's heart, but something in him had shifted. He was no longer defending himself against his enemy, now he was playing a cruel game.

Puahia stood bravely looking into the fired eyes of Makaha without flinching. Makaha, who wanted the blood sport to last longer, tossed his spear, plunging it into a banana tree. Puahia, left with his short spear and dagger, took heart. Makaha took out his dagger embedded with shark teeth and swung it menacingly over his head. Puahia took the challenge and stepped toward Makaha, jabbing his short spear near his heart. Makaha knocked the spear from Puahia's hand, using his dagger as a club, and sent it flying. Puahia pulled his dagger, and they faced each other in an ever-tightening circle. Makaha's muscles were slick with sweat. A wild animal unleashed, his savage intent unnerved his enemy. Puahia lost his resolve. Makaha sensed his weakness, lunged for him, tripped him with a swift kick in back of his knees that took him to the ground. Without hesitation, Makaha smashed the side of Puahia's head with the shark tooth dagger, shredding skin from bone. He took his neck between his hands and snapped the vertebrae. Puahia's spirit left his body with a whimper.

Not a sound was uttered as the villagers were afraid of what they had witnessed. Makahiki games were for testing and training of warriors, not for killing. Lako stood up and lifted his spear out of the blood stained ground marking the end of the battle.

"Today my nephew has shown himself to be a warrior of great skill and daring. He has more than just the strength of the body. The spirit of battle is in him. I make him the keeper of Ku."

An audible gasp escaped the thin lips of 'Ele 'ele, so

shocked was he at this elevation of his cousin's status that brought Makaha even closer to his throne. Koa tried not to let his anger show, but I could see the glint of humiliation spark in his eyes as he handed the feathered head of Ku to Makaha. Makaha took it and lifted the image of the war god high for the multitudes to see. He led the royal procession to the temple between the lines of prostrate maka'ainana and placed Puahia's limp body upon the sacrificial altar. Ku's altar was built upon the blood of a thousand warriors who were either smashed in battle or punished for breaking a kapu. Koa led in ritual chants that took many hours to recite. Handed down through generations, they told the story of the lineage of Lako and all the great chiefs before him. Today the honor to make sacrifices to the gods was bestowed upon Makaha.

Makaha left soon after that for his thinking spot in K'au. He told me he needed to digest his new position in life. There he would chant mele for many days, pulling mana from the heavens into his fingertips, supplicating Pele to keep his anger hot for the coming battle with Pano. It would be many seasons before I would know my tender lover again, for his spirit now belonged to Ku the snatcher of lands.

13
The Curse of Koa

When Makaha returned from K'au there was a great ceremony. The people danced with arms stretched to the sun. Boys and girls played in sunny yellow costumes. Everyone in the village gathered around when a blast from the conch shell signaled the beginning of the war dance led by Makaha. The men sat on a wooden platform. They each held a short stick that they flipped with one hand like a baton, hitting it on the floor in rapid succession while steadily pounding the floor with a tall pole in the other hand. Makaha pounded his spear with ferocious intent, sparking the men to a fury. It was a powerful spectacle that excited the multitudes.

The warriors began a haunting chant in long angry sounds meant to taunt the enemy. Their voices were aggressive, argumentative and hateful.

"Your family is a heap of stinks" came from one warrior.

"You are a pile of dung where pinworms are found" from another.

Jibes intended to wound the enemy's pride were used to break concentration.

The men wore red malos pulled up tight to their waists. Many had fearsome tattoos on their thighs. They danced to an angry frenzy, challenging each other with weapons. One swung a tripping club on the end of a rope in great circles. A practiced warrior could catch an opponent's legs with this weapon, taking his enemy off balance. They settled into a steady, repetitious rhythm, keeping their bodies low to the ground with knees bent, moving them quickly in and out. They danced until exhaustion. Then each dancer crept to the altar of Ku, keeping head bowed, and made an offering to the god they prayed to for protection.

Next morning at the pearly dawn an armada of bronzed 'Alapa warriors nurtured in the skills of war set off in the largest fleet of double and single hulled canoes yet to sail the Islands. Lako sat on the platform of the royal canoe beneath a thatched cover. His retainers included his spittoon carrier to collect spittle and other bodily fluids to prevent an ana'ana priest from collecting them and using them to pray him to death. This servant also tasted all of the high chief's food. The feathered head of Ku rode on the mast. Makaha and Mau, the commoner Makaha had decreed a warrior, shared a single-hulled canoe with five other men paddling in unison.

I watched the triangle tips of their sails until they looked like the fins of Mano upon the horizon. Then I went to Koa for his help. I yearned to feel the quickening of life inside my belly. I sought a potion that would help the seed of Makaha blossom into a son for us to share. Koa sat cross-legged rocking to and fro and chanting softly while he read the 'awa leaves in the bottom of my cup. He stopped suddenly and pointed a bony finger with curled yellow nails to the message.

"You must find the poison fish that dwells in the reef and bring him to me alive. I will make a medicine for you to drink that will kill the ghost spirit blocking the door to your womb."

The nohu fish has many bristling spines tipped with poison to protect him. His orange and white stripes make him hard to find in the sand beneath the swaying coral fans. I searched for many hours, diving deep into the reef, but only saw the bright yellow butterfly fish, the black masked triggerfish and shoals of blue striped taape. An eel with needle sharp teeth showed me his striped face from a tunnel in the finger coral. Sweet lobster crawled upon the powdery sand floor of the sea, but I was not interested in eating this day. I searched for many hours until at last I found the poison fish, snared him in my net and brought him back to Koa.

The wizened kahuna snapped the poison tipped spines off the living fish and tossed the rest aside. He blended them with secret medicines of which only he knew the making. Then he circled his brown hand with bulging blue veins over the cup and chanted a mele to help me conceive. He told me to take the brew in one swallow. I lifted the drink that smelled like crushed worms and gulped it down. The bitter taste lingered for hours, but I was smiling knowing that now I would soon present Makaha with a son.

That night I woke in a sweat. My teeth chattered with chills, but my head was hot and fevered. I reeled in fear when I found I had no feeling in my limbs and could not lift my arms or legs from my mat. I lay there staring into the dark wondering if this was a dream, for if this was real I feared I would not live to see the rising of the morning sun.

Burning images of Lono, Ku, Kane, Kanaloa lighting the night sky with flames appeared before my eyes. Sparks whirling in the hot wind fell upon me. I was choking. My eyes and mouth filled with ashes. The smell of burning flesh, hair and the smell of human oils dripping from the imu were strong upon me. I heard the din of the multitudes wailing. I saw a wahine running through a village with blood streaming down her face.

Huali heard my screams. She lifted my head upon her knee and wiped my face with a fragrant cool cloth and crooned a sweet oli in my ear. She sounded very far away. My belly churned as the potion Koa prepared did battle with the ghost spirit that had slipped inside through the soles of my feet when I was dreaming. She stayed with me until the cramping eased and I could sleep once more. I lived for many days in the hale where the wahine of the village stayed when they are impure. Blood streamed down my legs when I stood. I was too weak to walk so Huali brought bowls of rich poi. I kissed the black tears of Pele that I wore around my neck and prayed to the goddess for strength. When the battle inside me ended, I went to the sea and swam once more.

My body felt light in the soothing turquoise water. I fell into a seamless stroke that carried me far away from the village of

Kealakekua. I wished that I could just keep swimming and never return. Koa had revealed himself as my enemy. He was powerful, and I would have to be on my guard around him. 'Ele 'ele was jealous of his cousin, Makaha, who found favor with Lako, and he had seen a way to hurt him through me. The toothless bent woman had warned me of intrigues in Lako's court, but I had forgotten. I listened to the mewing voices of the whales calling to one another in the deep channel outside the bay. I wanted to follow them to the far away place they go, but I knew I had to return to my human world. I prayed that Koa's curse and the hard lesson he taught me ended here.

Smoke gray clouds crowded low on the horizon the day the fleet returned. From the shore where 'Ele 'ele, Huali and I watched, I could see that Lako's eyes were murky with sorrow. Over half of the brave warriors who set sail one moon ago did not return from Maui. A spy had warned Pano of their coming. He had plenty of time to recruit warriors from the chief of Oahu and had set a trap for them.

'Ele 'ele brushed the old chief's nose with his own in greeting, but Lako spoke no words. He silently embraced his son then went into the shadows of his hale to mourn the deaths of so many fine warriors. I ran to greet Makaha, but he too was filled with a brooding melancholy.

Mau's leg bore a deep jagged gash that severed the flesh from knee to hip. Because he could not walk alone, two warriors with head wounds wrapped in kapa cloth lifted him from the canoe and carried him to the shore. The maka'ainana man who had beaten the ali'i warrior would spend the rest of his days placing hot stones in the imu cooking for others. No more would he man his own canoe and sail free on the vast ocean.

That night Makaha made rough love to me, thrusting like a brute, then fell slack by my side. His sleep was fitful, and he woke with eyes wide, staring into the black of a starless night. I asked him many times to tell me of the blood that filled his dreams, but he would not speak of what had happened in Maui.

A full moon passed before Lako sent for Makaha again.

When he returned to me from this meeting his face was lean and drawn and his wondrous eyes downcast.

"What troubles Makaha? My love is strong enough. You can tell me," I said, knowing that the dark blood filling his dreams was like an inflamed wound in need of lancing. There could be no healing until this was done. But instead of talking he grew more quiet and inward with each passing day since his defeat at the hands of Pano. This day he stood with his broad back turned to me. His shoulders slumped as though the weight of his thoughts was too heavy to bear. He shuddered, took charge of himself, and turned to face me.

"Wai-nani ... you are my never-fading flower, but Lako has seen that in our time in the wedding bed you have not swollen with the bud of my children. He has decreed that I marry his daughter, Huali, the sacred bride, to carry his line."

My knees buckled under the weight of this news. The jealous dagger of Hina had found its mark. It was true that Makaha planted his seed in me each morning and night for the four moons of makahiki time, yet I had not conceived. I yearned with my whole being to blossom into motherhood and carry the child of Makaha, but my womb remained barren. I ached to feel each cell plumping with his life force surging through veins ripe, full in readiness, but it did not happen.

A demon whirled in the pit of my belly and rose to my throat and escaped with a great howling that left me weak. Though frightened by the gale force of my sorrow, Makaha tried to console me with soft kisses. But his lips were those of a traitor, filled with deceit. His touch felt like a hot cinder on my skin. I pulled violently away from him, seized by something more powerful than myself. I railed against this injustice, striking out at him many times, clawing at his face, tearing at his skin, pulling out clumps of hair. He contained my hands and held them tightly until I gave way to the tears hiding behind my anger.

"'Ele 'ele asked Koa to read the innards of a black pig. The message there was clear. I will not go against the ways of my people," Makaha said.

I ran from the hale and took to the sea, swimming away from my destiny. I would put poison in Huali's wedding cup. I would tell Lako of her eating of the kapu banana and bring disgrace and death upon her, even if it meant I would join her in the spirit world. I whistled to Eku in his voice, and he found me. I wrapped myself around him, clutching him with all my strength, twirling with him belly to belly until a wild tingling blocked all thought. Finding no happiness in the human world, I sought comfort in his forbidden love. I dreamed of growing fins and riding with him forever.

Laka's sleek frame emerged from the green in a silver streak of energy. She flashed past, brushing me off Eku with her snout. She circled back and, with the full force of her substantial frame, rammed me in the belly. I realized my madness had driven her to a jealous rage. I kicked frantically to get away from Eku before she charged again.

Dizzy with the pain, I started to sink. The world went black as my body settled into an upright position and my breath became shallow. Eku came to me, nosing me into a level position to keep me from drowning. He held me aloft in the water. Laka, sensing my helplessness, circled closer and helped Eku hold me out of the water with her snout. My mind closed like a sea urchin protecting its soft center of sucking tentacles from harm. I tried to hide my eyes from the wisdom of Laka, who had declared my actions foul. She looked back at me with an acceptance I can't explain. She held a calm indifference to the puny wahine invading her element. Dying would have been easy for me that day.

I returned to my human world to see that preparations for the wedding were under way. A newly erected tent of kapa stood upon a mound of pili grass surrounded by sweet-smelling clumps of golden 'ilima blooms. Koa chanted as he sprinkled the ground with olena water and circled the area with ti leaves. He placed four small staffs at the corners of the tent. Once the sacraments were complete, the royal procession led by Lako came forward. After Makaha entered, the old chief planted his spear in front of the wedding hale, signaling that no one was to disturb the royal couple.

The sacred chiefess, Huali, anointed with coconut oil, rested inside sitting upon her couch of finely woven lau hala surrounded by handmaidens. Her long black hair, tumbling in heavy waves, was brushed to a brilliant sheen. Her ivory body, dusted with the seductive pollen of the hala bloom, smelled of love. Wrapped in soft folds of white kapa with many leis of fragrant 'ilima, she awaited her husband. When Makaha emerged from the tent their union would be complete. The cold blade of jealousy was in my heart. The world did not fit. No joy was left for me in the village or in the wet arms of moana.

I turned away from the ceremony and walked for many hours. I looked down upon broad, strong feet and let them take me where they would. They led me to Hookena, my surfing cove, where I spied a lone swimmer bobbing in the surf. It was Mau. I settled beneath the tree that had shaded Huali on the days she had come to see me ride the waves with Eku. Mau seemed not to notice me as he did a strange dance in the water, lifting his wounded leg to his chest, alternating each leg, bouncing between each step. He chanted to Kanaloa, trying to regain his powers. When he saw me, he came forth from the water wearing a broad smile on his honest face that warmed my bruised heart.

"May I sit beside you?" he asked.

In need of comfort, I let him join me in the shade of the rustling palm. His time in the life-giving waters helped in the healing of the jagged purple gash on his leg, but the flesh pulled taut, made the injured leg shorter than the other. On land he walked with a stiff-legged lurch. We were both in need of mending. His wounds were visible, but mine were as deep and as real. He read the hopeless despair in my eyes. It was not a secret that I was cast out of Makaha's sleeping hale because I could not give him a son.

"We all have sorrows that we carry in our hearts," he said, sitting down beside me.

I knew that his young wife had died giving birth to his daughter Lana, and that he raised her alone, but I never heard him speak of it.

"Often our fate seems more than we can bear. The man who owns your heart carries his own troubles in silence," he said, and then went on to tell me how he had received his wound. "Our sail across the channel to Maui was peaceful, and it seemed all the omens were on our side. The soft wind filling our sails bristled the feathers of Ku on our helm. We had the best fighting men and left-handed warriors whose sling-shots missed not a hair on the head. Every one of our warriors are expert spear-point breakers and fearless. Convinced of our strength and that we would prevail, we were not ready for what Pano had in store.

"In the many months it took us to prepare for the battle, a spy took word to the Moi of Maui of our planned attack. In that time he gathered forces from other islands that lay in wait for us. When we touched the sands of Maui we were attacked by Molokai forces hiding in the hills, and those from Oahu from the sea. They pressed us into the hills where we ran through the furrows of potato fields, racing for cover from the shower of spears and rocks. Pano's forces formed a crescent-shaped wedge with men behind to the right and the left of us that pushed us to higher ground in the forest.

"According to our custom of war designed to save men for the work of the village, we expected that Pano would send his best man forward to wrestle with Makaha, our best warrior. We hoped that he would rest with that outcome when he witnessed our might, but he had no intention of settling the war that way. He did not offer his best warrior. Instead, we were driven like mullet by the sound of beating into the sluice gate.

"When we reached the cool shadows of the forest, we planned to turn and face our enemies crowding down upon us. Our warriors swarmed together for protection and formed a circle that would keep the enemy from our backs. Just as Makaha ordered the men to crowd in upon one another, the trap was sprung. Pano's men, hiding in the trees, cut the cords that held palms folded upon themselves. The great trees sprang back to their height, lifting a vine net buried beneath the sand at our feet. The world went upside down. We were caught clinging to the vines. From there the slaughter began. Many of the men lost their daggers and spears when the net snapped them off their feet. An arm or leg that fell through the vine net was hacked off by the warriors circling on the ground below us. Those who fell through the net were clubbed to death. The bodies of men with noses cut off and missing eyes were piled high.

"I scrambled to climb to the top of the vine net to get over the other side and into the trees. I leaped from the top of the net to a tree limb to get free, but it broke away from my weight, and I landed in a circle of warriors. A fierce joy flashed in the eyes of the men bearing down upon me. I pulled my dagger from its sheath and plunged it into the gut of the closest warrior and pulled his entrails out with a twist of the blade. This triggered the rage of the others. Deep red blood flecked at the corners of the mouth of the man I had struck. He buckled to his knees beside me. Six warriors circled about me now, intent upon revenge for their brother. I knew that Milu was opening the doorway to Po for me. I stooped low, hoping to wrestle my way out of the circle. One of the men lunged at me with his dagger. I held my belly to my back, missing death by a hair's width. They continued to circle around me, taunting me with insults to take me off guard.

"A toothless grin spread across the face of the largest warrior as he grabbed the vine I stood upon and yanked it out from under me, pulling me off my feet. His dagger found its mark, severing the flesh from the bone from my hip to my knee. This time I knew I was to meet a warrior's death. Just then, Makaha leaped inside the circle. Holding a long spear, he crouched to face the six men in a wrestling warrior's stance. The men paced slowly about him, looking for their time to take him down like a pack of man-eating dogs. He did not wait for their first move. Instead, he flailed the spear in a circle like a fire torch in a war dance and caught three of the men on the chin with his fast movements. Teeth and blood flew in the air, but the warriors remained intent upon their quarry. Makaha jabbed wickedly with the spear, catching one warrior beneath his breastbone, lifting him high until it settled in the man's heart. In moments, th warriors knew they were defeated and ran into the trees, leaving Makaha to collect his broken forces.

"Mist welled in his eyes when he saw my wound. No words were spoken as he sifted through the pile of broken, bleeding bodies to find a warrior who still had breath in him. Half-torn bodies hung limp on the vine net. Some were headless, some armless, all dripping rich red blood on the forest floor below. Those who managed to escape had run into the mountains to hide. Makaha lifted me and carried me back to our canoes. Once our men dared to leave the cover of the forest, we sailed home in silence with a sullen Makaha at the sweep."

When he finished speaking, I stroked the massive scar on his leg. My heart flew out to him and to all the brave Hawaiian warriors who had set sail that day. Once again, I was handed the burden of understanding my warrior husband and the hard truths he must carry.

14
The Leaping Place

Soon after wedding Huali, Makaha left for another campaign against Pano. Lako sailed with his warriors, leaving 'Ele 'ele and Koa in charge. 'Ele 'ele had made it plain he was my enemy when he whispered into Lako's ear that I was barren, but it was the kahuna Koa I feared the most. He saw me as a threat to the old ways. His potion had nearly killed me, and when that did not work he gave 'Ele 'ele the knowledge that would take Makaha from me. I knew to stay well away from his thoughts.

I looked for Huali in the women's hale. Our time in the hut always came together with the full face of the moon. But she did not appear. I don't know what I would have said to her given the chance. My heart was dark and bitter like the fruit of the ipu 'awa. Even though I knew she had no voice in her father's house, my rage against her was stronger than my reason.

I slipped out of the hut seeking solace in the wild darkness of the night and went to the bluff overlooking the sea where Makaha made love to me with the fire of Pele. The clouds were moving fast over the bold face of Hina, hiding the shame she must feel for being so cruel to me. A white blanket of stars cut a swath across the velvet sky. I hugged my knees, rocking back and forth, and told Hina, Goddess of the Moon, of my sorrow. I chanted and crooned mele to her for many hours. Rainbow rings of light surrounding her cast a circle in ripples across the sky. The clouds began to whirl with the colors of a soft pink seashell dancing with the moonbeams in a hula that stuck in my heart.

I rose, lifting my hands to pull the power of the great goddess in the sky into my fingertips and felt it move through my body like a river. The energy came up from the ground and down from the sacred sky, surging through me in great swells. I swayed with the music of the palm fronds lifted sweetly in the sea breeze. The curls of cloud mist dissolved and the bright rays of moonlight beamed upon me. The flow of the wind was in my breath. I danced until exhausted. Hours later, I awoke on the sand with the early rays of a coral dawn.

I went to the edge of the sea and felt the pulse of its heartbeat beneath my feet. The water was as warm as blood in the early morning mist. Bright breath of hundreds of dolphins returning after a night out feeding in wild waters rose like steam over the bay. At night when the yellow moon shines brightly down on black waters the dolphins forage in the deep. Still high-spirited from the danger of the open seas, their bleats, whistles and clicks filled the morning air. They did elegant leaps before coming to rest on the sandy bottom of the shallows. Here they settled in neat rows drifting with the surge of the tide with one eye open for the shadow of Mano lurking overhead. I felt sure Eku was among them, but after being disciplined by Laka, I left him to his brothers and sisters.

I spied Mau working in his fishing hut by the sea. He was left behind to mend nets while the warriors wearing red war malos sailed off in their canoes. He seemed content as he worked quietly, humming a chant to Ku'ula, the fish god.

"How is it with you, Mau?" I asked.

"It is good," he said, looking up from his labors with a smile on his wide, kind face. His leg was healing, but he still walked stiff-legged. His fingers were nimble with the bone needle he used to weave cordage in and out of his net.

"It is a fine day to fish," I said.

"Yes, it is a fine day."

I knew he could not man a canoe alone. It took two to paddle, cast a net and pop hands until the many colored fish were swarming, and then to pull them in.

"We could go together," I ventured.

"Fishing is not work for an ali'i chiefess."

"I am in need of doing. Please take me."

He gazed upon me with tender brown eyes for many seconds before answering. His loyalty to Makaha was immense. He wanted to help me, but he did not want to offend the warrior that had saved his life. Clouds of concern filled his eyes. He spoke softly when he finally answered.

"All right, you will help me fill my nets."

"You won't be sorry. I know the ways of the sea."

And so Mau and I became fishers of the sea together. He took me to the reefs where I dove for lobster hiding in the finger coral protected by the black spined sea urchin and the striped eel. Careful not to put my hand in a hole where eel could latch upon my wrist with needle sharp teeth, I collected lobster, crab and the wily octopus. Some days I collected opihi from the rocks. Shoals of brilliant yellow lau-hau, the rainbow butterfly with blue stripes down his fat sides, and triggerfish wearing bold black masks passed by me in dense swarms. When I waved my hand through their vast numbers, they moved away in unison as though I were shaking dust from a cloth. Sometimes, I fed them tiny morsels of food and they came too near my fingers, inflicting savage little bites.

Soon Mau was strong enough to help me cast nets. We waded into the shallow fish pools together, carefully spreading our trap. Then we circled about the fish, popping our hands to push the masses of tiny tang and blue-striped snapper into our nets. Pulling the line on our nets, we gathered more than enough for the village. The old women came to the shore at days' end to see what we brought in for their table. We opened the latches of our full calabashes teeming with fish.

"What get?" they asked, surveying our catch.

"Get plenty," we said proudly.

The kelu, or keeper of the fish, greeted us. He took the first fish caught and placed it aside for the priests to place on the Ko'a altar as a grateful offering to the fish god for being kind to us that day. After that the best fish were set aside for Lako and his ohana

Next the learned kahuna were given their share. Finally, the maka'ainana were allowed to help themselves to the remaining catch. Mau and I saw to it that no one in our village went without bounty from the sea while the warriors were away.

It was the tabu season for spawning aku and opelu, deep sea fish that moved in the oceans in vast schools. It was forbidden by the chiefs to take them at this time to assure that their numbers would always be great and the Island people would never be hungry. As Mau grew stronger, we sailed farther and farther into the deep waters where we could cast a line for sea monsters like mahi-mahi and swordfish. One morning he announced, "We will go to a spot blessed by Kanaloa."

Strong from the waist up, he paddled our canoe for many hours. The sun beat down from a cloudless sky as we stroked our paddles in unison. Bent to our labors, I thought only of the motion of my arms as I lifted and dipped, lifted and dipped my paddle into the heaving swells of deep blue water. Now, we were in the wilds of the live ocean like our dolphin brothers and sisters.

He pointed to a peninsula that jutted into the ocean like a long finger.

"There are mooring holes here made by the ancients."

A head wind came up as we paddled toward the point. Each of my strokes felt weighted. He leaned into the wind, bowing his muscled back to the sun. Instead of tiring, he was livened by the effort. Waves with a fetch of thousands of miles come to land here in a crashing fury. Undulating rolls of wave after wave crashed on steps of black lava. My shoulders and arms were aching by the time we were near enough to the point to tie on.

"You will have to do the tying," Mau said, handing me the line of plaited fibers and a spear. "You will find small holes four fingers wide made by our fathers when they landed here in the long-long ago."

I dove into the chop. The wind whipped, and the waves sloshed on the rocky ledge where holes were bored for mooring. Near the waterline I found the holes used to tie up hundred-foot canoes so they could drift in the deep water beyond the wave surge where the big fish dwell. I took the spear for holding the line, placed it in the hole and wrapped the line about it as tightly as I could. We drifted with the strong current until the line was stretched tight and we found our resting place. Mau baited his pearl-shell trolling hook and cast it into the water to let it drift in the deep waters where mahi-mahi feed on mackerel. He tossed tiny morsels of reef fish into the sea to bring the big ones up from the deep. We settled down to wait for a tug on our line and rested in the sun while our canoe lolled sweetly in four-foot swells.

"This fishing ground is protected by the spirits of our ancestors. It is the leaping place where thousands of our brothers have jumped into the afterlife. The fishing is always good here in this sacred place."

I fell to sleeping in the sun listening to his solemn chant to Kanaloa. When the big one hit the line hard, it nearly ripped the pole from his strong hand. But he was ready. He let the line go. Then he pulled back strongly, securing the hook in the great fish's mouth. The line whipped from one side of the canoe to the other. The sleek, silver monster broke through the sparkling sea and leaped for the heavens trying to free itself from the hook. For nearly an hour the fish struggled, pulling the line with all his might, but Mau stood firm. He nursed the line, keeping a steady tension. Slowly, with great patience, he worked the tiring fish close enough to our canoe to gaff it with a hook and haul it aboard with one swift movement. It bounced wildly, flinging itself from side to side on the bottom of the canoe. Mau took his dagger and slit the gill until life spilled from our gift from Kanaloa.

It would be a feasting day in Kealakekua. With the warriors occupied in battles, the villagers had not shared their favorite big fish since makahiki time. When we returned, children squealed with excitement and ran to tell their mothers about our catch. Hot stones were piled into imus by the kane while the wahine brought yams, breadfruit and purple poi to be shared. While Mau and I were at sea, Makaha and his warriors had returned. Our fish was to be shared by all. Banana leaves were spread upon the separate eating mats prepared for men and woman.

Nearly three moons had passed since Huali had left her hale. She hid from the sun since her coupling with Makaha. He sat by her side in the shade of a palm, holding her hand. I saw that her belly was full, spilling over narrow hips. Makaha's seed had fallen on fertile ground. She wore a modest kikepa dress tied at the shoulder instead of her pa'u. She seemed to me fragile and delicate like a wild bird, beautiful but not strong. I had no words for her. I watched the royal couple smiling and laughing from the corner of a jealous eye.

At eating time, Makaha joined Lako and 'Ele 'ele and the other warriors at the men's mat. Lako opened the packet of ti leaves to expose the eyeballs of our great fish steamed to perfection for his pleasure. He popped one of the the succulent trophys into his mouth, signaling our feast to begin.

Lako spoke of victory in Maui. Our warriors had secured my Hana home as a resting place between bouts with Pano. The lush forest on the far north tip of the island where I swam in the seven sacred pools is isolated from the reach of Pano's warriors. It offers the only safe harbor on the leeward side of Maui. Protected by my brother and the other fierce warriors of my father, it was not an easy target. My heart trembled at this news. I had to know of my family. I could not speak in front Lako for fear he would question my loyalties, so I clamped down my worries and waited until I could talk to Makaha alone.

Lako stood to speak.

"I am a happy chief today. The seed of my best warrior is budding within my daughter. I will know my grandchild before I pass into the spirit world."

'Ele 'ele squirmed with this news. It was he who whispered into Lako's ear of my childlessness. He wanted to bring unhappiness upon Makaha's house. Instead, he encouraged the marriage between his half-sister Huali and Makaha. Now he felt threatened by the unborn child too close to his throne.

Huali wore a white hibiscus behind her right ear and was radiant. But the powerful seed of Makaha caused her to be sick each morning. Her bones were light like a bird's, made hollow by the gods so they can sail on in the air. She floated like a mist when she walked. She was of the heavens and the clouds on the horizon, not from the sea like me. Dark shadows under her gentle brown eyes told me she was not sleeping. Still, she beamed, determined to be strong for her child.

When the village talk was over and the fire died to glowing embers, I went back to my sleeping hale where I lit the kukui candles above my feather mat and prayed softly to Hina for the strength to hide my tears. A shadow passed over me. I turned to see Makaha standing with strong legs spread in a warrior's stance, muscled arms crossed over his broad chest. He looked stern as he held me in his unrelenting gaze. The old rage I thought I'd buried in the moon came surging forth with the fury of Pele. It was as though I was standing outside of myself watching as I raised my arm to strike him across the face. He caught my arm before the blow landed and smiled with a fierce gleam in his eyes.

"My proud Wai-nani has not lost her fire."

I spat in his face. I knew he could snap my neck with one hand, but I was unable to swallow my anger. I should have been proud to be the second wife of a great warrior but could not accept my fate. He let go of my wrist and wiped my spittle from his face with the back of a broad hand. His countenance was calm, but there was darkness in his eyes that told me he would not be denied his pleasure. I struggled with all my might, but my desperate writhing seemed only to incite him.

He was not the same man I'd met in his thinking place two seasons ago. He was now the leader of men, used to having his orders obeyed and his needs met without question. He clenched me in a tight grip with one hand, whirled me about and took me in silence, butting me from behind like a dog. I cried out, but he held my head back with a great clump of my hair. His passion sparked mine against my will. He lurched and plunged until I was caught in the fever of his might. My lust was tinged with loathing for him and myself. I felt frightened by the flood of violent, painful emotions brought to me by the keeper of Ku. When he was finished he rolled onto the mat and looked to the ceiling, panting. I turned away from him, hiding my thoughts.

"What of my family?" I had to know. "Were they killed in the taking of Hana?"

There was a long silence as Makaha considered his answer. "Your father escaped with your mother. They are hiding on the flank of the House of the Sun. Your brother chose the death of a warrior."

I felt sick at this news. Mimo was in the blush of his beardless youth when I left him swimming in the match that would determine who was to be my husband. I could remember the hot anger in his eyes when he saw that it was I wearing his malo. What would he say today if he knew I shared the sleeping mat with his enemy?

15
Where the Gods Come Close

Grasping Lako was so fired by his victory over my Hana home he ordered Makaha to muster the largest fleet ever to sail the Islands.

"On to Wailuku!" he said bringing his long spear down hard on the ground.

Every hand in the village was bent to the war campaign. Warriors were sent to the mountains to find the perfect koa trees to carve into great double-hulled canoes. This time when Makaha sailed to Maui he was at the head of the largest fleet of canoes yet to sail from Hawai'i, manned with eight hundred 'Alapa warriors honed to military perfection. Their sails made a billowing cloud upon the horizon as they journeyed once more across the dangerous Alenuihaha Channel to meet the forces of Pano on Maui.

When Makaha returned after one turn of the moon, there were just two canoes left in his mighty fleet. When they entered Kealakekua Bay, Lako pulled on his nostril and wailed for the dead left behind at Wailuku. Women of the village sensed the sorrow at their door before the boats landed. That night the village was dark in the gloom of deep mourning. No fires burned in the kukui lamps. There began a great howling from the wahine left without husbands, joined by the crying of their keiki. Men and women fell to the ground, moaning, inflicting wounds upon themselves to show their suffering.

Makaha was missing his front teeth, and he had a purple

gash across his forehead. He did not speak, only stared with baleful eyes at the sorrow of the people over their great losses. I looked upon him with great pity. The slender man who spent his days in prayers and meditations stood battered and torn from battle, his heart weighted by his harsh destiny.

"You will go with me to Waipio," he said with the tone of a chief that told me there was no refusing. "We leave in the morning."

After two days' journey, we came to the lip of the precipice overlooking Waipio Valley. Ever since the long-long ago, ali'i had come to this water-rich home of the gods to catch mana. Clouds hovered on the far snout of the velvet green thousand-foot pali guarding the fertile valley. Protected on three sides by steep cliffs and shrouded in dense foliage, the valley had long been the resting place of great chiefs. Glistening streams cascaded down the sheer walls to the valley floor. I heard the thunder of a sparkling three-tiered waterfall tumbling down the verdant cliff. Silver veins of water lacing the valley floor merged to form the Waipio Stream that empties into the sea where it meets a wide black-sand beach.

With hand at his brow he scanned the horizon in silence. The waves breathing with an easy rhythm rose from deep swells to crash to a foamy white death on the curved shore far below. Legend speaks of the time when the water rose over the height of three warriors, filling the valley floor, leaving behind no trace of the thousands of Island people who lived in the valley. Uncertain currents here kept outsiders from approaching the secluded, sacred valley from the sea.

Makaha ducked down a twisting trail etched into the canyon wall. At spots it was so narrow we clung to roots and stepped into foot holes carved into the slick red mud. We descended into the cool, green darkness of a forest of giant ferns and mighty trees. The sun went out of sight, and the mist hovering in the treetops dripped wet life upon us. We scrambled back and forth across the slanting path until we reached a clearing overlooking the valley. I heard the happy laughter of keiki rising up from the village tucked in the shade of coco palms. A rainbow arced in the spray of the waterfall plunging into a rock pool from a high ledge in the canyon's wall.

"The rainbow maiden lives in the cave behind this rock pool," Makaha said. "She hides there from Lono. I know, for I have seen her."

I did not reply. I had not spoken since the knowledge that Makaha's men had killed my brother. Makaha too was sullen, and no other words had passed between us. Soon we were on the valley floor where children ran up to greet us while skulking dogs hung back in the shadows of the cluster of huts. A humpbacked old man with a withered arm emerged from his hale to greet us. He squinted at us through filmy blue eyes.

"Aki. I am Makaha," Makaha said.

At this the old one's eyes lit up, and he straightened his bent frame.

"I remember you. You wandered alone deep into the valley when you were a boy."

"How do I find Ka'eo?"

"He is tending his taro patch as he does every day," Aki said, pointing his stick to where we would find Ka'eo.

Ka'eo's patch was on the other side of the rushing river that cuts through the heart of the valley. The current was swift with deep channels. I stumbled on the boulders slick with moss, nearly losing my balance in the waist-high water. I looked upriver to see banana trees, palms and reeds forming thick impenetrable foliage along the shore. Makaha slipped through an opening in the green. The path led us through a tunnel of fanning ferns. Brushing aside huge fronds, I raced to keep up. A small point of light in the distance opened to a vast field of walled-in pools with neat rows of heart-shaped leaves.

Silver-haired Ka'eo tending his crop waded in knee-high water. He stood in the middle of a small pool mashing the roots of his plants with his toes to help them breathe and grow to great stalks. His leathery skin was burnished black from the intense sun. Intent on his labors, he did not see us until we were upon him. When he did feel our presence and looked to see who came to his garden, he shook his head and wiped his eyes to make sure he was not having a vision. Once he was certain that we were not workings of his imagination, a soft smile of wonderment spread across his kind face. He lifted both hands to the sky in greeting and raised knees high as he splashed through the water to meet us.

"My son has come home," he said, wrapping muscled arms around Makaha's waist and laying his head upon Makaha's chest. Makaha towered over the gentle kanaka who loved him as his own. Ka'eo's body shuddered with great aloha for Makaha. When he finally released his embrace, he came to me. His belly had grown from easy living since he'd rocked me in his arms in Kau three seasons ago, but his great heart still beat strong. His glowing warmth soothed my withered spirit, for even though I held love for Makaha the great warrior, my time with him had changed. I yearned for the somber youth with hairless lean limbs and tender eyes. I feared the moods of the man whose features had grown coarse with heavy brows and brooding eyes.

"Come. We will have a great feast. You will know peace in the valley and feel the love of my ohana," Ka'eo said, wrapping his arms about our waists and leading us to his village.

He introduced us to a lesser chief who bowed many times, prostrating himself to Makaha. Word had traveled island-wide that Makaha, keeper of Ku, the snatcher of lands, led Lako's warriors in many great battles. His wishes were only to be known and the people of Waipio would fulfill them. That evening the imu ovens burned hot, and a feast from the abundant offerings of the valley was given in our honor.

Ka'eo's many grandchildren clustered about him while fishes steamed under pandanus leaves. He rested brown hands upon the shoulders of the keiki and told them the story of the taro. "Two of the plant's roots became intertwined, and they would not be separated. They became lovers and tried to fly away from the imu. The plants prided themselves upon their rapid, perfect growth. The chief in the valley chased them, but they kept flying ahead of the enemy, starting new crops wherever they landed. That is how we came to have so many beautiful plants with many different shapes and sizes in our valley," he said, rubbing the glossy mane of a girl child resting her head in his lap.

I met Ka'eo's daughters Singing Land Shell, Shell Beautiful with Rainbow Colors, and Leaf of the Morning Glory. That night the "Shells" sang, and their voices stole their way into my heart, lifting me to song with them. Our voices mingled with the soft breeze stirring the palms and the sweet scent of ginger. The heaviness I carried with me dissolved into the sacred sky creamy with stars. After much music, dancing and laughter Makaha and I went to our hale that rested beside a waterlily-laden pond.

Makaha fell to a restless sleep, muttering curses, jerking like a dog chasing pigs. I lay staring into the dark listening to the thrum of the insects and the humming energy of the valley. Outside the full yellow moon cast a brilliant path across the night waters. I bolted upright when I heard a low guttural sound reverberating over the pond. Spirits of the ancestors whose bones were steamed clean and hidden in caves were talking to me. Thousands of spirits hovered in the valley. Ghost bodies drifted in the trees. They were everywhere, looking for a human body to re-enter—to slip through the soles of unsuspecting feet and move into the minds of the unwary.

Spirits of dead chiefs guard the entrance to the underworld. The gate to Po is here in Waipio, near a hidden sea cave. Spirits dwell there feasting, playing checkers, wrestling, doing all things that mortals do, but some are restless and yearn to know the warmth of the sun. Spirit catchers are sent out by Milu, ruler of the underworld, to capture those that wander from his kingdom and bring them back. They seize venturesome ghosts and carry them back to the spirit land, where they are punished for wandering among mortals. But sometimes in their travels outside of their world they catch a human body and play tricks on the world of the living. For many hours I would not let myself sleep for fear that one of them would enter my body. Mist was rising off the pond in the gray morning light before I finally found rest.

My time with Makaha in Waipio was filled with many long walks into the depths of the green valley. At the base of Papalua Falls, we looked up at the magnificent rush of water tumbling from the sky, sliding down slick rocks fringed with maidenhair ferns. A wooden stairway led to a rope ladder. From there a rope for balance was secured into the rock wall. Holding onto the rope, we stepped into the footprints of all those that had come before. Atop the first tier of the waterfall rested a wading pool nestled in ferns and soft green moss. Cascading water splashed into the pool, and a thin mist hung in the air. We shed our coverings and slipped into the bracing water. With a sponge from the sea, I washed Makaha's broad back, rubbing tense muscles rippling under his almond skin. We soaked in the pool, absorbing the ancient Island mana, and drank of the clear water trickling over rocks, taking its purity to our hearts.

Makaha reached for me in the amorous waters. I yielded to his yearnings under the splash of the falls. His embrace was powerful, his passion un-masked. Our love was furious. When it was over, we lay on the rocks, drying in the sun beside the pool adrift in each other's arms for many hours.

Makaha stirred from his long silence. "I have seen Lono," he said.

Our love in the waterfall must have brought the lonely God who Wanders the Sky to his mind for Lono caught his beautiful wife in a pool like this one with a young warrior and killed her lover with his own hands. Lono also received the lessons of healing in Waipio. His touch can bring the dead back to life. Before he set to wandering, looking for the runaway spirit of his wife, he was a farmer and loved the land, touching it with his hands, worming it with his feet.

"His spirit dwells here," I said.

"No, I have seen him. He is coming."

"Yes. He is coming. That is why we have makahiki each year." It seemed to me he was talking foolishly.

He sat up, pulling me with him and clutching my shoulders tightly as he spoke to me with fierce, dark eyes.

"Lono is coming. When I was in Maui, I saw the white clouds of his sails on the horizon."

"I believe you," I said, trying to calm him back into my arms, but our time of sweetness together was over. His thoughts had moved to greater worries, and I was left behind to pine for his tenderness. His eyes became glassy like a fish's as he looked inside his own mind, and he told me what he saw.

"When we approached Maui with our cloud of one hundred sails on our canoes filled with the finest 'Alapa warriors of Hawai'i, I believed Ku was with us. Our warriors wore the crimson capes of feathers and their helmets with brilliant plumes shone in the sun. Lako believed that the show of our mighty force would be enough to conquer Pano. I was ready to meet his best warrior and settle our differences, one-on-one, saving the lives of many warriors. Instead, when we landed near where we had been caught in the vine nets, there was no one to greet us, and we thought we had caught Pano by surprise.

"Beyond a sandy isthmus lying between The House of the Sun and Mount Iao before us lay Wailuku and the house of Pano. The cry arose from my lips 'On to Wailuku! On to Wailuku!' The strongest warriors with the bravest of hearts in all the Islands followed me as I ran headlong onto the isthmus. Onward sped proud chiefs over the sandy hills, racing to an easy victory in Wailuku. So fired was our force that when we met a dozen of Pano's men in our path we were not slowed a stride and trampled them beneath our feet. A few Maui warriors ran ahead, and we took them in chase, chanting our song of victory, 'We drink the water of Wailuku today.'

"Remembering the deaths of warriors snared in the vine net of Pano, I longed for revenge as our men ran the last mile to Wailuku. We reached the foot of Mount Iao looking over the Iao Stream. Suddenly, the Maui warriors we chased vanished from the path as it hit the base of a sheer rock wall. On the brow of the cliffs before and beside us hundreds of warriors rose up. In seconds, rows of them were behind us blocking our retreat. Once again we were sucked into a trap set by Pano. Our ranks were broken from the run over the sand hills, and to fight our enemy we had first to climb the cliffs surrounding us.

"Pano's men hurled heavy stones upon the helmets of our men and thrust long spears into those who clamored up the hillsides to reach them. Still, our brave men struggled up the loose sand mountains and steep cliffs, pressing the warriors back though the winding valleys. The battle went on and on under a heartless sun that filled the men with a raging thirst that drove us to the waters of Iao Stream. Pano's men were constantly replaced with fresh men while we were slackened from thirst and exhausted from the battle. I swung my war club with all my might, cracking the skulls of more of the enemy than I could count, but still they rose up. They came in ceaseless waves and each time I turned I saw another of our warriors lying broken and bleeding on the ground. I saw the shaft of a spear enter the chest of my best warrior and expose his still-beating heart. He gurgled 'On to Wailuku!' before he died.

"From the mounds of naked, torn bodies I saw broken arms of my men raised to fend off the hail of deathblows. Crushed helmets and blood-drenched feather cloaks lay trampled in the sand. Those who did reach the river were pounded to death as they clawed for water. The Iao Stream ran red with the rich blood of noble warriors of Hawai'i while Pano gloated. The sound of war clubs smashing skulls, limbs being twisted from their pockets, and the moans of men whose eyes were gouged out remains with me. Pano did not give us the chance to settle our fight without spilling the blood of so many good men. I must avenge them."

At the end of his telling, his great frame shuddered, and he turned to me with moist eyes. Our time in the valley was shared with the blood that ran red in his dreams, memories of battles, and spirits that haunted his visions. I wiped his tears with my hair oiled with fragrant flowers to soothe the ache in his heaving heart.

One day we woke to rain dripping on the thickly plaited pili grass roof on our hale. It pattered on the broad leaves of the banana trees. Water dripped into the ponds that had formed below the eaves of the hut during the night. Inside the rain, the crickets kept up their constant whirring conversation. I looked out to see large drops pounding circles upon the ponds. The palms bent to the will of a strong wind whipping the sea to foam.

For many days the steady downpour continued. Makaha carved flutes from bamboo for us to play. Listening to the raindrops, we serenaded one another with love songs and ancient chants. He taught me konane, a game of checkers. He chanced a game with another chief in the village and lost a bet to him to everyone's great amusement. Still the rain did not stop.

A more furious storm rose at the head of the valley. The wind spirits blew harder, lashing at the sea, struggling into a gale. They uprooted palms and ripped off the thatched roofs of many huts. Clouds gathered in heavy black masses. Jagged arrows lit the heavens and were followed by a bellow of thunder after they found their mark on land. The many rills and waterfalls emptying into the Waipio Stream bulged from their peaceful beds. The overloaded river pulled trees from the shore, shifted rocks in its course, and sucked hales into its race to the sea.

Higher and higher the waves rose until they reared far above the waters and met the winds from the shore whipping the curling crest into a shower of spray. Makaha climbed the rocks on the north end of the storm-blown beach.

"Tomorrow will be surf as you have never seen before," he said, grinning like a young boy.

I couldn't believe he was thinking of surfing in these treacherous waters. Milu, the guardian to the gate of the underworld, met his death here in the great pounding sea. The tow of the turbulent trough crowded him down to the sea floor while his olo, caught in the raging, struggling waters, was thrown out toward the shore. He was lost in the deep water.

Next morning when I awoke the rain had stopped, but the winds still bent the palms to the ground. The great ancestor Maui, said to have the winds of heaven concealed in his calabash, raised its cover once more to release a chaotic mass of fierce winds over the valley. Makaha was gone from his sleeping mat. I ran to the rocky shore to see him bobbing like a coconut husk in the giant surf. My throat went dry as I saw the suck of the rising swells pulling him deep into the belly of a foaming monster. He danced with the swift channel current with the courage of sky and sea in his heart. Half-man, half-fish, water was his home. He paddled hard on his giant koa board, trying to get at the right angle to catch the surf.

I came with the thought to stop him, but felt more jealous of his great courage than afraid. Mano was his ancestral keeper. The great shark god rode with him. That is why he held no fear and could find the perfect balancing place when he rode the waves. A crowd had gathered along the shore to watch him ride the water-mountains. The face of the waves, coming in sets of three, rose to amazing heights. The frothy head of the smoking bearded ones looked soft as it sprayed in the wind, but if one landed on his back it would drive him down as deep as the wave was high and hold him there. If it held him for two waves he would drown. The blue mountain rolled over his speck figure, and he reappeared behind its crush.

He moved into position to launch onto the next swell that was building far out to sea. He wanted to be at the lip of the wave when it crested. When the suck of the swell pulled him deep into its terrible belly, he paddled hard from the bottom of the wave then kicked with strong confident strokes up its blue face. Just before he reached the crest he turned to drop down into the middle of the open face to his balancing place. He plunged twenty feet straight down in the air to land in position on his board then skittered across the face of the wave like an arrow shot from a bow. He rode with right leg back, knee bent, rocking his hips forward and back. He turned the board back into the curl, faced the wave and dared to ride up the crest. The astonished crowd went wild. A split second kept him from getting clipped at the foaming crest of the giant that would show him no mercy if he made a mistake.

In my mind I saw my childhood friend who was dragged to the bottom of the ocean and pulverized by the churning water. He went numb from the waist down, tore ligaments in his leg, and suffered sand cuts all over his body. Still, I could contain myself no longer. I grabbed a short board from a nearby warrior contemplating the surf and ran in to join Makaha. I am born to life and death in the water. Slip my body into the waters of this chosen land and let me feed the birds from the shore. Let my body live and let me die by water. It was a good day to die.

Once beside Makaha my thoughts of death ended. I followed him to the cold blue bowels of a roaring wave. I could feel the pull of Milu as he tried to take me to his kingdom. I fought with all my might to paddle up the curving breast of the beast that dwells in the ocean. The churning rage over my head was about to drop on me when I slipped just under its snarling lip. I turned to make the drop and felt myself falling into eternity. I hit hard, nearly toppling over in the heaving swell. I shuffled back and forth on my board to regain my balance. Before I knew what was happening, I was encircled by an ice-blue tube shot through with light. I was inside the belly of the whale. Many moments passed in which I was lost to all but the immense power shooting me through the whorl of blue. It fired me out and down the face of the great wave.

I turned my board up and rode the crest to shore. When I emerged from the water my aura flew off of me in a halo of sparkling light. Pinpricks of light shot off my fingertips and the soles of my feet as I walked on the hard packed sand. The mystery of moana—the grand and vibrant sea—could never be grasped and made to stay still, I reminded myself. All one could do is let it go and live in harmony with it. I was content to live that day and did not re-enter the surf with Makaha, who continued wave-sliding for many hours like a dolphin born in water.

When the gods tired of the storm, the skies cleared to sapphire blue and three-colored rainbows burst over the valley. I took Makaha by the hand and led him up the canyon to Hi'ilawe and Hakalaoa, the twin waterfalls. These two streams plunging from the sky into a secret pool were once forbidden lovers. Rather than be separated, the lovers jumped off the pali together into the pool at the bottom of the falls to meet their deaths together. The joined water flows from the stream to the sea and supports the taro fields, feeding the fishes and nurturing the land.

"Like these streams our lives are forever bound," I told him.

"My brave Wai-nani, you are my never-fading flower," he said, rubbing my nose tenderly with his own.

"Your hard path is to be softened by the pure water of my love," I said. We held hands and turned to watch the silken tracks of the dying lovers.

16

Sisters in Blood-Sisters in Water

When Makaha and I returned to Kealakekua from Waipio, he left me to be with his sacred bride before going to the mountains to replenish the canoe fleet of Lako. Huali prayed each day to the gods for the safe entry of her unborn child into this world. She waddled under the weight of the child that kicked savagely against her ribs. In between bouts of pain she slept in the cool shadows of her hale. It gave me no pleasure to see her suffering. I believed that life was meant for the strong and that it was a cruel test of the gods for Huali to be carrying the fruit of Makaha's seed. It seemed even crueler when she came to speak to me of the future of the unborn chief.

"Wai-nani, how is it with you?" she asked with tender dark eyes.

After spending a season with Makaha in Waipio, my heart was even more confused about the child soon to be born. I remembered my time with Huali by the rock pool, eating the kapu banana, daring the gods to strike us dead. That we stood facing one another still was our bond.

"Love comes like a billow and rests before the eyes," I said, remembering love that left a constant yearning for Makaha before me.

"When love is given, love should be returned. Anger is the thing that gives no life," Huali said.

To hear my own thoughts come back to me and to receive understanding from one who should hate me softened the callus growing on my heart. For her to accept that while she was carrying the child of Makaha I was in the arms of her husband made her more to be loved in my eyes.

"I am afraid. I need your great strength," she said plainly.

"What is it you fear?"

"That I will die giving birth, and my child will be placed in the arms of someone not of my choosing."

"What is that to do with me?"

"I want you to promise me that you will take my baby to your heart and show him the ways of strength and kindness if I am not strong enough to live for him."

"You will be."

"My time is coming, and I am weak."

A fury was rising in me. I yearned to know the blossoming of motherhood. My own body with rich blood surging through blue veins was ripe, full with readiness. Why was weak and frail Huali chosen to be the vessel for Makaha's son?

"No task is too big when done together by all," I said, choking back fury and hiding my rage.

She took my hand in hers. "Come walk with me."

Huali never walked about in the full sun, to spare the suffering of those who might break the kapu of walking in her shadow. Instead, she walked like a ghost at dusk, wandering the trails by moonlight. She took me to a rock ledge overlooking small tide pools reflecting the last rays of sunlight. Wavelets purled into shore over the reef. She began a chant to moana, raising and lowering her voice with the wave surge. I listened to the breath of the sea and joined her in a prayer for her baby. Her voice was sweet and clear like a mountain stream. My voice was deep and far-reaching as I sent it to distant shores. We chanted together until our voices grew tired and the moon smiled brightly down upon us.

"In the morning I will come for you, and you will know the strength of the sea," I said. Tears gleamed in her long-lashed brown eyes, but she made no reply.

Mau and I took her to a sand-bottomed lagoon. The enormous child bloating her belly was so heavy she could barely walk to the water's edge. He steadied her as she waded into the quicksilver water. He tucked coconut husks from the nodding palms beneath her arms, so she could float. Once in the warm surf with the weight lifted from her bones, she laughed like a girl once again.

The dolphins, in from feeding, were sleeping in the shallows. I swam to their resting place and whistled to Eku, imitating Laka's call to him. Soon, he appeared with Laka and Puki at his side. They dashed in mad circles about me. Eku brushed his trembling skin against the back of my legs. Happily, I recognized the silken, clean feel of dolphin belly. Laka had forgotten or forgiven my bad behavior with Eku and skipped backwards on her tail, seeming glad to be reunited. Still, I was careful not to get too close to Eku. I needed Laka as a friend today. Puki did back-flips and summersaults of exultation. Once they calmed down, I made body motions asking them to follow me to the cove where Huali was waiting for me.

In my days at sea with my dolphin friends, I watched the family help a female give birth. They circled her for many hours, giving her waves of warmth with their emanations. They helped the mother give birth by stroking her flanks when her time came. Then they pushed the baby to the surface with their beaks so it could get its first breath of air. I knew the gentle ways of dolphins and believed it would help Huali to be in their presence. When I approached her with the dolphins behind me, her eyes grew wide with horror. The thought of the sea creatures plowing into her belly, killing her unborn child, filled her with dread. I told Mau to leave her alone in the cove because I knew that a strange male presence might upset the dolphins. She flailed helplessly in the deep water, trying hard to get away.

"I trusted you," she cried with welling tears. She feared that I had tricked her into this vulnerable state so that I could set my dolphin family against her.

"They won't hurt you. Stay still. You will frighten them away."

She had no choice but to be brave. Mau was back on shore

watching with great concern. He did not trust the sea creatures either. Eku, Laka and Puki circled Huali, blasting air through their blow-holes, frightening her even more. Involuntary sobs welled as she cried hysterically. Eku was the first to approach her, offering his dorsal fin. He looked at her with his globelike eye that saw to the bottom of her soul, and she felt his acceptance of her. She reached a trembling hand out to touch his fin. She saw no malice in Eku's tender eye and gave way to titters of relief.

The dolphins swam gracefully in wide arcs of figure eights around the cove, in and out through the warm water, creating a massage not of hands, but of water. Huali surrendered her body to the exhilarating tingling that penetrated her bones. A pleasurable prickling sensation caused her stomach to gurgle and set light bouncing in her brain. The dolphins twirled in a thrilling underwater dance for her, spreading waves of warmth that enfolded her body. They seemed to sense the second life inside Huali and became excited giving off high-pitched whines and squeaks that increased as they directed mana to Huali's belly. My whole body was buzzing in their presence. Suddenly, they skipped off, leaving a stream of bright bubbles in their path.

I went to Huali who was limp, nearly sleeping on her coconut husk floats. Behind half-closed lids her eyes told me she was in a far-away place. Maybe she had visited the underwater world of Po, where there is no human pain, and was coming back to have her child.

"Wai-nani will always be my friend," she said, then drifted back to dreamy silence.

Near the end of her time Huali was so weighted with her child she could not walk at all. Mau, with the help of her retainer, lifted her into her net chair and carried her to the surf each day. Eku, Laka and Puki sensed her vulnerability and nuzzled her tenderly with their beaks before performing their dolphin dance that left her dazed. The dolphin blips became a lullaby to the unborn child, rocking in the sea cradle. Huali sloshed beyond the breakers, lifted sweetly with the motion of the swells for hours, suspended between sky and earth on coconut husk floats.

"My child will be a water baby like you and Makaha," she said smiling. All of her thoughts went to her child. She had no concern about her own suffering. She worried that her baby would be strangled by the umbilical cord while still in the womb. She felt inadequate for the task ahead and at fault for being weak.

"If only I were strong like you, Wai-nani," she would say, as I combed the lustrous hair that drifted to her ankles.

"You are strong like the green tree that bends but does not break," I told her, but the deepening circles beneath her sad eyes told me she was not sleeping. Her breathing was labored, and secretly I feared for her life. The child was too large for the vessel the gods had chosen for its journey into the human world. I slept with her in her hale so that I would be with her when her time came. She awoke in a feverish sweat, moaning.

"He is here... is here."

With the help of Mau and her retainers, I took her to the rock pool where she had first taken me when I entered her village. I dreamed that the baby was to be born into water. Instead of digging a pit filled with pandanus leaves that she would have to kneel over, I saw her lifted by water. The life-giving waters of Kane would take the burden off her bones and help ease the child into this world. Mau and I lifted her from her chair and placed her gently into the warm pool with water to her waist. She smiled, trusting us with her life and that of her baby. A stab of pain clouded her dark eyes. The child would wait no more to squint his eyes in the morning sun. She clung to the mossy rocks lining the pool and clenched her teeth.

I jumped into the pool beside her and began to massage her stretched and swollen belly with long lomilomi strokes. Lifting each arm, I stretched the muscles down to her hips, trying to coax them to be more giving. Beneath her heart, I felt the child bursting at the skin struggling to get out. Mau took her hand. She held tightly to him and wailed the ancient cry of motherhood. The movement inside her body increased in intensity. She puffed and panted for breath, while I massaged harder and harder, pushing, trying to press the baby down the birth channel. But he would not come. The baby ripping and tearing her flesh had only one purpose, to come into this world. He needed to leave the womb behind an empty sack, stripped of nutrients, bleeding and cast aside like a chrysalis. The worm must shed its skin to become the beautiful butterfly.

As nature churned forward with no regard for the vessel, Huali prayed for the strength to see the spirit stir in her child's eyes. There was no anger in her, just enduring mother's love. I placed my hand where the head should be and found that, yes, the top of his head was trying to emerge, but it was too large for the opening. I was afraid to pull on the soft skull, fearing I would mar the unformed bones. I felt certain that it was a boy, for it twisted fiercely, kicking to be free.

"Take him from me," Huali wailed, not caring about her own body, only needing the birthing to be over.

I reached deep between her legs and cupped the skull of the newborn in my hands. I pulled ever so gently to nudge it from the womb, while Huali pushed with all the strength left in her body. Together, we brought Makaha's son into the world. The large head had torn her flesh. Rich red blood gushed into the pool as I quickly lifted the newborn chief from the water. The piko, his naval string, was wrapped twice tightly about his neck. I snipped it with my teeth, uncoiled it from his lifeless form, and handed it to Mau to place it in the waiting calabash. The new ruler's face was as blue as death. I dangled his turgid, purple body by his feet, waiting for his spirit to snatch his first breath. He scrunched the wrinkled, wizened face of an old man. The toothless mouth opened exposing a wiggling tongue. His body shuddered, and he let out a wail that could be heard by the ancestors. Huali, exhausted from her effort, fainted and fell limp in Mau's arms. As I rinsed the afterbirth from the baby into the rock pool, Huali's dark blood curled about my knees.

Dark clouds raced across starless heavens. Droplets splashed into the rock pool, foretelling a coming storm. I clutched the wet baby to my breast, letting my own salty tears splash into his murky eyes. I placed his seeking, toothless mouth upon my dry nipple where he sucked with no reward until he broke away in a shuddering howl. Mau looked at me with disapproving eyes and took the baby from my unwilling arms. He wiped the infant with a cloth scented with herbs, rubbed his body with oil and then wrapped him in soft kapa.

He held the child to Huali's breast and let him suckle there. The sacred bride awoke to see her son siphoning life from her aching breast. A jagged light tore the heavens, followed by clanging thunder that echoed through the mountains. The rain fell in floods, sweeping mud down the hillsides. And so it was that Nohea, first son of Makaha, was born of two mothers while the swollen rivers ran red marking the birth of an ali'i chief of the highest caste.

"May he receive water and flourish," said Mau.

My heart felt as hollow as the bones of birds, but I could not fly away.

17

Taking the Piko of Nohea to Ka'u

Soon after the birth of Nohea, Makaha returned from the mountains and declared a week of feasting to celebrate the coming of his son. He held Nohea high upon one huge hand for all to see. His heart burst with pride as he chanted blessings upon his son.

To the chief belongs the whole land
To the chief belongs the ocean and the land
The night is his; the day is his;
For him are the seasons—the winter, the summer,
The month, the seven stars of heaven now risen.
Let this chief live forever! Evermore a chief!
Let him be borne forth gloriously with the short gods and the long gods.
Let him go forth fearlessly, the chief holding the Islands.

Makaha spent many quiet hours with Huali, who was still weak from the birth of Nohea. She hid from the sun, coming out only to sit beside her husband while he chanted the blessing over Nohea. She was as ashen as a ghost spirit, but the calm of a deep pool rested in her dark eyes. I no longer felt jealousy for her, only a yearning to be part of their joy. The naval string of Nohea remained wrapped in mulberry bark cloth in the calabash. I found Makaha at dusk sitting alone staring up at a half-moon and spoke to him of the planting of the piko.

"It is a happy day for Makaha and all the Island people," I said, daring to interrupt his thinking.

"Huali spoke to me of your part in the birth of Nohea."

"Huali is not strong. I want to go with you to plant the piko of Nohea. I can go in her place."

"No. It is a dangerous journey across the fiery heart of Pele to Ka'u."

"I broke the cord between Nohea and his womb life. I should be part of his re-connection to the father sky and mother earth."

"You defy me?" Makaha said with a look of amazement that held no malice.

"I am twice his mother in love, once in my love for you and again in my love for Huali. I am to be a part of his living time."

Makaha fell silent for a set of seven waves. He watched the quicksilver of the moon captured by the curl of the waves landing softly on the sand, spreading a luminous path along the shore. He gave grave consideration to my request before he answered with the measured voice of a great chief.

"You may come with me, Wai-nani, but you must keep up. Pele has a jealous heart. If her mountain people see you, they will want you to become one of their own."

"I am not afraid with you."

"I am one warrior against many."

"We will stay well hidden."

"I leave when the sun shines pink on the water," he said, turning his gaze back to the sea.

For this journey he wore his white malo. Tied to his waist he carried the calabash containing the navel string, a carving stone, a small gourd for water and cooking, some poi and two pairs of fiber sandals.

"Mahalo, and safe journey," Huali said, standing beside the doorway of her hale with Nohea suckling contentedly at her breast.

It would take us three days and two nights to traverse the island on the trails of the ancients leading to the lava rock field where our ancestors etched drawings into rock with sharp stones

Hundreds of small holes carved into the porous lava rock in Pu'uloa hold the piko of young chiefs to assure their long life and a connection to the land. Makaha set out at a steady, even pace, letting long arms dangling down his side swing with the gentle rhythm of the runner. I fell into his track, but keeping up with his giant stride was not easy. My breath is good from swimming, but he could run for hours never needing to drink or rest in the shade of a palm.

The trail struck up through the pie-shaped ahupua'a, stretching into inland valleys where farmers toil in the taro and sweet potato fields. Terraces framed in rock walls and fed by a diverted stream made beds for the taro plants growing in different stages of life. Maka'ainana stood in the knee-deep water pressing the roots of the taro with their toes to stimulate growth. From the upland slopes growers walked down to the sea on this trail to make gifts of their harvest to their fisherman relatives and receive in return the ocean's bounty.

The trail pounded into the lava crust by the feet of the ancients was hot and dry but easy to follow. As the trail took us higher, it opened to vast, lush grass meadows overlooking the sea coves far below. I could see the white scalloped shore with clear turquoise lagoons wrapped in the shadows of coral reef where the rainbow colored parrotfish play. The water went to a deep-sea blue fading to dark purple on the horizon. A cool breeze licked up the mountainside bending knee-deep grasses.

Stopping only to drink from a trickling spring Makaha kept his pace until the afternoon sun was setting behind purple mountains. He handed me a bowl of three finger poi which I gratefully ate, licking and smacking my lips with deep satisfaction. Before he slept he set a snare for birds so that we would have food in the morning. I dreamed of the menehunes, the little people, who dwell in the highlands, hiding in the shadows of the cool forests playing tricks on passers-by. I saw the shriveled body and wrinkled face of a girl staring at me through a twisted knot of a tree and heard her tender sighs in the wind as I drifted to sleep.

In the morning Makaha stuffed hot rocks into the belly of the nene goose he snared for eating. The succulent flesh that fell from the bones gave us strength. After several hours of climbing, we walked in the shadows of a forest of ohi'a trees. Laka, the Goddess of Dance, lived in these trees that sway with the weight of heavy red and yellow flowers in their crown. A red apapane bird, the honeycreeper, dipped its beak in the brilliant red blossoms looking for nectar.

In their flowering season woodlands were gay with red and yellow blooms, and the creeping vine, the 'ie'ie, was aflame with color. Birds had kept this flower garden alive with motion and with their song. The black 'o'o whose wings hide the rare yellow feathers used for the royal mantles of chiefs were gathered here and ohi'a trees were in full bloom to the very tops, while the undergrowth of berries and ferns were too thick to pass through.

Mist hung in the treetops. As we climbed higher the fog turned into a cooling rain. I kept close to Makaha as he brushed aside palm fronds shading the path. He ran quickly through the green jungle of tree ferns standing four times my height. I wanted to collect some of the golden fibers growing at the base of the fronds for a bed that night, but Makaha was slipping out of sight. A creeping plant covered the forest floor, making it hard for me to see the trail. He stopped only long enough to see that I was behind him, then sprinted on as fresh as when we started.

"Please wait," I cried, breathless.

He waited for me to regain my strength before pressing on. Through a small clearing in the tree canopy I saw billowing dark clouds rising above the fiery home of Pele.

"We are nearing Halema'uma'u where Pele sleeps," Makaha said. "We will rest now and travel under the cover of the night sky. We can skirt the mouth of her home, take the rim trail and cross through the heart of Pele's land on the Iki trail in the sleeping caldera."

I feared the awesome power of the goddess born of sky and earth but yearned to look into the fierce eye of her temple. Raised on the story of Hi'iaka performing the first hula at the urgent request of her sister, Pele, the words of the ancient hula chant kept going over and over in my head.

There is Pele in Hawai'i
Dancing at Maukele
Rumbling and creaking of the lava as it flows
Devouring the land of Puna
A thing of beauty from the sea
Reflecting over the cliffs
In the name of Hi'iaka-in-the-bosom-of-Pele.

"Can I look on the goddess while she sleeps?"

"No," Makaha said sternly.

"But, she will know we are here. If we don't make an offering, she may not let us cross through her dark heart."

Makaha fell silent, considering this thought.

"We will go long enough to lay the fruit of the 'ohelo bush on her doorstep, but if her people see you, that is not all she will have."

As we climbed up the wall of the volcano crater we collected clusters of the juicy red berries along the way as our offering to Pele. When we reached the rim of the giant caldera, I looked down upon the plumes of hot breath rising from the lungs of the goddess. Keeping concealed was not a problem along the walls of the crater lush with foliage, but the volcano floor was an open space, scarred like the face of Hina. We traveled fast across it with only the light of a sliver moon to guide us. Crawling on our bellies, we crept up to the resting place of Pele. Before daring to look inside the caldron, bubbling with her hot fury, we shoved our offering of berries to the lip of the caldera.

Makaha chanted softly to her and asked for her blessings. Pele's ash-rimmed, red eye stared up at the star-struck skies. Lava bubbled in heaving swells that burst open in a magenta spray of sparks. A white-hot fountain of cinders shot to the heavens with each of her melodious snores. At rest, her power to send fire miles into the sky to form molten rivers of lava that devoured forests was stilled, but my heart trembled. I prayed to pull the power of Pele into my lungs, bones and bowels. I hoped to steal her mana, storing her explosive energy in my heart for times needing courage. I yearned for her grace and beauty in my dance. Makaha signaled me to crawl backwards away from the crusty lip of Pele's bed. We kept our foreheads respectfully to the ground. When we reached a safe distance, we ran with legs no longer tired. I flew over the crust of cooled black lava to the cover of the forest on the crater wall.

Makaha led us to steam vents where we stopped long enough to sooth muscles that remembered our long journey. We skirted the village on the west flank of the crater where the mountain people live and took the trail that zigzags down the inside wall of the Iki caldera.

In the stillness of the first light, I heard birds twitter from glistening treetops, wet from rain. We emerged from the tangle of ferns and sweet smelling 'awapuhi onto the lava lake floor into bright sun. The womb of all creation was not warm and soft as I expected. Instead, the air was crisp and clear, and a cool wind whispered in my ear. The volcano floor rose up and down with mounds of caked black rock that once oozed masses of lava and spewed hot coals.

"Put these on," Makaha said, handing me the pair of fiber sandals from his bundle. He put on a second pair he brought for himself.

"Stay within my footsteps. There are soft spots in the crust where the volcano still lives."

He followed stacks of rocks marking the trail. I felt the heat of the volcano floor through my sandals. I became Makaha's shadow, stepping exactly in his footprints. Hot mist smoked from mounds of lava that looked like breasts with steaming nipples. Their breath drifted in light clouds clinging to the volcano floor. Great chunks of broken lava lifted and heaved when Pele rolled over in her fiery bed, leaving great gaps in the caldera floor. Frozen rivers of brittle lava cascaded down the side of the crater.

By midday we reached the other side of the caldera and

scrambled up the steep ascent to the rim. In a dripping lava tube with moss covered walls, we found shelter from the fat sun blazing down upon us. The entrance to the immense cavern, framed in fern fronds, was hidden from view. From inside we heard the voices of the children of Pele. They were coming back from a hunt, carrying a pig on stakes back to their village for cooking. They lived close to the fearful noises, the muttering and sighing, the groaning and blowing, every agonized struggle and mighty action of Pele. Fired by her bloodlust, they were to be feared. We lay very still until they were well away from us.

When the air was quiet again, we headed for Pu'uloa, "The Hill of Long Life," where we would plant the piko of Nohea. The far side of the volcano is ragged and scarred with many lava rivers. The blue-sky dome curls over the sea, and there is nothing in between earth and heaven. We ran down the flank of the crater on a reddish trace winding between billows of pahoehoe lava fields. Makaha fell once again into the steady runner's stride, swinging his long arms in an easy rhythm, while I struggled not to lag behind.

We neared a field alive with hundreds of drawings carved by our ancestors. This bed of flat, porous stones holds the stories of the Island people. K'au is the raw beginning place where Hawai'i is still being born. The burning rivers here have created forests of lava trees twisted into ghost statues as they churned down the flank of Kilauea to the sea. Mushrooming mountains of steam mark their death where they meet the sea. Ka'u is where the land swells and is called "the breast that nursed them." This charred land is a solitary place of great mana. That is why Makaha wandered here listening to the voices of the past.

We leaned into a strong wind coming off the spray-whipped ocean. Golden tufts of long-stemmed grass were all that lived between the rocks in the field of drawings. Among the drawings were a family cluster of man, woman and child of high rank, dogs, turtles, canoes, sails and fishhooks. A fisherman catching a fish was etched into the rocks. Some pictures looked like footprints. These drawings began when our ancestors in the long ago, guided by the stars, arrived on the south tip of Hawai'i in their great canoes.

Makaha spotted a cluster of circles with dots inside marking the places where others had planted the piko of a newborn chief. He paced about the spot, noting the position of the sun and the direction of the wind. He took from his bundle his carving stone and sharpened it on the edge of the rock where others had made their marks. He polished the stone and rubbed it warm with his hands, speaking softly to it, empowering it with the force of his spirit. He chanted while he carved the circle of life for Nohea. The strength of the day passed over us while he made preparations for the connection of his son's spirit to the breast of the earth.

When the sun rested in a flaming sky, he lifted the navel string from the calabash and placed it carefully into the hole he had scooped out of the middle of the circle. He covered it with a rock to keep it from animals searching for food in the night. Makaha arose and began to dance, pulling mana into his fingertips. He chanted to the gods for long life of the newborn. With knees bent, hands lifted to the heavens, I joined him in prayer for many hours to ensure that Nohea would live to be a great chief.

When we had completed the ceremony, he turned to me and said, "Nohea is twice blessed with two mothers to guide him."

18

A Time for Talking

Sullen 'Ele 'ele sat coiled like a sea worm beside Lako. His skin was nearly white, for he never went into the sun, ventured into the sea, or walked the mountain trails. He knew all of the chants of the priests and the order of his society. He looked at me with a mixture of undisguised contempt and secret longing.

His mother Ohaha lay beside her husband resting her chin in the cup of her hand. Her great hulk rose and fell like a live mountain with every breath. Koa sat cross-legged before Lako. I sat on the right hand of Makaha and Huali sat on his left, closing the circle Makaha had called together to share his thoughts. Talk is the way to find answers to troubles. It could take many hours to sort through a problem and to hear all sides of an argument. Retainers fanned the royals with plumed brushes, batting flies out of the heavy air.

"We must make a peace with Pano," Makaha said. "My warriors have no heart left for war. A wise man knows not to argue when he has been worsted."

"Pano is the enemy of our people and always will be. You only give him time to grow strong," said Lako.

"He has never sailed to our shores. We have always gone to him. Our forces are weak. We need time to mend, to build new canoes and to make new weapons. We need to know our children, to strengthen our hearts as well as our bodies. It is a time for re-thinking. No canoe is defiant on a stormy day. It is not wise to venture into the face of danger when the gods are not on our side."

"Pano will come while you are sleeping. Better to die in battle where one will have companions in death than to wait for death to come silently to your door," said Lako, whose greed only grew stronger with age.

"He has never advanced here because the currents go against him. His forces are tired like ours. He will listen to talk of peace," Makaha persisted.

"Has our best warrior grown weak in the knees?" 'Ele 'ele sneered through the narrow eyes of a tree rat.

"He speaks a truth that we should hear," replied Ohaha as she tried to rise to a sitting position. The old chief turned to listen to his wife. She struggled to escape her prison of flesh, stretching her spine to find a balanced position. Her retainer came to her aid. She spoke in a mighty, powerful voice seasoned with wisdom. "I know my brother. He is wickedly wise. He will fain remorse and take this chance to rebuild his forces. If we send 'Ele 'ele to ask for this peace, he will honor his high caste and do him no harm."

'Ele 'ele, stunned at his mother's suggestion, shifted on his knees and looked to his father for help.

"What are the signs?" Lako asked Koa, who was intently reading the bubbles in the bottom of Lako's 'awa cup.

"They say to swim quietly in shallow water when one is not sure of the reef."

"There is more," came from Makaha. "As I was leaving Maui in the red of sunset, I saw the clouds of Lono's canoe on the horizon. There was no mistaking the forest of white sails. He was moving toward Kauai, but he will be here soon. He is coming."

"It is known he is coming, that is why we have makahiki," said 'Ele 'ele, who had finally found his tongue.

"No. This is not an invisible god. This is Lono riding on his floating heiau. He is coming, and we must be ready. We need to set the tax collectors to their progress and have them bring back tenfold what they would normally bring back to Kealakekua. We must be ready for the return of Lono. It is with his power that we will conquer Pano. I have seen it in my dreams."

Lako looked to Koa, who handed him a wad of rancid pig

flesh that he had chewed soft for him. Lako took of the flesh provided to give him wisdom. He chewed upon it for many moments without speaking, thinking on the news of Lono's return and the call for peace from Makaha. He spat the chewed meat into the spittle bowl before speaking.

"We shall seek this peace you speak of. 'Ele 'ele will go with Makaha to the court of Pano. He will take the most magnificent feathers of the mamo for his cape as an offering. Meanwhile, the mountain people will gather breadfruit, taro, banana and the fishermen will set nets for sweet mullet and all manner of moana's rich bounty. When you return we will have rest and feasting for the warriors while we wait for the promised return of Lono.

"What of Wai-nani?" blurted 'Ele 'ele. "Her mother was once the favorite wife of Pano. Why does she not talk the peace for my father?"

Ohaha shifted her innards and lifted her massive breasts off her belly before answering Lako's cowering son.

"She can go with you. It is true that my brother favored Ha'aheo above all women. The presence of her daughter will soften his heart."

I kept silent, while the screaming inside my head muffled all sound. Pano, the most feared enemy of my family, chased my parents through the mountains. He sent them to hiding in a lava tube while I was being born. The truce with my father was based on their mutual defense against the forces of Lako. With peace in the wind he would no longer need my father and his warriors. What would stop him from killing them and taking me to the sleeping mat made with memories of my mother? Even with Makaha at my side, I would be vulnerable. He was one warrior against Pano's many. He would not be able to stop him if the Moi of Maui decided to take revenge upon my family through me.

"Is she to be trusted? Will she not tell her father of our talk?" asked Koa. His voice against me was dangerous. War cannot be declared or peace made without the blessing of the gods through their messengers the priests.

"Wai-nani is loyal to me," Makaha said with unshakable confidence.

"But is she loyal to the ohana of Lako?" 'Ele 'ele scoffed. "She spends her time with the maka'ainana, Mau, and his ohana, when you are at war with our enemies. It is said she breaks the kapu of separate eating when she is with them."

Makaha looked upon me with stern disapproval. Above all he respected the ways of the ali'i and upheld their traditions.

Huali came to my defense. "Wai-nani shared in the birth of Nohea. She is my sister in water and blood."

Makaha was visibly disturbed by these accusations. Instead of asking me if they were true or giving me the opportunity to explain, he did something that I even now cannot forgive.

"It shall be kapu for any man, maka'ainana or ali'i, to lie abed with Wai-nani. Their punishment will be death on the altar of Ku," Makaha decreed. "That will end this talk. Wai-nani will observe the ways of our people."

When the talk ended a bright moon high in a black velvet sky painted a bold path across the dark waters of Kealakekua Bay. I slipped into the water warmer than the night air and the soothing world that caressed every nerve. In the world of humans I needed to be on guard against what others were doing and thinking and to be aware of wrong moves. The sea was a place where I was safe from intrusion upon my thoughts and eavesdropping on my talks with the sacred bride and my true friend Mau. I listened to the sounds of the sea, hoping to hear the squeak or whistle of Eku. But instead my own thoughts rose from the bottom of the sea floor like bubbles in a quiet pool. In this place of solitude, I watched them come to the surface of my mind.

My fear for myself was only surpassed by my fear for Makaha. What would prevent Pano from killing him, the long prophesied threat to his kingdom? Did he know that Makaha was his son? If he did know, would that stop him from setting his many warriors upon him? Would it be too great a temptation for him to put an end to this talk for now and ever with Makaha standing helpless before him? This was a journey of great peril, for Pano's heart was the most deceitful of all things.

Stretching muscles, I felt the anxiousness trickle from my body through my fingertips into the living sea. I heard popping in my skull as my body became light and buoyant. As I followed the white swathe of light cast by the moon, I heard the voices of ancient navigators. They gave me courage as I stroked rhythmically for hours, unafraid of Mano skulking on the sea floor waiting for easy prey.

19
The Way to Wailuku

Two double-hulled outriggers made ready for our journey bobbed in the bay waiting for the winds to be right. A rectangle of mats placed beneath palm trees were arranged for the farewell ceremony. Seated on a mat behind the large 'awa bowl was Lako. Sitting at his left was 'Ele 'ele, and to his right Makaha. Facing each other in long lines were twenty-four warriors chosen for their strength and endurance to paddle. The mellow sounding of a conch shell announced the beginning of the ceremony.

Koa, clad in a long white robe, moved about the ceremonial spot chanting a blessing upon the peace progress. Makaha and the other warriors wore white malos and crowns of forest fern. Dipping a coconut shell into the wooden bowl, Koa offered the bitter brew to each of the warriors. As each one sipped from his own cup, Koa waved the white feathers of a kahili over their heads, anointing them with blessings of the gods. He lifted a male figure carved from a gourd and handed it to Makaha and chanted a mele over him. He then gathered the image and carried it to our waiting canoes where he tied it to the finlike stern of the larger ship. Again the conch shell sounded, ending the ceremony, carrying the message that we must wait for the wind, but that ou spirits were ready.

I was not allowed to join the men in this ceremony, but I wa elected to go on the journey with them as "chief witness." W finally set sail when the space directly beneath the heavens wher the seabirds fly flamed red. A soft Kona wind at our back fille the large plaited pandanus sails. The canoes lifted gently, moving sweetly with the blue swells. 'Ele 'ele sat on the platform in the waist of the boat beneath the shade of a thatched cover. He held the white-plumed kahili spear of peace in his right hand and wore a regal red and gold feather cape and crested helmet.

Makaha steered the canoe, placing it at the right angle to move the swiftest through the cobalt blue depths. He understood the sea and flowed with it. It was a gift. He could feel the movement of the currents and shifts of the ocean's thoughts, and he could read the water paths made by the currents. Twelve paddlers in each ship bent to his commands, working in perfect unison, while 'Ele 'ele's retainer beat the shark-skin drum setting the pace for the warriors.

It was an uneventful sail beneath clear blue skies. Soon, Maui loomed green on the horizon. Haleakala, House of the Sun, looked down upon the island. Our warrior announced our arrival with the blast of a conch shell. A gentle landing on soft sand allowed our warriors to lift 'Ele 'ele's platform onto their shoulders and carry him through the foaming surf to the shore, where we were greeted by an escort of Pano's men, sent to lead us to his village.

Our man went before the progress announcing the arrival of 'Ele 'ele, a chief of most high mana, calling out "Kapu Moe!" All the people along the way prostrated themselves before 'Ele 'ele. Not a sound came from the villagers as we passed them by. Under the rule of Pano, who enforced all ancient laws with strict severity, kapu breakers were burned until their bodies were reduced to ashes, or they were strangled or stoned to death by priests.

The warriors led us up a narrow footpath along the brink of tremendous precipices. Makaha looked down upon the sacred Iao Valley and the mountain trail with the keen interest of a predator as he tried to commit everything he saw to memory. His men had never reached the fabled, lush valley from which Pano ruled his island realm. Winded from the ascent, we stopped to rest. Grumbling clouds clustered about the cinder cone of a crater that guarded the approach to the valley. The Iao River whispered

Island meles as it wound its way through black lava boulders, feeding banana and palm trees, breadfruit, and all manner of sweet-scented flowers.

Once on the valley floor we were taken to Pano's court. Two muscled warriors wearing black malos and adorned with black geometric ancestral tattoos stood with legs astride, blocking the door. Their fearsome faces were covered with fantastic designs. Black bands arched their eyebrows then fanned from their noses and cheeks to their chins. Each mark had been etched into the skin by a sharp wooden mallet with blades made of albatross bone to raise the warrior's threshold for pain. They lifted the kapa covering the door to Pano's meetinghouse, inviting our progress of peace to enter.

When 'Ele 'ele's platform was lowered to the ground, even the guards prostrated themselves before him as he passed. The striated patterns stretching across their loins and thighs undulated with their movements. They stood once more after he entered the chamber of the Moi of Maui. Snarling dogs guarding the entrance snapped at my heels as I passed by them. Makaha and I quickly went to our knees and placed our foreheads on the mat before Pano. 'Ele 'ele went to the center of the room, where he sat cross-legged before the chief who held our lives in his hands.

Behind the most feared chief stood eight warriors, each holding a tall feathered kahili that spoke of their status. A giant warrior with his arms crossed over his chest stood directly behind Pano. I guessed him to be Keo, the legendary warrior who grabs his enemy by all fours, lifts them over his head and whirls them until he hears the snap of their back. Beside him in the line of warrior chiefs I saw the eyes of my father. His splendid body was stamped with the tattoos worn by the warriors of Maui, and a jagged scar went from his forehead to his chin. He stared forward, unblinking, pretending not to know me. The grim carved image of the Poison God rested on a platform beside Pano.

Pano's stern countenance was unmoved as he surveyed the three messengers of Lako. He was strong and sly enough to resist the many invasions from the island of Hawai'i. He added to his strength when he took the island of Oahu from his own foster-son, then killed him and sacrificed him to his war god. Pano was all-powerful on Oahu. He ruled Maui and the small islands of Molokai and Lanai, and he had a working agreement with his half-brother who ruled Kauai. If the Islands were ever to come under one ruler, it seemed Pano, not Makaha, was the chief chosen by the gods. Finally, he spoke to 'Ele 'ele.

"What brings my nephew to the house of Pano?"

"You have beaten the warriors of Hawai'i severely and soundly. We seek a peace, for Lako is a tired chief."

Pano did not speak to what 'Ele 'ele said. Instead, he turned to Makaha.

"So this is Makaha. The kahuna have said your cloud shall rest over all the Islands. You have given my warriors a good test. Why should I not nip this poison gourd in the bud today?" he said, spreading black lips into a sinister smile.

"Because you are the Moi of Maui, most powerful of chiefs, with nothing more to fear from me," Makaha replied, careful not to take the challenge.

Pano grunted. After a moment's reflection, he laughed. The shark teeth encircling his navel opened and closed with his wicked glee. One half of his body from head to toe was tattooed black. Any person taken in crime who passed on his dark side escaped with his life, those who did not, died. It was not certain whether he would set his warriors upon Makaha and end the threat to his rule or take the peace that was offered. He turned his calculating gaze upon me, looking at me with intense scrutiny, trying to understand his vague sense of recognition.

"And what is this? Why does Lako send such a fragrant flower to me?"

"I am Wai-nani daughter of Ha'aheo... wife of Makaha," I said, letting the cruel Moi of Maui know that if I was not treated with courtesy there could be repercussions. "I am sent as a witness to the peace between to the two great chiefs, Pano and Lako," I added, keeping my eyes respectfully averted to the floor.

Pano smiled wide as recollections of days with my mother

flitted across his face like cloud shadows upon the sea. He knew I was the seed of the marriage he had fought with all his great might. His face settled into a dark frown, with tattoo coils turning downward, making his grimace even more brutal.

"This is a tidy bundle," he said. "Your father now stands behind me, while your mother hides in the mountains because of your warrior husband's attack on your Hana home." He spat into the empty skull beside him.

Cold wind blew through the hale, threatening to lift the rustling pele-grass roof from its rafters. Blazing light flashed, illuminating the dark corners of Pano's face, followed by a blast of thunder that shook the ground. It echoed far into the mountains. I trembled at the great might of Pano, who worshiped the thunder god and prayed to powers of the night. I searched for resemblance in his features to that of his son but could find none.

He laughed loud then turned his gaze upon Makaha. I could not tell if he knew him to be his son, but was relieved to see his interest in me passing. It seemed he was more concerned with making the peace than anything else being presented to him that day.

"And what of Hana?" Pano asked Makaha. "Your warriors cannot remain so close to my resting place," he said.

"They will return with me to Hawai'i with the news of peace," Makaha said without hesitation, even though the lives of many warriors were lost to claim this toehold on Maui.

Pano seemed satisfied with this. "Before you leave I invite you to share my leaping place. We will fly together to seal this peace."

Pano was a famous leaper, sometimes from a height of six hundred feet or even higher, and it was said he could climb cliffs that no other person could ascend. Though I considered Makaha part water creature, I had never seen him dive from rocks into the sea. His great feats were performed on the olo board. Makaha knew that he had to take this challenge or it could mean death to the peace he sought.

"Pano and Makaha will be joined in flight before the next sun sets," Makaha said.

Satisfied, Pano then turned to 'Ele 'ele, who had remained silent during the talks.

"I will take this peace your father has offered." With that he opened his arms, signaling 'Ele 'ele to come to him. 'Ele 'ele went to his uncle on hands and knees, then curled into his lap like a small child. Pano rocked him gently as they both wailed over the deaths of warriors and friends on both sides of the war that had ravaged Maui for many seasons. Pano stroked him like a pet dog. He clapped his hands, dismissing all but 'Ele 'ele, who was to remain with him.

It was known that ever since my mother had left the Moi of Maui and all his court could offer, he had turned inward. His sleeping house was high on a point overlooking the village where he could keep a watchful eye on his chiefdom. He liked solitude and separated himself from the other chiefs. He feared spies, and no woman could enter his hale. 'Ele 'ele was to go with him to his lonely house all that dark night, while Keo the giant stood guard at his door.

Once dismissed from the meeting, I slipped away from our warriors to find my father drinking 'awa with the men in their eating hut. The heavens swirled with a furious wind that bent palms to the ground. I sent one of our warriors into the hale to tell my father that I waited for him behind a rustling palm. I sat for many hours listening to the wind voices beneath the broiling night skies. Jagged spears of light flooded my hiding place. Winds churned and rocked the heavens. Grumbling thunder rose to clamorous bellows. Finally, my father appeared before me with red-rimmed eyes, dimmed from drinking too much of the bitter root.

"How is it with my mother?" I asked.

"She is still the most beautiful of flowers, but she pines for her children."

"Tell her that I am happy with my husband."

"That you sleep in the arms of the warrior who killed her son will not console her."

"What do you mean?"

"Mimo was killed defending your Hana home from Makaha's warriors."

My heart grew numb. "Makaha is destined to rule..." I stammered, but the words seemed hollow and foolish as I looked into the sad face of my father who had lost his first son to the wars of Lako. The knowledge that the death-club that killed Mimo may well have been wielded by the hand of Makaha left me stunned.

I gathered myself enough to say, "Pano is a cruel chief. He is your enemy. He will have no use for you in a time of peace. Leave him now. Collect my mother and come with us. Lako will welcome my family in his house."

My father looked at me with tired eyes. "Wai-nani has learned what it is to be a woman. You have your mother's brave heart and fiery spirit." His eyes grew tender, letting me know that his aloha was great for me.

"You and my mother can meet us at the point as we sail by Hana Bay on the way back to Hawai'i. Wave the white flag of peace, and we will know it is you."

"Have I any grandchildren?" he asked, ignoring my plea for his safety.

"No, Father. My seed is stuck in my womb, like a pearl polished by sand in the belly of a clam."

He placed his large, brown hand upon my head. "It is no matter," he said. "If my line ends with you, I am still proud."

Tears streamed from my unbelieving eyes. I clasped him in a warm, sad embrace. At last I knew my father's love for me.

At first light our party was escorted to Pano's leaping place. 'Ele 'ele's face was devoid of expression. He either could not or would not speak of the night before. No one dared to lock eyes with 'Ele 'ele. Makaha wore a white malo. Pano wore his black malo and was carried upon the shoulders of the giant Keo until we reached the steep face of the cliff.

I looked straight into the sun shining off the torrent of water plunging over the lip of the pali hundreds of feet above where we stood. The cascade thundered into a huge rock pool so black I could not see to the bottom. A misguided jump from the ledge above would find a man's body broken upon jagged edges of the lava rock, or the diver's skull could be crushed on boulders hiding in the dark water.

Pano began the arduous climb, placing bare feet into indentations in the rock wall. Clinging to vines the size of a man's arm, he pulled himself up to the top. Even though many years were upon him, he scampered up the steep face like a boy. Makaha followed him closely so that he might step exactly into the footsteps of the man he did not know to be his father. Once aloft Makaha looked down for a brief moment then lifted his gaze to the heavens. He raised his arms, entreating the gods to give him mana and the knowledge to gauge the depths of the pool below. Pano stood beside him. The sun cast burning halos about their heads.

The blast of the conch signaled their time. In one swift movement, with arms spread to the wind like owls, they flew out across the water. Makaha arced then turned his body down, pointing his toes, plunging like an arrow shot from the sky into the murky depths. Pano, practiced at the art of leaping, was at home in the sky and made a pretty plunge. I held my breath for endless seconds until Makaha's swirling dark mane appeared upon the surface and he burst forth from the depths laughing with bright white teeth. Pano rose a second afterward from the raging current and blew from his nose.

"So we both live today," he laughed loudly. "Go back to the Moi of Hawai'i with your peace."

On our parting Pano gave Makaha a manservant, a gift to assure our safe passage. I did not want him among us, as I was sure that he was a spy sent to inform Pano of any plans to break the peace. He would tell Pano if my parents joined us on our return to Kealakekua Bay.

The sky was shut in with heavy mist when we left Wailuku. Storm clouds were flying while the wind picked up speed. By the time we reached our waiting canoes, Kanaloa's fury clamored to stop us but we could not risk a change in Pano's mood. We set sail from shallow waters protected by the reef into the disturbed waters of the Alenuihaha Channel. Soon we were pitching in ten-foot seas of the notorious channel and drenched in spray.

We sailed past the red cinder cone of Ka'uiki Head that marks the entrance to Hana Bay. I looked for the white flag of my father on the point jutting into the turgid waters. He was not there. A fleet of six outriggers sailed from the protected shores of my Hana home and slipped in behind our progress. This would be the last safe harbor between Maui and our passage along the sheer sea cliffs of the Hamakua Coast. Swells rose to twelve feet when we reached the mid-point of the channel. Blue-black clouds hung low in the sky. Gusts of wind pushed us back, but Makaha held a steady course for Kealakekua Bay.

We pressed along the northern coast of Hawai'i in the face of winds that would not die. The men were exhausted. When we reached the western coast, the heavens opened up in a fury. Winds whipped the sea into twenty-foot waves that slashed over our hull. Rains twisting down from the black sky in thin fingers made it impossible to see. An angry spear of lightning opened the sky long enough for us to find our other canoes struggling to stay in sight. 'Ele 'ele was curled up into a ball below his platform trembling like a dog and hiding from the storm. Makaha held the steering sweep and rode up the face of monster waves as we twisted over the crests, then plunged down into the trough of the next mountain of water. Our canoe slammed down hard after each rise, threatening to shatter from the pounding. Makaha ordered me to the front of the boat to put more weight in the bow. I held fast while waves tried to knock me from my perch. But when Maui opened the latch of his calabash wider, letting loose an even more violent wind that ripped the thatched cover of 'Ele 'ele's platform off, I moved to join him on the floor.

For many hours we plunged up then down the cresting monsters. Our canoes rode the storm with dignity, but the wind and waves were driving us toward the rocky sea cliffs of the Hamakua Coast. Now our choices were limited to two. Hold steady in the storm or turn back to Maui. Our boats could be smashed on the ragged lava edges jutting into the sea, captured by the currents that guard Waipio Valley. Our paddlers were weakening, but kept heading into the wind. The high hull of our boat pitched and acted as a sail. The canoe went broadside, turning sideways to the oncoming swells. We lost sight of the other outriggers when they dipped into the valleys of the wild sea. 'Ele 'ele cowered beside me as green as a parrotfish and let loose his innards.

Night descended, bringing more terror. The blanket of clouds blocked out the moon and stars, and we were left to drift in the void. Without stars to aid Makaha in wayfinding, we could become lost or snatched by the currents. The warrior assigned to the sharkskin drum was forced to take a paddle, as the other warriors were weary and needed replacement. I grabbed the drum and began to beat out a steady rhythm for the paddlers, who alternated, giving each other rest. The wind driving us to the shore did not relent. The men paddled hard, but we did not move forward. They were barely able to maintain the position that kept us from being sucked to the shore.

A big wave smashed into us. Our canoe lurched and pitched into a giant wave that plowed over us. It lifted 'Ele 'ele from his hiding place and washed him overboard. Without hesitation, Makaha dove into the black brew and swam to him, thrashing wildly in the swells. He wrapped a muscled arm about 'Ele 'ele's neck and tried to pull him into our canoe, but he made no progress against the raging storm. He swam with the current to the canoe trailing behind us. A warrior on that canoe extended his paddle to Makaha, who grabbed it before the swift current swept him and 'Ele 'ele past the boat into the land of Po. He pushed 'Ele 'ele into the waiting arms of a warrior who lifted him from the water by his shoulders. Then Makaha scrambled aboard the canoe unaided. In our canoe the twin, 'Ele 'ele's manservant, took the steering pole and I picked up his paddle so it would not fall into the deep. I pushed hard to keep up with the tiring warriors, remembering my lessons from Mau.

Makaha took the steering sweep of the new outrigger and yelled over the storm, "We are one boat. One people."

All of the warriors began to chant, "We are one boat, one people." We paddled in unison, chanting against the wild storm. During the night it blew itself into the waiting arms of Mauna Kea. When the sun lifted its smiling face, a rainbow arced across the heavens. My senses were tingling. The fleecy white clouds in the blue vault overhead looked like a crown upon earth. This vast scene was animated by a pod of dolphins surfing on our bow, challenging us to race. Seagulls flew close by, scavenging victims of the storm. Shore birds raced wing tip to wing tip over the energized water. The storm had passed quickly. It was as though nothing happened in the night while the world was being reborn.

We sailed onto Kealakekua Bay bringing our joyous message of peace. Huali stood on the shore with Nohea in her arms. The villagers waved a greeting and beat a welcome drum. When we touched the sand, Makaha jumped into the water and waded to his wife and son. He took the boy is his hands and held him high for all to see.

"We bring a time of peace to our children," he said with a rare, broad grin.

Then he put an arm around Huali and walked with her back to her hale. I ran to find Mau at his fishing house. Though I had accepted our trio of love, the reality was hard to endure. I found Mau filing shells to fine hooks. He saw the tears welling and held me in his strong arms. Even though Makaha had declared love with me kapu, Mau sheltered me from the confusion swirling in my heart. My tears flowed like the rains of Nopopo. When the great storm washing over me was stilled, all I heard was the beating of his heart.

He released his grip and slipped his mouth down to suck on my still breast. He picked me up gently and carried me to the lapping surf. His lameness vanished when he entered the water where he was as free as a dolphin. We swam together to deeper waters, away from the eyes of the village. I felt my limbs slip their fetters and my body become as light as I stroked with rhythmic harmony across the shining sea.

Mau stroked evenly with me until it felt as if we were one

body. When I rolled upon my back in the water, he came to me with the sweet whisper of love. He embraced me and entered with a gliding and rolling motion. I braced myself against the water with paddling arms. The world slowed down. I felt the tingling in my belly I had only known when I was near Eku. I never felt so alive in my own body. It was as though our lovemaking would never end. I felt at peace inside the thunderclap of our love that smelled of tears.

20
Orono, Lono

When Nohea was one year old, Makaha took him with him on his outrigger into the bay. He tossed the boy into the turquoise water to teach him how to swim. Instead of treading water with arms and feet, Nohea sank like a stone. He sputtered for air, while Huali and I watched with horror from the shore. She ran back and forth along the sand, clutching her stomach and moaning. The infant chief nearly drowned before Makaha jumped into the water and lifted him high in the air to show us he was alive.

Though his son had disappointed him, Makaha laughed loudly. He held the sputtering boy upside down by his feet and patted him on the back. Though Nohea was howling, Makaha did not end the swimming lesson. Instead, he stayed with him in the water, balancing him in one hand so he did not sink, and floating him in a circle. Soon Nohea was smiling and Huali and I were laughing again.

While we were watching Makaha, a forest of sails like fast moving clouds appeared on the horizon behind him. The heiau of Lono had come to rest just outside of Kealakekua Bay. Our people gathered upon the shore to greet the lonely god. For nearly a day no signal was given by Lono of his intentions. In that time another floating heiau appeared beside his.

Throngs of villagers watched frozen in mixed wonder and terror at the sight. Twitching Lako, palsied from the affects of 'awa, leaned on his staff staring at what was before him. Makaha told him of the coming of Lono, but now that it was upon him i did not seem real. He ordered the people to ready their canoes and to fill them with gifts for the wandering god. Maka'ainana tending the taro patches terraced up the hills brought mounds of their crop to the village to be mashed to poi. Mountain people brought breadfruit, bananas, and fruit from the trees. Pigs and dogs were killed and dressed for warming imus, while the fisherpeople harvested their ponds for the makahiki harvest feast and the return of Lono.

"It is time," Lako said. "Lono wants us to come to him and assure him he is welcome on our shores. Koa will go first and give him our blessings. Then we will take him to the heiau where Koa will perform the ceremony of welcome. Makaha will come with me in my canoe. We will go to greet Lono together. The rest of our village will follow with our gifts to show our great aloha for Lono."

"I want to go with you in your canoe," I said. I heard the words come out of my mouth, but it was as though someone outside me was speaking. I trembled at the thought of knowing a god in flesh and bone, but my curiosity was greater than my fear.

"No!" Makaha said sternly over his shoulder. "Stay with the other wahine."

Lako countermanded him. "She can come. Lono pines for Ka-iki-lani. Wai-nani would be a fitting offering to a lonely god."

Makaha threw me a scorching look but had to accept the decree of the old chief. The kapu he set upon anyone who bedded me did not apply to gods. I had not intended myself as an offering, but the words of the Moi of Hawai'i could not be overturned. And so it was that Koa, dressed in his white robe, holding the white feather kahili of peace, stood in the waist of the canoe filled with pigs, breadfruit and poi and sailed with his paddlers stroking in unison chanting "Orono, orono."

In our outrigger Makaha stood tall in his white malo. His black hair was flattened to his scalp with oil, heightening his bold features. Standing behind him, I wore a lei of 'ilima flowers and my most beautiful p'au tied at the hip. Lako draped his finest feather cape upon his frail shoulders and wore the crested red and yellow feathered helmet of the ali'i.

The floating heiau of Lono loomed large before us as we approached. His canoes made of wood were massive with enormous banks of sails and rope lines to pull them to the sky. As we neared we heard the creak of the wood in the vessel rocking in swells as it strained against the tide. Our steersman announced our arrival with a loud blast from a conch shell.

Lono's warriors leaned over the rail of his great canoe and smiled down upon us. Their faces were white from their years without sun in the underworld. They wore clothes covering their entire bodies, hiding their skin from the warmth of the sun. They draped a rope ladder down the side of the boat and waved us greeting. Koa climbed the ladder first. Makaha helped Lako, shrunken with age, out of our bobbing outrigger and up the ladder.

Lono appeared before us wearing a stiff covering with golden shells and a red kapa tied tight at his neck. His helmet was three-pointed like the white flags of Lono sailing over his heiau in our village. All of his flesh was hidden from the sun except his hands and face. His faded white skin was splotched with red scaly patches, and his eyes were the color of a pale blue lagoon. His sorrow and long search for his wife had wrung the life from him and twisted him into a fearsome god that looked nothing like our imagining. A blue-eyed warrior named Little King spoke for him.

"Welcome aboard His Majesty's vessel the *Resolution*," he said in a tongue that sounded like that of our ancestors.

Koa bent his head low in the direction of Lono, who stood before us on the wooden deck of his great canoe. Lono extended his hand marked with a jagged scar to Koa and said, "I am Kapena Kuke."

Koa trembled, bent lower to the ground, avoiding eye contact out of respect, and murmured, "Orono Lono, orono Lono."

The rest of our party took his lead and chanted along with him, "Orono Lono, orono Lono," hoping to gain Lono's favor. Lono raised a hand to silence us and wrapped an arm about old Koa's shoulders and led him to the heart of his floating hale.

We followed them into a chamber below the deck.

Makaha's eyes darted wildly as he tried to take in the wondrous things he saw. He was fixed upon the dazzling gold fixtures and polished knobs everywhere about us. Lono wore a shining long knife draped from his waist. Glittering objects from his hale in Kahiki—land of the gods—decorated his floating heiau. Koa placed a red cape over the shoulders of the long-awaited god. He stepped back and gave a talk, thanking Lono for his blessing to the harvest of the people of Kealakekua Bay.

Lono took a splendid cup from his calabash and filled it with a red drink. He sipped of it first to assure Koa that it was not poisoned and handed the peace offering to him. Koa, whose eyes were red and sore from drinking 'awa, squinted at the strong taste, but he swallowed the liquid so that he would not offend Lono. Lako came forward and, bending even lower than Koa, handed Lono the feather cape off his shoulders. Lono nodded with respect to our withered chief and draped a covering of splendid cloth over Lako's trembling shoulders.

Lako straightened his body, then took me by the hand and offered me up to Lono as a gift. I cringed inwardly, not wanting the touch of the ghost man before me. He may have been a beautiful warrior in his past life, but now he stood before me drained of vitality. I feared he would suck the mana from my bones and squeeze the blood from my flesh to waken his lifeless limbs. A wistful smile crossed quickly over Lono's face. He and Little King laughed loudly. I didn't know whether to be hurt by their laughter or grateful when Lono declined the gift of Lako. Koa indicated to Lono that he wanted him to follow us to the heiau built for him and Ku, the great war god. Lono agreed to come with us to the shore.

When we sailed away from the vessels with him aboard, the rest of our people knew that Lono was pleased with our gifts. They came singing and shouting in great numbers. They paddled to the heiaus of Lono then swam about them like shoals of fish, clambering aboard the *Resolution* and her sister *Discovery* until they threatened to tip over.

Once ashore the party was met by four warriors carrying

short sticks tipped with dog hair who went before them chanting, "Orono Lono, orono Lono." The people cleared the beach. Only a few remained in sight, lying flat to the ground in a posture of respect as the gods passed by. The escorts led Lono and Little King to the heiau built for him high on a platform of leveled stones supported by wooden scaffolding.

Lono stared at the skulls of dead warriors lined up on a railing as though he had never seen a sacrificial altar. He stopped to gaze upon the twelve images of our gods carved from koa wood that towered over the heiau to protect it from intruders. As the procession passed them, Koa stopped to acknowledge each one, taking extra time at the image of Lono draped in white kapa. He prostrated himself to the image and motioned to Lono that he should do the same. Lono was confused to be asked to bow to a carved image when he himself was standing before us, but, honoring Koa, he went to his knees and placed his forehead on the ground.

Koa took Lono by the hand, indicating he should follow him up the scaffolding to the inner chamber of the temple. Lono seemed hesitant to follow our kahuna up the wooden ladder, but he did. Once inside, Koa said prayers to our ancestors, reciting the genealogy meles for many hours. A procession of the priests of Lono entered carrying a meal of baked pig, breadfruit, coconut and poi. The priests performed many long chants while the 'awa makers chewed the root, removed it carefully mouthful by mouthful with their fingers and put it into a drinking bowl. Lono and Little King tasted of it, and then Koa rubbed their faces, heads, shoulders and hands with chewed coconut wrapped in kapa. When it came time to eat the consecrated pig offered, Lono declined it, even after Koa had politely chewed the flesh for him.

Lono told Koa he wanted to be called Kapena Kuke. He requested that he be allowed to set up a place to chart the stars by the heiau at Kekaua. He wanted a kapu placed on the site to keep trespassers away. He also wanted a guide to take Little King into the mountains to gather cuttings of plants so that he might take them back to his world and start his own taro patch. He was tired of wandering and needed supplies. He wished to trade pigs, poi, salt and water for the gifts he had to offer.

All of his wishes were granted. The makahiki festival began with Kapena Kuke presiding over a grand feast prepared for him and his warriors. Lako clapped his hands for the hula dancers and musicians, which he greatly enjoyed. With outstretched hands he moved stiffly to the music and called to the drummers for "More excitement. More excitement!" Much laughter was shared between our people and the white gods.

The party went long into the night. Kapena Kuke set the skies aflame with lights that streaked through the starry sky. Makaha looked wistfully upon the sight, wanting to know how Lono had captured the power of Pele. His thoughts were fixed upon the long knives and daggers of Lono's warriors. With these things he could defeat Pano. He schemed on how to acquire them.

Lono invited the ruling ohana of Kealakekua to dine with him aboard his heiau. I was included along with Huali and 'Ele 'ele. Makaha was disturbed by the fact that the ancient kapu that said women could not eat with men was being broken. Lono, who lived on the sea, ignored the rules of the land on his floating heiau. Ohaha, who sat in the platform of our outrigger, could not climb the rope ladder up the side of the ship. Lono's warriors lowered a net to lift her aboard. Many of Lono's chiefs sat at the table with us. The short and limping Kapena Van-ku blew smoke in the air from a fire in his mouth, and a pig-faced warrior named Bligh stared at my breasts until I felt shame at my nakedness.

During our meal Makaha spoke of the objects he desired and talked of trade with Kapena Kuke. There would be no more gifts of pigs or poi from the people of Kealakekua Bay. There would be one nail for one pig. There would be a dagger for a dozen. Kapena Kuke agreed. He saw how eager Makaha was to know about his weapons and agreed to give us a fire show the next day after the wrestling matches.

The dry food offered to us stuck in my mouth. Our men refused the pork because it had not been consecrated. Women were never allowed pork in any event, but I did sip of the liquor in the shining cup that Kapena Kuke offered and found myself giggling. Lako tried it along with Ohaha and 'Ele 'ele, but Makaha did not take it to his lips. Huali, following the lead of her husband, took a small portion to be polite and left the rest behind. Thinking that Lono may prefer a boy-girl for a gift, Lako offered him a mahu for the night. Once again Lono declined. It seemed his heart belonged to his lost wife and no other.

During the days that followed, many of our wahine spent nights aboard the heiau of Lono. Even though Kapena Kuke made it kapu, the women of the village sought the mana of the gods in their offspring. They stole aboard his ships at night and left with the first rays of light. I did not like the rank smell or the hairy bodies of the haoles but I was curious to know more about them.

I volunteered to take Little King to the mountains. He asked about the flowers, birds and animals of Hawai'i as though he had known nothing other than the cold underworld of Po. I spoke with him in his broken pattern and used my hula hands to tell him as much as I could about the way we used plants to make kapa, cordage, roofs for our hales, and nets for our fish. We traded many words. He told me the golden fixtures on his canoe were made of brass. The shining long-knives were called swords. Kapena Kuke came from England, a cold island ruled by the white ghost king. Little King had sailed with Kapena Kuke to Tahiti, land of our ancestors, where he learned to speak in our words. A season ago Kapena Kuke and his warriors had sailed from Kauai to a long-away place in the north world where ice had sealed them in and they had nearly died. They came to find the sun in Kealakekua, and to replenish their supplies for their journey back to the cold island. He asked me to take him to a fresh water stream that met the sea where Kapena Kuke could easily fill the water calabash on his ship.

He followed me up the mountain through our taro patches and breadfruit fields. Along the way I plucked a handful of pili grass.

"This we thatch closely together to keep rain out of our

houses. In the low mountains grows the ohi'a, a large tree where bird-catchers snare the honeycreeper for its crimson feathers used to make the cape of a chief. Images of the gods are hewn into ohi'a posts and rafters for our heiau."

We entered the thick tree canopy where the koa, the largest tree in all the Islands is found. "Koa is made into canoes, olo, paddles and spears and has many other uses," I explained to Little King, who listened with great interest.

When we reached a bluff that looked down upon Kealakekua Bay, we could see the heiaus of Lono, *Discovery* and *Resolution* resting just inside the reef where Eku and his family drifted in sleep in the early morning hours.

"You can see more with this," he said, coming close behind me. He reached his arms around my shoulders and spread his long-eye for me and told me to look into it.

Through it the world came close. I could see the men aboard the ship washing the decks and working on the lines of their masts. It was as though I had the sight of the sea bird flying high over blue waters. I felt the warmth of his body. He did not smell like the others, but was as fresh and sweet as a milo blossom. He did not breathe smoke, and his face was clean of stiff bristles. I turned to face him and looked up into aquamarine eyes lined with long black lashes. They held tenderness for me, and I felt his yearning.

He leaned down, placed his mouth upon mine, and moved his tongue inside. It felt strange, yet this touching stirred tingling in my belly. I followed his tongue with my own then reached to feel the rising ule in his long malo. When I touched him there, he jumped away from me as though he'd been bitten.

"I'm sorry," he said, "I have a wife."

"Why are you sorry? I have a husband." Although I did not tell him it was kapu to be with me. I believed this tabu did not apply to white gods.

He laughed with pearl white teeth. "She is different than you," he said.

"How is she different?" I truly wanted to know.

He hesitated for a few seconds, trying to decide the right answer. He brushed my hair away from my face with a gentle hand and said, "You are more honest."

I took this as another strangeness of the haoles. How can someone be more honest? They are either honest, or they are not, but let it rest. That ended my time with Little King, who wanted only to know about flowers because his wife was not honest.

21
The Death of Kapena Kuke

It seemed the haoles had been with us for many seasons, but it had been less than a turn of the moon. Kapena Kuke's warriors had eaten nearly all of the crops collected for makahiki festival that would have lasted for four moons of feasting. Lako sent the people of his district out again to collect tribute of vegetables, bundles of kapa, a large herd of pigs and red and yellow feathers of the kind used to make cloaks and helmets. He kept a third of the bounty and gave the rest to Lono to fill his ships' calabashes and bless his safe sailing back to the underworld.

Makaha and the other young chiefs grew angry at the generosity of the old chief. This was supposed to be a time of resting after a hard-won peace and years of warring. The day of the wrestling matches came. Our warriors were eager to display their skills against the greedy white gods. Kapena Kuke's warriors were left behind in foot races, out-matched in wrestling, afraid of sledding, and many could not swim at all! It was no challenge to beat them at our games.

An old seaman drawn down under with 'awa dared to test his strength against a young chief. The warrior easily out-danced his wild swings. He captured him, picked him up and whirled him over his head. The crowd roared with laughter as the warrior pretended to plunge the seaman on the waiting spear at Lako's feet. The fright he gave him caused the old seaman's heart to stop beating, and he fell dead in front of the entire village. We were stunned at the sight of a dead god. Lako ordered that the man be laid upon the stone platform of the heiau. Kapena Kuke said no. The seaman was to be buried in a grave. He spoke his words over the body, and the grave was filled by the priests of Lono with sacrificial pigs, coconuts and bananas.

That night Kapena Kuke ordered a fire show to remind us of his power. His war chiefs lit comets that rose into the sky like fiery rooster tails and exploded into sprays of green, blue and red light. Colorful circles filled the black heavens with sparks that drifted down to us and died on our heads. When the skies had gone back to black, Kapena Kuke turned to his ship, raised his hand and dropped it down. The smoking mouth of his heiau opened and spit a fireball that screamed through the night, smashed on our shores, and sent the villagers running for cover. Lono, who had captured Pele's anger, could direct it against his enemies. The village people backed away and hid in terror from the sight, but Makaha stood firm, arms clasped across his broad chest.

That night after Kapena Kuke left our shores with his warriors and went back to his floating heaui rocking sweetly in the swells of our bay, Makaha called for ho'oponopono—a time for talking. Lako, his high chiefs and kahuna gathered to hear him speak.

"Gods do not die," Makaha railed. "These are men of our flesh, and they bleed as we bleed," he said with fierce authority. "Our weapons are not as strong as Kapena Kuke's, but we are many. We can take his canoes and sail them against Pano."

The house of Lako went silent as stone at the thought of killing Lono and his warriors. Though the death of the seaman showed weakness, our people still feared that the haoles were gods.

"Gods respect the kapu of other gods," Makaha continued. "Kapena Kuke has broken our eating tabus. He has no respect for our ways. He is not of our ancestors. The haoles come from a faraway place called England, ruled by a white ghost king. Kapena Kuke is not Lono," he concluded.

Earlier that day Lono had requested the carved image of Ku

that stood at the base of our heiau to replace his broken topmast. It is a hard march into the mountains to get the koa wood, and Lono said that he was preparing to sail back to the underworld and wanted to leave soon.

"Gods do not take the images of other gods and use them for fittings on their own temples," Koa said. "Gods know the power of other gods and fear them."

Lako listened to all that was said before he spoke.

"Lono has said he is leaving us. We will gather more crops to fill his calabashes for his journey. He has given us the gift of metal and shown us the power of Pele. He is a god. He wants Ku to protect him on his voyage. He may have the wooden image of Ku to ride on his heiau."

At this decree, Koa let fly a glob of black spittle into the filth pot.

Makaha's eyes blazed. "I am the keeper of Ku," he said defiantly. His face was twitching with rage. I had never witnessed the full extent of his ferocity. The veins beside his eyes bulged as he strained to keep quivering hands from seizing the old chief and shaking the life from him.

"You are still my nephew, Makaha, and though you are my best warrior, you are not the Moi of Hawai'i. I say Kapena Kuke may have the wooden image and that we can carve another. The image is an image. It is not the great Ku, snatcher of lands. He rides in the upper heavens with Kanaloa, Kane and the rest of the gods. The coming and going of gods is unseen. Their breadth, their length and all of their dimensions are unknown. The carving is only the image of our god in our dreams."

Makaha bristled at the proclamation and looked to Koa for support but found none. Instead the priest said in voice that ended the talk, "Kapena Kuke is not a god that we know, but you are our chief, Lako, and we bend to your wisdom."

The next morning Kapena Kuke's men came ashore in their canoe and proceeded to remove the wooden image of Ku from our heaiu. The stunned villagers ran to hide, afraid of what could come from this act. Nothing happened. The men trimmed the tall piece of koa, laid it atop their boat and took it to the *Resolution*. Supplies were heaped on the beach for Kapena Kuke's journey. The ships' water calabashes were filled to the brim with sweet spring water. Before he left Kapena Kuke, along with Little King, came to the long house of Lako to thank him for his kindness.

"Your aloha for us has been very great," Kapena Kuke said.

"You have asked us for many things," Lako said. "Now, there is something I want in return."

"If it be in my power to grant your wish, I will," Kapena Kuke replied.

"Leave Little King here with us so that we may learn more about the ways of the haole."

Little King looked to Kapena Kuke in silent desperation to see what his future held.

"I'm sorry. Lieutenant King is a free man. It is not up to me. It is up to him."

Lako looked to King. "Will you stay here with us? I will give you land and a wife of your choosing."

King looked down for along time then looked back at the frail old man before him. "I can't stay, but will you have this?" He handed him the long-eye as a gift. This made Lako smile wide exposing toothless gums.

Kapena Kuke received an escort of our canoes when he left Kealakekua Bay. Our women jumped from the ships and swam back to our shores, and we waved aloha with great joy in our hearts to see him leave. Kapena Kuke ordered the billowing white forest of sails unfurled. The warriors of the *Discovery* and *Resolution* left our waters with a cold Kona wind at their back.

The Kona wind begins as a gentle breeze but can build into a furious gale. The leaves of the opua pointing downward told me that a big storm was coming. Soon the sky was entirely shut in with thick, heavy rolling clouds that spoke of high surf. An opening in the cloud, like the jaw of the swordfish, promised rain that would cleanse our village of the footprints of the haole.

All that night the wind tore at the pili grass roof of my hale. The rain poured in blinding sheets and gushed down the village paths. Palm trees thrashed in the gusts off the sea until they were ripped from the earth. High surf beat down hard on the shores of Kealakekua Bay, breaching the lava rock wall guarding the village. My thoughts went to Little King and Kapena Kuke on their floating heiau in the frightening storm let loose from Maui's calabash. Daggers of light flashed across the heavens all through the tide of sleep.

When a glimmer of light colored the mountains and the curtain of night parted, the storm had passed. We were sorry to see Kapena Kuke's heiaus returned to our bay. Kapena Kuke with Little King and nine other warriors sailed toward our shores in three small canoes once again. In the long-glass Makaha saw that the topmast wearing the face of Ku was splintered and the sails attached to it dangled limp in the still morning air. It seemed clear to us that Ku, the war god, had sent the shaft of lightning that tore the mast in two. All rules had been broken, and Ku had responded with his great fury.

Lako could no longer control the young warriors of the village. Makaha was among those gathered upon the shore dressed in black malos of war, holding daggers, clubs and spears, awaiting Kapena Kuke. The great chief was no longer welcome at Kealakekua. The people hid in their huts or ran to the mountains, for they were afraid of this morning. The village was empty, save for the warriors lined along the lava rock shelf telling Kapena Kuke to go back to his ships. Still he came forward, landed his small canoe and walked through the angry men to Lako's long house.

Kapena Kuke entered Lako's hale and said that he was to come with him to his ship. The old chief was greatly confused. He wanted to keep peace, for he feared the power of Kapena Kuke. Whether he was the god, Lono, or a great chief, he held the power of Pele. He agreed to go with Kapena Kuke and walked outside of his hale with him. Ohaha was so frightened that she would never see her husband again, she grabbed him by the waist and pulled him down to the ground with her great weight and pinned him there. Just as Little King was trying to convince her that no harm would come to the old chief if he came with them, a shot echoed across the bay. One of our warriors had cut the cord of one of the small canoes tied to the ship and tried to steal it for its weapons. While he attempted to sail it to the shore, one of Kapena Kuke's warriors had reached out with his gun and killed him.

A great crowd of warriors gathered about Makaha and pressed close so that Kapena Kuke and his men had no room to move. Lako, sitting near the water's edge looking dejected and frightened, did not know what to do. One warrior came out of the crowd with a long iron spike at the tip of his spear and held it in Kapena Kuke's face. Kapena Kuke fired his long gun. The ball stuck in the warrior's heavy body mat. Some of the warriors threw stones, sending Kapena Kuke's men to the water's edge. A chief made a pass at Little King with his dagger. Kapena Kuke fired his second barrel, loaded with ball, and killed him. My people threw more stones. Kapena Kuke ordered his men to fire. When they stopped to reload, Kapena Kuke turned toward his heiau, holding his hand up to stop his men from firing, and was struck from behind. Then he was stabbed in the back of the neck with one of the English daggers traded for pigs. When the warriors saw the red blood of a human, not a god, they fell upon him in a wild frenzy. Kapena Kuke lay face down in the shallows, where he was stabbed and clubbed to death.

Four of the haoles floated dead in the water while the rest jumped into their canoes and escaped. Many of our warriors died from the gunshots from the men in a small canoe waiting in the water. Makaha pulled Kapena Kuke's body from the blood-washed shallows. Lako was stunned. He crawled to Kapena Kuke's body, leaned over him and let out a great howling. He grieved for the death of such a great chief and feared what would come from this most sorrowful day.

"Kapena Kuke will receive the rites of an ali'i chief," he decreed.

It was decided that Lako would be hidden so the haoles would not try to take him hostage again. He would be taken to a cave in the cliff guarding the village and kept alive with food let down to him on ropes. Before he left he put a kapu on the village and sent the people to hide in the mountains, leaving Makaha and his warriors in charge.

As Lako had ordered, the body of Kapena Kuke was prepared for burial. Because a corpse is tabu and can only be handled by a priest, Kapena Kuke received the ceremony reserved for the death of a great chief from Koa, who took a part of the flesh of his body to be used in the incantations and then wrapped his body in a garment of banana and taro leaves. A shallow pit was dug, where the body was buried about a foot below the surface and a fire was made on the ground the whole length of the grave. This was kept constantly burning for many days, during which time a prayer for the dead one was recited. Then the bones where mana is stored were separated from the flesh, and worship was performed to secure their deification. The bones were then arranged in order, with those on the right side in one place, those on the left side in another and the skull bones placed on top. They were all made into a bundle and wrapped in kapa. Decayed parts of the flesh were declared unclean and tossed into the ocean. The bundle of Kapena Kuke's bones was prepared to be taken to a cave where they were to be hidden from time and enemies.

While Koa was away performing the ritual burial of Kapena Kuke, the remaining war chiefs of England made demands upon our village. First, we were to deliver the body of Kapena Kuke to them immediately. Second, we were to return the canoe stolen by our dead warrior. Third, we were to allow them to come ashore to mend their mast with the remaining rails of wood of our heiau. We sent 'Ele 'ele, holding the kahili plume of peace, to speak with Kapena Van-ku, who declared himself the new chief of the haoles. He said if Kapena Kuke's body was not returned, he would fire upon our village. 'Ele 'ele promised Kapena Kuke's bones would be returned to them even though Koa had not completed the proper ceremony for a high chief. He told him the canoe could not be returned, as it had been burned for the nails inside it. However, the haoles would be allowed to come ashore and repair their mast.

The village was empty when they came to take the remaining wood at the heiau. It was a tense truce. All that night fires flared in the darkness of the hills. An eerie wailing for the slain warriors and the haole chief of the cold Island echoed through the valleys and mountains. A bright moon traveled fast through the dark clouds swarming overhead. Grumblings that spoke of a coming storm joined the voices lifted in sorrow. I looked to the goddess Hina for help, for I was afraid of the anger of the haole toward our people.

Next morning the blowing of conch shells along the cliffs signaled the arrival of more warriors in canoes. Our warriors threw stones from slings at the men aboard the ships of Kapena Kuke. One even showed them his backside which further incited the haoles to revenge upon our deserted village. They opened the mouths of their cannons and fired them upon Kealakekua. Their men who were ashore working on the masts lighted torches, and set fire to our hales. Makaha, who had remained in the village to protect it from the haoles, was wounded in the battle fought from the ships. Kapena Kuke's men killed two maka'ainana as they fled. The angry haoles cut off their heads and took them back to their ships as trophies.

Finally Koa returned with the bundle of Kapena Kuke's bones. The haole met him with a procession of drums and white flags along the beach. Koa handed them the remains. The scarred hand left with flesh on it wrapped in kapa told them that this was their chief. Makaha put a kapu on the bay, the haole burial service was given, the ship's cannons were fired in salute, and Kapena Kuke's bones were let down into the silent waters. When the haole finally sailed away leaving our village in ashes, our fishponds empty, our hogs slaughtered, and our calabashes dry, we hoped they would never return to us and would remain forever on their cold island ruled by the white ghost king.

22

The Dividing

The first year after Kapena Kuke's ships left us was spent rebuilding our village. The people planted more taro and refilled the fishponds. The devastating wars with Pano had resulted in the loss of the 'Alapa warriors and left the spirits of Hawaiians weak. To add to our sorrow, the curse of Kapena Kuke was upon the Island people. Many of the villagers had open running sores on their previously unmarred bodies. Warriors howled from the pain of a swollen ule, while many others went pupule and died from disease left to us by the haole.

One season after the foreigners left, Lako brought together his kahuna and high chiefs for the dispensation of his chiefdom. Shriveled with age, he knew his time to meet Milu at the gate of the underworld was at hand. 'Ele 'ele was to be Ali'i-Nui, the divine ruler over all of the island of Hawai'i. Makaha was entrusted once again with the war god Ku, the snatcher of lands, and handed the feathered image with a snarling mouth full of sharp teeth. In addition he was given lands in Kohala and the beautiful Waipio Valley, most treasured resting place of the ancients, to govern. Keli'ie, Lako's other son and half-brother to 'Ele 'ele, was given the district of Ka'u.

Lako's dispensation of power created a tense trio. 'Ele 'ele, though the heir apparent, was not well loved by the Island people as was Makaha. Even though Keli'ie, who resided in Ka'u, never had a strong presence in the court of Lako, he believed he was the better choice to lead. Genealogy was critical, but a warrior could achieve authority through valor and prowess. Makaha, prophesied to rule, was a proven leader, but his time to be chief had not come. Lako, the defeated chief who was unable to bring the Hawaiian Islands under his thumb, died in his sleep leaving anarchy in his wake.

The muddled villagers wailed to the gods for guidance. Koa performed the burial ceremony, chanting genealogical meles as the bones were prepared for hiding. They were placed in a cave that lay to the south of Kealakekua Bay with those of other ancient rulers. High chiefs 'Ele 'ele and Keli'ie, dressed in resplendent capes of bright red and gold feathers, sailed with his bones on the royal barge and took them to their final resting place.

When they returned, a human sacrifice was to be given over to his spirit to assure his safe journey into the spirit world. A captive warrior from the battles with Maui was delivered up to the lele altar. Tradition dictated that 'Ele 'ele was to inflict the deathblow. But before 'Ele 'ele could take the dagger to the man's throat and slit it as though he were a pig, Makaha stepped between them. He sliced the warrior's throat with the blade of an English dagger, scooped the eyes out of their sockets, and presented the sacrifice to the god Ku. This was a bold affront to 'Ele 'ele's divine authority. 'Ele 'ele was much angered by Makaha and decreed that he was to leave Kealakekua Bay and spend the rest of his days in Kohala.

Makaha snorted in defiance but obeyed the edict. He left Kealakekua Bay, taking his growing retinue and warriors, as well as the altar and trappings of the war god Ku. Huali, Nohea and I were to go with him on this journey. On the way to Kohala, we stopped to rest in Waipio. We found the sacred valley rich with the bounty of summer. The morning sun spread over the majestic pal jutting green arms into the blue sky. Wild, shaggy growth on its walls kept strangers from invading the neatly planted bottomland.

Upon our arrival at the valley floor, the people of Waipic gave a warm aloha to their favorite son and new ruler. A grea feast was held that lasted long into the night. The valley was onc again filled with the fragrance of flowers, succulent pork an vegetables in steaming imus and the scent of smoke from the kukui torches. The pandanus leaves placed upon the eating mats were piled high with the bounty of the valley. Makaha reclined to eat one pig and a small dog, to show his pleasure to the people who loved him so well. When all of our progress had eaten their fill, Ka'eo stood to make an announcement.

"Makaha, who wandered the paths and swam in the white-fringed surf of Waipio when he was a boy, is now our chief. The bright star that trailed a fiery plume behind it the night he was born has come to shine upon us. It is he the gods have chosen to give us peace. His cloud shall rest over all the Islands. The people of Waipio Valley give to Makaha the magic of the conch shell, Kiha-pu."

With this he presented to Makaha the famed shell, studded with the teeth of defeated chiefs. Chief Kiha of the misty past brought the shell with him to the Islands. When blown with the proper spiritual mana, it invoked the aid of the gods. If the sea was without fish it brought fish. If the calabashes were dry it brought water. If blown in battle its haunting music filled the hearts of the enemy with fear, assuring an easy victory. For many years Kiha-pu was secreted in Waipio Valley. Makaha's somber brown eyes glowed with this gift.

"Your new chief learned his lessons as a youth walking slowly through the deep clefts of the canyons of Waipio where the gods come close. I surfed at the black crescent beach, learning the lessons of Kanaloa here in the churning belly of moana. Now I receive the lesson of love from the people of Waipio. This gift marks peace to all who live in this sacred valley."

With that Makaha took the magic conch, placed it to his full lips, drew a breath deep from his belly and let the mana he collected in Ka'u at his thinking place fill the vessel. The wild, deep-throated voice of the shell echoed through the shadowy recesses of the encircling mountains. Our hearts were captured by the spell of the sound. I lifted my voice to the heavens and was joined by my sister, in water and blood, Huali. Young Nohea entwined his sweet man-boy voice with mine. Earth spirits joined us with their voices in the winds, the rhythm of the surf, the thrum of the night insects and chatter of the mountain streams. Together we sang the praises of our new chief and danced until the sun lit the tops of the swaying palms.

Blessed with the gift of the powerful talisman, our hearts full to brimming, we left for Kohala. It was a two-day journey by land from Kealakekua Bay or one day by sea. I had wanted to swim with Eku so that I might live with him there, but Makaha wanted me with him when he arrived in what would be our home for four seasons. So I left my dolphin family behind with their brothers and sisters sleeping in Kealakekua Bay.

Huali traveled in a net hammock carried upon the shoulder of her retainers. Nohea rode on the shoulders of the seven-foot warrior given him at birth. I preferred to walk so that I could feel the warm red earth between my toes.

"You will talk to the people of Kohala for me," Makaha said. Even though Makaha was a bold and fearless warrior, he did not like to speak to the multitudes. When we arrived in Kohala, the people living in the wild mountains and small villages by the sea gathered about our progress. They prostrated themselves, bowing deeply to our caravan of royals. Normally they would see only Lako's tax collectors from Kealakekua and give the appropriate tribute. They knew that the arrival of Makaha was about to change their world and they prayed to their gods of forest and sea that it would be a change for the better.

I was not a practiced orator, but I looked into the intense eyes of honest people and began. "I am Wai-nani, born of royal parents in Hana. I come with my husband Makaha, the new chief of Kohala. He is tired from warring with Pano and no longer wants to carry on the battle plans of our dead chief Lako."

The people murmured, expressing a mixture of relief at the words of my message and a curiosity about me.

"It is the ali'i chiefess who swims with dolphins," I heard a woman say.

"It is she who wave-slides with warriors," a voice across the crowd confirmed.

"She fishes for the great ones in deep waters and brings them home to us for our imu," called another voice filled with fervor and excitement.

"It is Wai-nani, the one who loves the ways of the maka'ainana and is the protector of the people," came from behind me. It was Makaha speaking this time for me. Whether he said this from his heart or to gain the trust of the people of Kohala did not matter to me. That he chose to stand beside me in front of the rest filled my heart past overflowing.

Once we were settled in Kohala, Makaha set the villagers to work terracing the hills with taro patches and building a watercourse to Iole from Waipio to water his crops. He enlisted every able-bodied man and woman, maka'ainana and ali'i alike, to work on his projects. They bent willingly to the tasks, for their hearts were filled with great aloha for him and for me.

"I will build a heiau to Ku more wondrous than any other. Ku has deserted me in battle because he has not been loved well enough. My warriors' muscles will grow strong and their hearts will be fired in the making of it," he said.

All who lived in Kohala were set to the task of building an immense heiau within a few miles of the seashore at Pulukohola. It was to be three hundred fifty feet long, one hundred and fifty feet wide, and its wall thirty feet thick at the base, eight at the top and fourteen feet high. The rocks for the construction of the monstrous walls were to be passed from Pololu, the valley of the stones, twelve miles away. Slaves, maka'ainana and warriors stood the whole distance in a line to pass the stones to the sacred enclosure.

Mau, loyal to Makaha, remained behind in Kealakekua Bay to spy upon 'Ele 'ele. He was often gone for days searching for big fishes in the sea, and his absences were not noticed, his movements not watched. He traveled across the waters to bring us news from Kealakekua then returned there with his calabash filled with fishes.

"'Ele 'ele and Keli'ie are coming for you," he told us. "They have war canoes and many warriors." 'Ele 'ele and his half-brother did not forget the prophecy that Makaha would one day reign over all the Islands and they plotted to rid themselves of this threat. They landed on our shores with a small band of warriors with only the bright moonlight to guide them. A trap was set for them. In the skirmish 'Ele 'ele was clubbed to death by one of Makaha's chiefs. Keli'ie escaped and fled, taking the body of 'Ele 'ele with him. I was not sorry to see my long-time enemy gone. The death of 'Ele 'ele left Keli'ie dangerously close to absolute power over Hawai'i, but Makaha chose to remain in Kohala, declaring once again that this was a time to heal.

Makaha oversaw the work on his temple and concentrated on the obstacles encountered in building the watercourse. The water lay in a ravine two hundred feet below the land level, and the problem was how to take the whole stream from the head of the ravine where it fell and carry it to the land below. This was to be done by building an embankment from the bed of the ravine, allowing the watercourse to flow down upon the lands. The last half mile of the channel was to be hewn through solid rock with stone axes and sticks of wood. During this undertaking, Makaha strengthened his forces, building war canoes, making new spears and clubs. He kept all of the metal objects, nails, daggers and guns from the battle with Kapena Kuke in his war chest and used them to create more deadly weapons.

During this peace, he took two more young wives and fathered children with them. His tenderness in lovemaking belonged to them. Even Huali, his sacred bride, was ignored. But as the mother of his heir, she remained in special favor. He often went to her hale, where she lived in seclusion, to play with Nohea. Before entering her hale he had to drop his malo out of respect for her sacred bloodline and to allow his son, who was of a higher caste than himself, to sit upon his chest. He doted over his firstborn son and spent happy hours giving him lessons of navigation by stars, the art of war and the rituals of the Island people, preparing him for his day to rule.

Often, when he made a decision of great importance he sought my counsel, but he no longer saw me as beautiful. He respected my opinion and spoke of me with great favor, but in love he was distracted like a humping dog. Still, he kept the kapu of death upon any young chief I might choose to lie abed with me.

During makahiki, Makaha enjoyed the love game of kilu. To keep blood strains pure, only those of the ali'i caste were allowed to enter into this game. Without a war, the energies and spirits of the young chiefs were filled to bursting. Makaha believed lovemaking to be good for his warriors. In this game five men and five women sat in a circle opposite one another. Each person sat behind a pob, a wooden cone with a broad base. Each player received a kilu, a gourd cut in the shape of an egg that they would use to try to strike the pob of the person they wanted to leave with at the end of the game. A tally keeper presided. When ten strikes of the pob were counted, the winner crossed over to the chosen one and kissed her or him. During these days of rest and plenty when the game was played under Makaha's watchful eye, I was allowed a lover.

I chose 'Iwa-lani, a young chief with a splendid body and daring dark eyes. As each couple found partners, the circle grew smaller. When all the matches were made, the beat of the shark's skin drum began the dancing. 'Iwa-lani bent his knees low and flung them in and out close about me. I undulated in slow, sultry movements designed to fire his passions. Out of the corner of my eye, I saw Makaha enticing his youngest new bride. Her back was as straight as a cliff, and her breasts were round moons. I looked back into the dangerous eyes of 'Iwa-lani and let the fire in his gaze ignite my desires.

Upon the blush of the new day, Makaha found me lazing beneath a palm listening to the white-fringed surf. Instead of being mild from a night of love, he was agitated and tense.

"You are not to join in love games," he declared.

"But, why? I have done no wrong."

"What treachery did 'Iwa-lani whisper in your ear?"

"None. Few words were spoken."

"He knows that Wai-nani knows the secrets of Makaha."

"I am loyal to you above all people," I said, fearing an even more restrictive kapu. For even though Makaha said he distrusted 'Iwa-lani, an ambitious chief with a large retinue of his own, I could see it was jealousy that raged in his heart.

"It is kapu! No one shall lie abed with Wai-nani while I live," he said with finality. He spun on his heel and left me to stare out to sea in stunned silence.

While he spent his days with his son and his nights with young brides, I searched for a lava tube in the mountains. I found one with the opening hidden behind lacy maidenhair ferns. I lined the floor with sweet-smelling pili grass. This I covered with lau hala for a comfortable bed. Kukui candles placed in notches of the porous walls filled the tube with a yellow glow. Each time Mau came with a message, I took him to my secret place and savored the generous love he had for me there. His embrace was always tender. He rocked me sweetly into dreams made fitful from fear of discovery. Death would meet us if Makaha found out, but my sex in full flower would not be denied.

Our village prospered, our storage houses were full and our village was filled with the laughter of happy keiki. My people hoped never to see haoles at our shores again, but Kapena Kuke's men told the ghost king on the cold island that we lived in plenty. Soon many traders arrived wanting the same things as Kapena Kuke—meat, fruit, vegetables, firewood, salt, water and women. But these men came with weapons to trade, not six-penny nails. They were greeted with a mixture of respect and suspicion. Makaha bartered with them freely, collecting an arsenal of powerful weapons.

The early traders armed all of the warring chiefs. They sold guns to Pano on Maui as well as Makaha on Hawai'i. Often the guns they traded were broken and the gunpowder mixed with charcoal blew off a hand or the side of a warrior's face when he pulled the trigger. Bad feelings grew between the Hawaiians and the foreigners. When the word came from Maui that an English captain of a sailing ship had murdered with his cannons a hundred singing natives who had sailed out to greet him, revenge was an easy step. The Island people seized a small schooner that was the sister ship of this boat for their own.

Makaha secured the schooner in trade. "Now, I need a haole to teach us their ways." He wanted the knowledge needed to build the ships of the foreigners and to know more of their ways of war. When Lako had asked Little King to remain with us, he refused. This time Makaha did not ask. Instead, he abducted two haoles. With them at his side to man the big guns on the schooner, an armada of double-hulled outriggers with cannons and many warriors trained in the use of guns, he was ready to return to Maui.

He pressed all of his retainers to complete the heiau of Ku. Even senior chiefs were set to carrying stones from the seashore for the floor of the massive temple. When the temple was completed, a tall kapa cloth was draped over the oracle tower. Three altars stood within the sacred enclosure, and images were placed at the corners for Lono, Kane, Kanaloa and Ku. Empty notches in the rock walls awaited the poison god of Maui held by Pano, the gods of Kauai, Molokai, Lanai and Oahu, for Makaha never stopped believing that he would one day rule over all of these islands.

Many human sacrifices were normally made to consecrate a new heiau. But Makaha, trying to rebuild his forces, slaughtered three hundred pigs and only eleven kauwa for the ceremony. Their blood was used to consecrate the wooden images guarding the temple. When the chanting priests had finished their part, Makaha placed two abalone shells in the carved holes intended as eye sockets for Ku, opening the way for the god of war to receive mana creating oneness of spirit.

At the completion of the ceremonies Makaha sent a runner to Chief Keli'ie, who lived in Ka'u, and invited him to Kohola to talk out the problems between them. It is hard to understand why Keli'ie accepted this invitation. He knew Makaha had 'Ele 'ele killed. But dressed in his fiery feather cloak and the crested helmet of the ali'i chief, he sailed into our cove with twenty-six high-ranking chiefs beside him.

Makaha awaited him in his war canoe manned with the new

guns. He stood with a crescent of warriors armed with guns lining the shore at his back. The yellow feather cape draped over his shoulders flared in the wind. He raised the magic conch shell to his mouth, and the wild song that came from its deep throat made my skin ripple with blue flesh. When it stopped the air was filled with an eerie calm.

"Here I am," Keli'ie called out in greeting.

Makaha believed that the spell of the Kiha-pu shell and the blessings of Ku had brought his enemy to him. He saw Keli'ie's deliverance of himself and his men as an omen of his appreciation of the heiau built to his war god. When Keli'ie stepped down from his canoe, a warrior under the orders of Makaha sank his spear into the young chief's chest, wounding him fatally.

All but two of Keli'ie's men were slaughtered. The body of Keli'ie was taken to the heiau of Pulukohola and placed upon the lele altar as a sacrifice to the war god Ku. The two remaining men were sent back to Kealakekua to spread word island-wide that Makaha was now the Moi of the island of Hawai'i.

23
Revenge of Pano

Makaha now had a schooner and a pair of skilled haole seamen to sail her and to man her cannons and swivel guns. Plus, he had a host of double-hulled outrigger canoes paddled by trained warriors armed with muskets. While Pano was on Oahu negotiating with the chiefs on that island for more warriors, Makaha decided it was time to return to the shores of Maui where Pano had left his son behind to defend his village in Wailuku. Makaha consulted the priests, who read the entrails of a freshly slaughtered pig, and told him the omens were good. With the feathers of Ku bristling in the wind, we set sail with his cobbled armada fashioned out of the old and the new ways.

When he reached the shores of Maui, he was greeted by a band of warriors standing on the shore. Pano's son had sent Keo, the giant warrior, to face the enemy in one-on-one combat. Our people had suffered great losses from constant wars among chiefs and the revenge of Kapena Kuke continued to ravage our people, taking many lives. This way of battle would spare our warriors for the work of the land. Makaha chose to take the challenge himself. The defender of Maui stood half a head over him and smiled down upon him with the tyranny of stature.

Makaha's features, grown coarse in his manhood, were fearsome to look upon. He relished the chance to avenge his warrior brothers caught in Pano's traps. His bloodlust rose as he smiled wide at the giant towering over him.

"Keo lumbers like a whale with blubber around his belly," he goaded.

Keo remained calm, crouched into a wrestler's stance, and began to circle about Makaha looking for his chance to strike. "Who is this boastful little man who dares to fight Keo?" taunted the famous giant. Makaha locked eyes with Keo, rounded his back and danced his way around his cumbersome enemy. If Keo tripped Makaha and caught him by the ankle, he would snatch him by all four limbs, clasp them together, arch his body high over his head and swing him until he heard the snap of his spine, then throw him lifeless to the ground. For a time there was no motion. Suddenly, in a clamor of squirming limbs obscured by a cloud of sand, the warriors were locked in a wrestler's clench. Each bent around the other with straining muscles, neither having any advantage. The least loosening of one's grip opened a chance for the other to strike a paralyzing blow, so they remained entwined, moving slowly in a circle.

Makaha swept one foot with terrific force against Keo's leg and pulled him to one side. But in the half second that Makaha was off balance, Keo caught his arm and twisted it neatly behind his back. He was about to give a final hitch that would rip it from its socket when Makaha bent between his legs and bit the giant there. Keo roared with this insult, letting loose of Makaha, who turned to face his enemy in a whirlwind motion. Blind with rage, Keo lunged after Makaha, who jumped away from him. The giant dove into the dirt trying to grasp Makaha's ankle so that he might gather his limbs into his death grip, but Makaha stepped down hard on the center of the giant warrior's back, then delivered a fatal blow to the base of his skull that left him limp and lifeless.

Shouts of praise rose from the circle of warriors watching. But the death of the warrior at Makaha's feet did not settle the score for the legion of 'Alapa warriors systematically slaughtered earlier by Pano's men. While the life drained from Keo, Makaha raised his hand to his army and sent them forward into battle. They chased the warriors of Maui inland and pushed them back into the narrow steep-sided valley of Iao. The fleeing warriors were shot in the back while they clamored up the dunes the 'Alapa could not crest. This time it was the blood of Pano's men that turned the Iao River crimson.

From the decks of the schooner, the haoles fired upon Pano's men with Lopaka, the big gun. Though Makaha's actions betrayed the noble custom of settling disputes, revenge upon his life-long enemy Pano tasted as sweet as the nectar of the lehua blossom in his mouth. When his warriors reached Wailuku, they burned the houses of Pano, stole the coveted poison god resting there and delivered it to Makaha.

A message of two stones, one black for war, one white for peace, was sent to the great Moi of Maui. The answer came quickly, "Tell Makaha when the black kapa covers Pano and the black pig rests at his nose then is the time to cast stones."

While Makaha remained on Maui with his warriors to secure his supremacy, I returned to Kohala with the wounded where I was greeted by Huali with Nohea at her side.

She and I determined to make the progress overland back to Kealakekua Bay. Huali yearned to see her stepmother Ohaha, and I, even though I could whisper it to no one, not even the night wind, yearned to be with Mau. He still lived in his hale by the sea with his daughter, Lana, whom he raised with the help of his mother and sisters. His days in Kealakekua were spent tending the fires of the imu, cooking meals for his ohana, mending his nets and playing with his daughter. He sang with his family in the evening around the night fire and was content.

Our legs grew weary as we traversed the many gulches on this journey. First we descended into shadowy depths then climbed the winding path through trees dressed in thick vines. The third day brought dark clouds clustered on the shoulders of the mountains. The sky shut in around us. We heard the rumble of a cascade in the center of the pali as it leaped to the valley floor on its way to the sea. What was just a stream when we passed here on the way to Kohala four seasons ago was now a gushing river. A cold wind whipped up from the sea lashing at the rocks below us. Grumbling clouds, snarling surf and the din of the crashing river drowned out the voices of the trees and birdsong.

The purple sky opened up, and rain came down upon our heads in a great fury. Rivulets carved the center of the trail, collecting stones on their way to the bottom of the ravine. Rocks knocked on our shins and tripped us. We scrambled to keep from sliding down the pali and were soon covered in the rich red mud coursing toward the river. Newborn cascades sprang from the walls of the steep ravine. The river we were to cross bulged beyond its banks, carrying trees with it to the angry sea. Huali trembled at the sight, fearing Nohea would be drowned in the rush. Even sitting on the shoulders of his seven-foot servant he could be swept away from us. He was not a strong swimmer. If he fell from the giant's shoulders I might not be able to save him from the turbulent waters.

"We can take shelter in Waipio until the storm passes," Huali said, pleading.

The entrance to the sacred valley was not far behind us. We turned and headed for the hale of Ka'eo where we knew we would be well received.

When we reached the valley and looked down upon the curving shore where the surf breaks hard upon the sand, our hearts were glad once more. Flecks of sun flew off the cascade that cut through the center of the valley where Makaha and I once stood holding hands as lovers. Dew dripped from the giant ferns lining our path, and birdsong filled air fragrant with blossoms. When we reached the hale of Ka'eo, he burst forth to greet us. With strong arms he pulled me to his chest and held me close, where I listened to his heart pounding hard in his warm breast. I melted into his embrace, joyous to return to his ohana.

The Singing Shells rushed to me and took turns holding me in a glad embrace. Shell Beautiful with Rainbow Colors placed a lei of black kukui nuts upon my shoulders. My eyes went moist with happiness when Leaf of the Morning Glory held her infant son out to me to hold. I took the round-faced boy in my arms. He blinked at me with wondrous dark eyes and gurgled sweetly as I tickled his plump belly.

Ka'eo signaled to the people to gather gifts for the royals. Steaming imus were soon filled with pigs and dogs roasting to succulent perfection. Sweet freshwater shrimp were gathered and served beside mullet from the sea. Bowls piled high with three-finger poi were laid out for us upon shining ti leaves. Young boys staggered along in couples with sticks between them, supporting clusters of bananas. Others brought coconuts, breadfruit and apples from the mountains that surrounded the lush, cherished valley.

Huali was given a hale with Nohea, and I was to sleep with Singing Land Shell. We spent lazy days resting at the sea shore, surfing and gossiping about all that happened in our time at Kohala. Huali sat beneath the shade of a coco palm watching Nohea roll the maika stones with the other keiki of the village. She smiled wide as she watched her son—too long alone or in the company of adults learning lessons of the ancients—having fun with the children of Waipio. Ka'eo drew a mock maika course where the surf meets the sand and showed the young ones how to roll the stones in the shape of a wheel chosen to fit their size. He demonstrated the sling to the older boys and showed them how to gather smaller stones so they could practice hitting a marker placed in the sand.

I sprawled in the shade of the coco palm beside Huali, gazing upon the horizon, half-dreaming of my days in the surf with Makaha. A slight movement that looked like a fin caught my eye. As I strained to know the source, it loomed larger and dark against the cloudless sky. It was the first of many crescent sails to cluster just outside the wave surge. At first I thought it was Makaha returning from Maui with his fleet of canoes, but these sails were black. It was his father, Pano.

Never before had the Moi of Maui dared to come to the shores of Hawai'i. Now his band of outriggers carrying foreign guns and manned by ferocious warriors had arrived at our door. Makaha's dishonorable assault upon his chiefdom had so enraged his father that he came for revenge.

"Take the children and the old ones to the Place of Refuge," Ka'eo shouted to me.

"Huali, you and Nohea will come with me. We will hide you in the mountains."

Waipio, with the natural defense of steep pali, had never before been attacked from the sea. The bones of Umi and other ancestors held in high esteem were hidden in caves peppered throughout the mountain walls. The caves were filled with feathered kahili, helmets and crests of the gods, war clubs and calabashes filled with gifts to long-ago rulers and kahuna. The bones of these chiefs in sennet caskets were the sacred vessels for the highest, holiest and most powerful mana. The ghost spirits of these rulers whispered from each rock, tree and flower in the valley.

An unguarded Place of Refuge lay hidden in the depths of the valley. There was no need for warriors to be here to defend it because the country people of Waipio lived in peace, sharing and caring for one another. In fact, there were no warriors in Waipio at all since Makaha had gathered all who could do battle to go with him. A few beardless youth, many elders, women and keiki were all who were there that day to protect us from Pano.

"Gather the slings and stones," I told young boys practicing to be warriors. "Follow me to the Place of Refuge. We will make our stand there."

The Singing Shells ran through the village gathering up the little ones too small to go with Ka'eo. I grabbed two little ones on each hip and made my way through the valley to a hale behind a stick wall guarded by the image of Lono. The little ones huddled together on the floor while the boys and I piled our stones high and made ourselves ready for the oncoming attack. Ka'eo led those who could climb the steep cliffs to hiding places in the mountains. The village was deserted except for a few dogs, confused at the happenings, when Pano landed his forces.

He did not come straight for us, but instead went to the burial caves. His warriors pillaged and destroyed the burial sites and stole all they could carry. Defiling the honored dead was the most onerous insult Pano could commit. When the looting was done he entered the village looking for live victims. His men set torch to our hales while their snarling dogs attacked all that moved on the ground. They tore the throats from our dogs and pigs; and they killed our chickens in their search for children. The dogs sniffed the air to find our scent. Pano and his men followed the dogs up the canyon to the banks of the river that winds through the heart of the valley. Sensing we had crossed the river to lose his pack, he pointed his spear, signaling his men to charge forward through the rush of water.

I saw them coming at us, their eyelids turned inside out and held up with sticks. Only their eyeballs and teeth were left in a natural state. Their black malos were girded up tight to show their war tattoos, and their demon yelps filled my heart with terror. Pano himself was running at the head of his forces with his long spear ready to fly.

"Put your stones in your slings," I whispered to my brave boys.

My brother had taught me how to hurl a stone, but I was long unpracticed. I prayed his spirit was with me today. I took aim but held back my blow until the hot breath of Pano was nearly in my face.

"Your mark is the forehead. First six slings will fly, and then while they are reloading another six will fly," I told them. I stood, signaling my young warriors to rise and let go their stones. My stone found its mark. The stunned warrior fell to his knees, another grabbed for his eye where the stick he used to hold his eyelid had turned inward. Blood spurted through his fingers. The rest came strong upon us as my warriors continued their volley of stones. It is kapu to enter a place of refuge, but I was not sure that Pano would not break this kapu after this awful day of dishonor and defilement.

"This is a Place of Refuge," I yelled from behind the fence surrounding the heaui.

Pano held up his hand, signaling his warriors to stop.

"What wahine dares to defy Pano?" he demanded.

"Wai-nani, daughter of Ha'aheo," I declared uncertain if this knowledge would save or condemn me to a swift death.

At this Pano threw his head back and laughed loud. The shark's teeth surrounding his navel closed and opened with glee.

"The wife of Makaha hides behind the walls of the Place of Refuge." At this he howled. His men dared to laugh with him. After what seemed an eternity he seemed to decide not to kill me that day.

"Tell your Makaha that Pano will meet him on the sea." With that he whirled on his heel and ordered his men back to their boats.

Once the warring ali'i were well away, the defenseless country people came back to rebuild their ravaged village. Ka'eo sent his fastest runner to give Makaha the message from his father. We continued on our journey to Kealakekua, afraid of what Makaha's answer would be to Pano's wrath.

24
Stolen Love

My desire to see Mau had doubled. With Makaha's kapu upon me it would be too dangerous for him if I spent time on his fishing canoe or at his hale. Yellow-chinned Koa might take tales to Makaha when he returned, so I schemed to find another way to be with my sweet maka'ainana man. As I traveled along the well-worn path that runs along the bluff overlooking my old surfing cove at Hookena, it came to me. Nohea was about the same age as Mau's young daughter. I would call to Eku, Laka and Puki and bring them to the sandy cove. Then I would invite all the keiki of the village to swim with my dolphin family. Nohea, being of a high caste, was sheltered like his mother. He needed to breathe in the sweet sea air and feel the sun warming his shoulders. I would help him become brave in the sea and be with Mau without raising whispers in the village. I couldn't wait to set my plan in action.

When we arrived in Kealakekua Bay we were greeted by laughing keiki running in circles about us. Huali lifted the flap to the long house of Lako where Ohaha lay on her side in her dank smelling hale. Six seasons had gone by, but she still mourned the death of her husband. She had three deep gashes on her cheek where she had inflicted pain upon herself. One mark was for the death of her husband, one for her son 'Ele 'ele and one for her nephew Keli'ie. Her sunken eyes were ringed in dark shadows. Her hair hung in greasy strands down to her shoulders. Huali went to her and knelt down before her. She took her hand and held it to her own heart.

"How is it with you, great Mother?"

"Birdsong does not reach my ears. They are closed to the sound. Your Makaha has kicked in the door of my house, bringing great sorrow."

I knelt down beside Huali and placed a hand on the graying chiefess's shoulder. "Let me take you to the sea. You can sit beneath a palm and listen to the sweet talk of the leaves rustling in the breeze. You can watch the keiki playing with Eku and me. Children's laughter will bring sun in to warm your chilled heart. The voices of the wind rushing off the water and the whisper of the foaming waves will give you peace."

"There will be no peace for me until I join my husband in Po, but I will go with you," she said, as black pearl tears rolled down her drawn face.

And so it was that Ohaha agreed to be lifted by four retainers into her manele and to be carried to the seashore. The blessing of the aging matriarch allowed all of the children of the village, maka'ainana and ali'i, to come to the cove to swim with the dolphins. Mau came with Lana, who played in the waves with the other keiki, while we built a raft that we anchored beyond the wave surge. Then we tied together coconut husks to keep the small ones afloat.

I went to where Eku sleeps while the early morning mists were rising and whistled to him. Many times I made the sounds I heard Laka make to call him. Finally, he popped from the placid water, arcing over me like a silver rainbow. He bobbed his head to me and clicked his jaw. After a couple of frantic circles, he offered his dorsal fin in welcome. I rubbed him firmly on the belly and patted the bulbous melon on his forehead. Soon, Laka and Puki appeared. Puki still swam at the shoulder of his mother. Next season he would swim with the other young males and look for a mate of his own.

Once I got the dolphins to the cove Mau tossed them pieces of fish from the raft to keep them playing about us. One by one we brought the children out to the raft. Eku happily slid his nose upon the float to let the little ones rub it. Laka, always a bit shy made mad dashes back and forth past the raft. When she flew high out of the water, we rewarded her with extra fish. Soon she was doing all manner of flying tricks.

The squealing children were ecstatic with their new playmates, especially Puki. He brought toys up from the sea floor and tossed them into the air with his nose. Even old Ohaha, who hadn't smiled since the death of Lako, burst out laughing at his antics. He slipped into a piece of kelp he wore like a cape, draping it over the leading edge of his fluke. Then he let it slide off his body, picked it up with his mouth and pushed it into Nohea's hand. He threw it up in the air and Puki jumped out of the water, caught it on his nose and wore it like a fern lei upon his head. Nohea stood on the raft trembling with excitement but would not enter the water to join his new friend.

It took a full turn of the moon to give all of the keiki time in the water with the dolphins. They floated on the coconut husks while Eku turned onto his back and let them rub the sleek skin of his belly. While playing with my dolphin family, I learned that Eku liked to imitate my movements. If I waved to him, he would wave back with his dorsal fin. If I rolled over while I was in the water with him, he would do a complete revolution. Soon Mau and I had a series of signals that he understood. It seemed he wanted to talk with us. He liked playing with humans, especially the small ones. He would skip backwards on his tail, do complete circles in the air, charge back to the float, slide half his body aboard, and smile sweetly waiting for fish.

Lana slipped into the water as carefree as a mermaid. I showed her how to roll in the water and how Puki would follow her lead. If she lifted her hand up high, he would lift his head up high and bob it wildly, squeaking and clicking his happy sounds. When she swam straight, he swam in line with her and offered her his dorsal fin. She grabbed hold and was ferried about the cove. She seemed to know his language. When she rolled her hands, he rolled in the water. He let her ride astride his back. When the ride was over, she patted him on the belly for a reward. Mau smiled wide at his daughter's happiness.

At day's end when Ohaha had gone back to her hale and all the children had gone home, Mau and I stole the pleasures of love. He pretended to leave the village for an evening of fishing, while I swam to the entrance of the sea cave where he waited for me in his canoe. We dove together into the aquamarine water down to a narrow tunnel through the orange coral reef that opened into a hidden grotto. A waterfall bubbling through the cleft of the rock tumbling over mossy boulders awaited us. There we rolled in the bed of moss beside the laughing water.

He gave me lomilomi massage with strong knowing hands, stretching my arms out of the socket gently and rubbing all the muscles along my side. While I lay on my back, he lifted my leg, bending it at the knee then rotating it at the hip joint. He tapped the bottom of my feet with his fingertips, sending pulsing pleasure through my limbs. I floated happily in the bounty of his love.

While we shared one another's love, Makaha caught Pano just outside of Waipio Valley. A sea battle was fought with cannons from both sides. Makaha saw the white teeth of Pano gleaming in the flash of gunfire and heard his evil laughter over the roar of the cannons.

"Next time you will not slip through my net," Pano yelled across the lashing seas as he caught the trade winds in his sails and steered his vessel away from the fight. But he never ventured to the shores of Hawai'i again.

Even after Makaha and his warriors returned victorious, Mau and I continued our tabu pleasures. We knew Makaha would crush our skulls with his own hands if he knew we were sharing the secrets of love, but we did not stop. I was resting in the women's hale when my retainer came to warn me. "You must run." She had heard Koa wagging his tongue to Makaha. "He saw it in the 'awa leaves that you and Mau have broken Makaha's kapu."

At first my heart went numb. Makaha would be upon me in seconds. I remembered his fierce combat that crowded out all tenderness. I knew my only chance to live through his anger was to swim to the Place of Refuge where I had met the crone plucking crabs from the tide pools.

"Tell Mau to take Lana and sail to Hana. Tell him to find my mother. She will hide him and take his daughter into her heart." Then I ran to the sharp rock ledge that lines the Kealakekua Bay and dove into still waters.

25
To Live and Die by Water

It is forbidden to chase an enemy past the massive rock walls that surround the safe haven that is the Place of Refuge. Warriors have been slain at the doorstep with the carved images of Lono, Kane, Kanaloa and Ku looking on, but if they had made it inside the gates, the ancient laws would have protected them. To get inside the sacred walls before Makaha reached me was my only hope.

It was a half-day's swim with no stopping for rest. I extended my arms and legs to their fullest and moved into a rhythmic stroke, concentrating on a steady pattern in my breath. I tried not to think of what violence would befall me if I could not out-swim my husband's rage. I hoped to reach the place in my swimming that takes "no thinking" and that I could make it to the refuge faster than Makaha could follow in his canoe.

Once outside the shelter of the reef the winds from Maui made the water jumpy. The fighting winds created a squall that slowed my progress. But I caught a strong current that carried me in the direction I wanted to go. Even though swimming for my life, I felt free to be in the sea once again. The terror in my heart flew out my fingertips, giving me speed in the water. I was balanced, gliding close to the surface, fast losing myself to the pulse of the liquid world. Many nights in my dreams I was not human but aquatic with gills and fins and flew through the water like Eku. Once I was an octopus with red suction cups, jetting through the sea squirting ink in my elegantly elusive wave. If only I had that power of disguise to save me today!

I slowed long enough to look over my shoulder and saw the triangular sail of Makaha's outrigger. He stood at the sweep, a lone warrior with black mane tossing in the wild wind. His anger flared like sparks from the volcano. If he caught me in this time of wounded pride and rage at my refusal to obey, he would crush me like a crab in his strong grip. Powerful in physique and a capable navigator, he could steer the sweep and man the sail of his canoe alone. The winds were working to my advantage, making his progress slow, but he was gaining on me.

His canoe rode up the face of the chop and thudded down in a pounding progress. I was better able to ride the waves in the water. The bumpy water and low clouds spoke of more wind that he would have to sail into. If this happened, I would be able to make it to the rocks walls of the refuge and climb over to safety. I sealed my mind to the fear in my heart and concentrated on swimming. I rolled over on my back, sliding into an easy, fast flowing stroke and closed my eyes to the bright sun. I saw my old allies. The ephemeral light behind each of their cone shaped heads outlined their bodies. They each placed a hand on my heart until ten hands were stacked one upon the other. I felt the burning power of their mana giving me strength as I swam.

The voice of the wind did rise, keeping Makaha well behind me. His sail was becoming smaller now, and I could see the point of the jetty where the Place of Refuge rests upon the horizon. This bad dream would soon be over. Makaha, who respected the old ways, would honor the kapu of the Place of Refuge, and I would be safe. The storm in his heart would pass, and he would become calm once more like the sea in the morning. As I comforted myself with these thoughts, I caught a glimpse of a white fin slicing through the chop. My bruised heart nearly flew out of its cage at the sight of Eku! A miracle had brought him to me. In my flight, I didn't have time to call to him, but now I could ride with him above the waves and escape the anger of Makaha. I turned to clasp my old friend in rolling embrace but pulled back in horror.

Instead of the warm luminous eye of Eku, I saw the onyx black eye of Mano the shark staring at me with glasslike calm. Though terrified that a thirteen-foot man-eater was swimming with me, I could not help but be mesmerized by his power. I had never seen Mano this close—his pointed snout and five large gills. Only in the fishing boat with Mau had I seen one this large circling in the distance, preying upon the sailfish and mahi-mahi. This one was twice the size of Eku with a short white fin that sat high on his back.

The threat of Makaha's wounded pride drifted back in my mind. He could be talked to, but Mano knew no reasoning. The flood of fear rushing through my tired limbs gave me new strength. He swam slowly, moving beside me. I decided to show no concern, but to keep stroking as though going for a walk with a friend. He came close so that I could see sharp, pointed teeth jutting from his lower jaw. His mouth was made for catching slippery fast-swimming fish, not slow plodding humans. This was not the great white, the most feared of all the monsters in the sea that carved a scar in my brother's belly, but a smaller cousin. The creature was content to swim alongside me and brushed against my body with rough skin, scraping the flesh on my thigh. I felt the sting of the saltwater on the wound but continued stroking and kicking towards the point, now coming near enough for me to see the oracle tower covered with kapa cloth.

I prayed my blood in the water would not stir Mano's appetite. Not only was my leg bleeding, I was full into my time in the women's hale. Instead of attacking, he simply swam with me as though he were my bodyguard. I determined that he must be an 'aumakua. It is known that a fallen spirit will find a body to inhabit if it wants to join the mortal world again. I believed the spirit swimming beside me was that of my brother, Mimo, now floating in the underwater world of Po. He must have seen my trouble, taken on the shark's skin and arrived to protect me against the fever-pitch fury of my husband. He stayed with me until I reached the fish ponds and the tiny white sand cove of the Place of Refuge that opens to the sea. Then he circled about me twice, fanned his tail and swam back to the deep waters. I watched his white fin slice through the water and thanked the spirit of my shark brother for giving me his great strength.

Makaha's sail was now close behind me. I ran inside the walls of the heiau to find the good priest, A'ala, to ask him to hide me there. There are no questions asked of the weary and desperate who make it inside the sacred gates. He gave me a pa'u to cover my nakedness. "You can hide beneath that rock," A'ala said, pointing to a shallow ledge supported by boulder legs. "I will tell Makaha that even he cannot enter in chase. When your trouble has passed, I will come and get you."

I trusted the kind, old priest and did as he told me. It was a tight squeeze, but I stretched out flat upon the ground. My heart was pounding like a thunderclap. I shuddered with fear when I heard the sound of heated voices.

"Where is she?" demanded Makaha. "I know she is here."

"It is forbidden for you to enter," the priest said.

"She has broken my kapu," Makaha bellowed. "I am Makaha, keeper of Ku. Get out of my way," Makaha said, brushing the priest aside. I trembled with fear when I heard his footsteps. He was sniffing about like a dog looking under rocks, in the sea caves and around the tide pools trying to find my scent. I felt his presence through the rock ledge I hid under. Before I could run he was upon me. He routed me from my hiding place and dragged me out from under the rock by my hair. His body shook, and his eyes were ringed red with rage. His mouth curled into a snarl.

"Wai-nani has made a fool of me. You have broken my kapu for the last time." He growled, reaching for my throat. He held my neck with both hands, stopping the air. I clawed at his face but grew weak. The world was going black. He shook me violently, lifting me off the ground, cutting off the blood to my mind.

"Makaha is a cruel chief who has lost his mana," I sputtered. "Ku rules your heart." I felt my face swell purple, while tears spurted from my eyes.

"Your father is Pano," I blurted, desperate to say something that would stop him from killing me. At this, he dropped me like a hot cinder.

"You are lying."

I choked on my words but got them out before the world went black. "You are the seed of the Moi of Maui."

Stunned with this revelation, Makaha slumped to the ground. His entire world was built upon his genealogy. The knowledge that he had been at war with his father, blood of his blood, his entire life knocked his knees from under him.

"You say this to save your life."

"Yes, but it is a truth that I have carried with me since our days at Ka'u where Ka'eo put the burden of understanding upon me."

"That is why Pano did not kill me when I stood before him."

"Yes. You have become who you hate," I dared. To fulfill his prophecy as ruler of all the Islands, he would have to kill Pano, whom he now knew to be his father.

Makaha went silent. His massive head dropped between his knees as he tried to comprehend why he had been given this hard destiny. He could not find the answer. I sat down beside him upon the cold stone floor of the heiau and pulled him close to my heart. I stroked his wild mane and pressed my thumbs gently on his throbbing temples. He gave way to the agony welling deep inside his giant body. His shoulders lurched with heaving sobs that he let flow like the rains of Napopo. I rocked him there in my arms until the orange sun sank into the black water. His heart finally grew still, and he could speak once more.

"Wai-nani is my never-fading flower."

His tenderness to me had returned, so I tried to explain. "There is no one above you, but no hala fruit shows its color in the darkness of night. My flesh is one with the sea and the sky and the pulsing ocean. The mana that flows through me cannot be contained just as water will not stay in your hand. It must be enjoyed. There is no more."

"I cannot let you love Mau. You make me look foolish."

"Your kapu is cruel. Makaha has many wives. Your truth remains with me, if you let Mau live."

He turned to face me, brushing my hair back from my face, smoothing it down with a gentle, giant hand. A tender play of confused emotions softened his wondrous eyes. He took my hand and led me to the tide pools where I met the old woman who gave me the black tears of Pele to protect me against danger. We watched the lapping waves until Hina's tinkling laughter lit up the heavens, and then we set sail for Kealakekua Bay, together once more. Makaha stood at the steering sweep and rode the heave of the waves with his eyes fixed upon a cluster of stars in the heavens pointing to the way home. I sat in the bow, leaning into the soft warm wind. The night air was sweet, gentle and cool upon my skin as we rocked upon the silver path cast upon the luminous waters by Hina smiling high overhead.

26
Two Minds One Heart

Makaha did not give chase to Mau, who fled with his daughter to Hana. Instead he made the journey to his thinking place in Ka'u. In the stark lava fields where the wind bends golden grasses low to the ground, he found solace. There he lifted fingertips to the sky and chanted mele for many hours hoping to receive mana and gain the wisdom to deal with his new truth. When he returned to Kealakekua Bay, his face was solemn, but his features were calm. His resolve to conquer his father's forces and gain control over all of the islands was greater than ever before.

He did not punish me further for my love of Mau, but he did assign a humpbacked dwarf to follow in my footsteps. This irksome shadow was to report back to him if I should smile at another chief. If I were found in another's arms, the dwarf was to be put to death. In this way Makaha freed his mind of angry thoughts, and he could go back to the pressing matters of war.

After Makaha's victory over the Mauin forces, Pano sailed back to Oahu and built new storage houses and a great army there. Makaha determined that he would take his armada of shallow-draft, double-hulled outriggers and the cannon-equipped schooner to Oahu and crush his father's power now and for all time. Testing his strength, he took his fleet to the two smaller islands of Molakai and Lanai and easily brought them under his command. He sailed home victorious and even more resolute to build naval forces strong enough to take Oahu, the last military stronghold between him and absolute authority over all of the Hawaiian Islands.

Our world changed rapidly during the years of Makaha's rise to power. The foreigners brought us many things both evil and good. Our borrowed haoles not only taught our warriors how to kill with modern tools of gunpowder, cannons, muskets and cutlasses. They gave Makaha lessons in foreign dress, customs and language. They acted as translators and taught Makaha all the tricks of trading with the ships that often came to our shores. The ships from England brought beautiful cloths from tight looms and fitted clothes made by fine tailors. We had acquired furniture, steel tools and new breeds of pigs, goats and sheep. The visitors also brought us tobacco and alcohol that caused our warriors to lose their minds.

Makaha was able to take the good and leave the bad offered to him by the haoles, but many of our people were not as strong as their leader. He made it kapu for our people to drink the haole's liquor, but this kapu did not apply aboard the foreign ships. Our wahine swam out to the boats holding their kapa skirts overhead so they would not be destroyed in the water. Once aboard they ate kapu pork and bananas, drank liquor and sang and danced with the men until the curtains of night parted. They swam back to our shores in the morning mists carrying gifts to their families from the sailors.

It was a far different world from the one Kapena Kuke sailed into in haole year 1778 that Kapena George Vancouver we knew as Kapena Van-ku found when he returned to Kealakekua Bay in 1792. This time when we saw the tree forest of masts and white billowing sails of *Discovery* resting on the horizon, we set out to greet the ship on our trading barge. Makaha wore the splendid white shirt given to Lako by Kapena Kuke and the long black trousers worn by foreigners. On his broad shoulders rested his magnificent cape of yellow mamo bird feathers that floated to the ground. On his regal head rested the crested yellow and red feather helmet of a great chief. The royal spittoon carrier to capture all of his bodily fluids never left his side. Even though he was the all powerful Moi of Hawai'i, he feared his enemies would give bait to ana'ana priests to direct evil forces against him.

I sat beside him wearing a fragrant, double lei of 'ilima flowers, a forest fern crown and a brilliant pa'u stained with the colors of the sunset. Several of his other wives joined us in the parley. Our haole was there to talk for us, and Koa, now the oldest and most powerful priest in Hawai'i, stood beside Makaha wearing his white kapa cape, holding the white kahili staff of peace in his hand. Our barge, powered by thirty-six paddlers, was laden with gifts for our visitors; eighty pigs, a dozen dogs and mounds of breadfruit.

Makaha ordered the multitudes to greet the ship. Like shoals of fish our people swarmed the bay. More than thirty thousand of our people in canoes filled with gifts circled *Discovery*. Thousands more lining the shore dove into the water holding a small pig or a bird above the waterline to bring to the ship. The beat of shark drums, tap of sticks and the wail of nose flutes made a swell of music greater than that of any birdsong. Once we were aboard ship, our offerings were piled high upon the deck.

Kapena Vancouver greeted us, not as a fake god, but as a human with a broad smile. He wore the royal flame red jacket of war, but his piercing blue eyes crinkled with good humor. He lifted the three-corner hat from his nearly hairless head, swept it grandly in front of his body and bowed deeply to us. He was plump from a plentiful life. His rosy face was damp with sweat, and droplets of moisture hovered above his lips. When he clasped Makaha in welcome, his bulging eyes met Makaha's piko knot. Makaha bent down to brush Kapena Vancouver's nose with his own in greeting. Vancouver stepped back and offered his hand. Our haole spoke for us.

"You are welcome in Kealakekua Bay."

"I bring gifts from England where His Majesty King George the Third sends greetings to the great chief Makaha."

Kapena Vancouver ordered his men to bring forth a huge beast with long sharp horns. It pawed the deck and swayed its head back and forth surveying its enemy. Steam came from its slimy flared nostrils and its dark eyes, ringed in white, were shot through with red. Makaha extended his hand to touch the thing. It snorted lowered its head further and moved toward him menacingly. A great athlete, Makaha jumped into the rigging of the ship where he swayed from a safe vantage sizing up the strange gift of King George. Four cows were brought forth to keep the monster bull company on our island.

"They give sweet milk and are good eating," said Kapena Vancouver.

"These large pigs will feed many at one time," Makaha said, jumping down to the deck to get a closer look at his wonderful gifts. "How is it with King George on his cold island?" asked Makaha.

"He prospers and has sent Makaha many seeds and cuttings of new vegetables and fruits to show his aloha for the Hawaiian people," said Kapena Vancouver, wiping the beads of perspiration from his lip with a lacy kerchief pulled from his sleeve.

"What weapons do you have to trade?" Makaha asked.

"I will give you the same answer I gave to Pano," he replied with a broad grin. "None, you will prosper more in peace than in war."

"Then why have you come to our harbor?" Makaha asked, annoyed that Vancouver would not give him what he wanted.

"His Majesty has commissioned me to take the islands off Nootka Sound on the Northwest coast of America back from the Spaniards."

"Then you have weapons for your war."

"Yes, but they are not for sale."

"What good are you to me then?"

"I am your friend."

"You are also the friend of Pano."

"A wise leader knows the heart of his enemy as well as his friends."

Makaha was silenced with this, and there was no more talk of guns.

"Won't you join me in my quarters?" Kapena Vancouver asked, waving us to follow him.

We stepped over the chickens in coops and piglets that ran

free on the deck, and went down a wooden ladder to the same cabin we had shared with Kapena Kuke fourteen years ago. Kapena Vancouver offered a lavish meal of fowl, fruit and cheese presented to us on fine china. I drank dark sherry from a silver chalice and laughed loudly into the night. We played checkers, the game much like our konane. Kapena Vancouver lost the wager of a pearl necklace and an exquisite looking glass to me and challenged me to another game. Makaha nodded to let me know it would be all right for me to return to the ship another day to meet his challenge.

We left *Discovery* with our canoes laden with gifts from King George. Makaha was delighted with his huge "new pigs." Villagers lined the shore and looked on them with terror in their eyes. Once they were upon the sand, the animals broke loose and galloped on the beach, kicking their heels. Our people ran for the sea and plunged in while others shinnied up coco palms to hide from the monsters. Some scrambled up rocks to flee the snorting bull and none would approach the cows. Two sailors, given to us to tend to what they called cattle, collected the beasts. The bull was not in good health from his long journey from the cold island and needed special care, so Makaha ordered that a place be built for him.

The masts of *Discovery* swayed in silhouette against the orange sunsets over Kealakekua Bay for two turns of the moon. George Vancouver asked to see where Kapena Kuke died once more. We took him to that place across the bay.

"Has King George forgiven the Hawaiian people for the death of their great chief?" Makaha asked. He lived in sadness because of the misunderstandings that took place between our people and the wandering chief.

After many silent moments of prayer for his lost chief, George Vancouver replied, "Yes." He had been on the deck watching through his long-eye the day that Kapena Kuke was killed. Makaha, eager to make amends, gave our guest the same place that was given to Kapena Kuke to set up his star-gazing eyes and made it kapu for anyone, especially women, to enter the area. Makaha built the sailors a sleeping hale beside the area, so wahine could visit the men when clouds crowded the stars out of sight during their long hours charting the heavens.

While I was sitting under the branches of a cloth tree built for me by my attendants, a seaman dared to sit by my side. He did not know of the kapu placed upon me and was not afraid of the eyes of the dwarf who shared the cool air of my servants' fans. I continued to string puka shells for a special necklace while he spoke to me of his travels.

I did not spend nights on the ships like the other wahine, so I was curious about the haoles. I asked the seaman to lift his shirt so that I could touch the swirls of soft blond hair on his belly. The skin on his back was covered with brown and red blotches and curly white hair. Patches of skin fell off his nose leaving cracked, bald red places. I tied some red ribbons in his golden hair to help his appearance. When I requested to see the whole of his body, he pulled down his long pants. I was shocked to see a tattoo that resembled those of our ancestors imprinted upon his right buttock. I sent my retainer to get Koa so that he might read it for me. Koa came quickly, bent down to examine the markings closely, then looked up at me with a sly grin.

"It is the mark of the pinworm."

All who heard gave way to gales of laughter. The red-faced sailor told us that he had been stamped with this insult by a kahuna in Tahiti. I placed a crown of forest ferns upon his head to thank him for this knowledge. He confirmed for us that our people came here in the long-long ago from the island of Tahiti. Our legends tell us that they were guided here by an ancestral guardian shark named Kalahiki. They did not come to harm or fear death, for he led them over the black oceans like beloved children. When it was stormy and the ocean was rough, he swam in front of the canoe fleet. If they lay becalmed at sea with land out of sight, he lay with his head in the direction of Hawai'i that rests beneath the brightest star in the heavens.

The haoles had many gleaming instruments to help them cross the seas between the cold island and our island home. They were able to retrace their steps, to stop at Tahiti for supplies, and to find us in the vast ocean world at will. The ships of traders that followed came using their maps. Kapena Vancouver was happy to answer all of Makaha's many questions about these charts. He spun a round toy world on its axis and pointed his finger to what he called "The Sandwich Islands."

"Grid lines of latitude and longitude are used to pinpoint a spot on our world map," he said. He brought out a wooden box and opened it for us to see. Inside resting in plush silk lining was a ticking face.

"With this clock I can tell time at sea. It is always set to the time in England. With it I can calculate the longitude. The secret of knowing where you are is to know what time it is," he said.

Makaha was in awe of the ticking timepiece and immensely respected the sea knowledge of the haoles. Vancouver showed him how to use the log line, a fifty-foot rope with knots at intervals let down to drag behind the ship in the water. Counting the knots told him how fast he was sailing and allowed him to calculate a dead reckoning. He also used lunar tables to read the angle between the moon and the stars, and that is why the men were set to measuring the heavens on land, free of the sway of the rocking ship.

"I see the currents moving and watch the drift of the clouds," Makaha explained. "If a cloud is plump and yellow and hangs low on the horizon it is a sign of calm weather. If the sky in the west is blue-black at sunset it will bring high surf. If there is an opening in the cloud like the jaw of a swordfish, there will be rain. The kona from the south is a withering wind that will cause waves to rise up." For many hours Kapena Vancouver and Makaha shared secrects of moana, the grand and vibrant sea.

When the day came for the promised checker game with Kapena Vancouver, the annoying dwarf and one of my female retainers were assigned to watch over me aboard *Discovery*. The game went well and my winnings piled high. I laughed loud and drank much of the sweet liquid George Vancouver shared with me. Kapu lines became blurred, and the tabus of our people were often broken aboard the ships. Kapena Vancouver sensed from my recklessness that I was hiding sadness behind shining eyes.

"Wai-nani, is something troubling Your Highness?" he asked. "Can I be of service?"

I don't know why, but I found myself telling my troubles to this strange man who seemed to want only to be a friend to the Island people. "Makaha has not touched me since I told him a sorry truth that he cannot bear. He wants me at his side to speak for him and to stand tall before the people, but he does not want me in his arms. I stir up bad thoughts for him. It is kapu for any warrior to be with me, yet he does not come to me. I wish he had taken my life quickly in a fury rather than to kill me slowly like this," I said, letting frozen tears roll.

Kapena Vancouver rubbed the stubble on his chin, trying to find an answer. Finally, he went to his wooden sea chest, lifted the round, leather-bound lid. He dug deeply until he came up with his solution to my problem, a bolt of blazing red silk.

"This was a gift from a Chinese warlord," he said. "If you were draped in this splendid cloth no mortal man with red blood in his veins could resist your charms. Come back here at dusk tomorrow. I will hide you in my master's quarters. I will send an urgent message to Makaha. He will come, and I will leave him alone to find you."

The plan frightened me, but I was desperate. What if it should fail? Makaha would be angered, and I would never know love with him again. I brushed my black hair until it shined with moonlight and oiled my skin to burnished copper perfection. I brought out the red paint pot that I had traded for a mother of pearl comb and daubed it on my lips. Then I placed a crimson blossom behind my ear, the sign of readiness for love.

That night I trembled with excitement in the shipmaster's quarters. When a knock came on the door, I almost didn't answer. I opened it slowly to see Makaha dressed in haole finery. He wore a white shirt with ruffled lace cuffs, open at the neck. The stiff collar stood in sharp relief against his dark mahogany skin. On his chest rested a whale-tooth necklace braided from human hair.

The bulging muscles of his thighs pressed hard against the cloth of his knickers and silk stockings. I held my breath in the red dress stretched tight across my anxious breast, waiting to see if he found the picture before him pleasing. His stern gaze froze upon me for tense seconds. Then he took my hand, held it in his own and kissed the tips of my fingers.

"Wai-nani is my sweet, never fading-flower," he said, as his eyes danced over my body igniting the fires that burned most brightly for him. He took me in his arms. I lifted my mouth to his and kissed him deeply with a probing tongue. He jolted back, shocked at the sensation. It was not the way of our people, and it made him think about my past lovers. Then his black eyes softened to pools of tenderness. He gave way to all the fierce love he held for me in his heart and kissed me back with a wild searching tongue. After the storm of our passion had passed, we floated adrift in a glassy lagoon of love. I laid my head on his heaving chest where the beat of his royal heart was loud in my ear. I listened to the creak of the rigging as the ship rocked in gentle swells and the rush of the surf searching for the shore. The morning air smelled of ginger, seaweed and the sharp tang of the sea. My most beloved, the magnificent Makaha, rested at peace once more in my loving arms.

27
A Flash of Hot Light

Kapena Vancouver, who told us to call him George, talked with Makaha about the ways of the cold island until the glimmer of color lit the mountains.

"I have many wives and King George has only one. It is better for me," Makaha declared.

"I can't argue with that. Our laws are to protect the king's line."

"Ali'i only have children with other ali'i," Makaha explained. "Ali'i are the descendants of the gods. Their blood remains chaste."

"Our god does not call for the blood of humans. Our god is a god of love and mercy. If you take our god to your heart he will see your way to heaven and save you from the fires of hell," Kapena George explained.

"When I see you jump off a cliff and be saved by your god, I will believe in him," Makaha replied. "Until then, I remain the keeper of Ku."

This ended the talk of religion. Makaha's burning interest was in the ship itself and the tools of navigation. He had an abiding love for the sea and was determined to build a mighty fleet to conquer Pano and maintain control of our island world. Kapena George showed him his maps, his compass and how all the brilliant metal objects worked on board *Discovery*, but still refused to give arms to Makaha. Instead, he asked us to take shelter in the protective arms of King George the Third.

Before he set sail George called a meeting aboard *Discovery*. Makaha and a party of high chiefs assembled in the captain's cabin. Kapena George proposed to us that if we let King George's flag fly over the islands, he would protect us from warring island chiefs and bring us more cattle, sheep and seeds to plant along with all of the other treasures the world of the haoles had to offer.

"Leave us one of your vessels with guns for our protection," Makaha countered.

"I can't do that."

"If I agree to your request I would be protecting your property until you return from the cold island," Makaha pointed out.

Still Kapena George would not leave weapons for the Ali'i-Nui of Hawai'i. But he did agree to leave men with the tools, skills and supplies to build a great ship if we let him fly the flag of Britain over our heiau. Makaha agreed.

When the day came for Kapena George to leave us, we went to his ship on Makaha's great barge for the last time. Moist eyes met one another aboard *Discovery*. The wahine wailed when our warriors pulled them from the arms of their sailor lovers. During the warm nights aboard ship in the moan of the swells, the ghost gates of more than one wahine had been knocked down. Soon we would have many hapa-haole keiki running through our village. In time, we learned that the cow that chased the people up the coco palms was also fat with calf. Makaha's eyes glowed with great aloha for Kapena George when he placed upon his shoulders a splendid cape of feathers that had taken a hundred years and thousands of mamo birds to create. It was his gift to King George to thank him for the bull that he gave to us, even though the bull had died the day before the *Discovery* caught a crisp wind and left Kealakekua Bay.

Fired with new knowledge, material and skill of the English workmen, Makaha set our industrious people to work building hundreds of the great pelelu canoes. The master canoe designers were sent deep into the forest to select trees that would become the hulls. The priest, with prayers and offerings, blessed the wood before they were felled. Then the trees were carved and shaped and polished to a fine finish. When they were complete they were put on rollers to be delivered to the sea.

He embarked on a campaign to unite the people of the island of Hawai'i and to bend their labors to his purpose. With a retinue of singers, dancers, musicians and chanters I journeyed with Makaha, Nohea and three young wives of Makaha, on an island-wide progress designed to fire the people to his cause. Nohea was carried upon the shoulders of his retainer. I was offered a net hammock but preferred to walk at Makaha's side. When we arrived at a village, Makaha would introduce me to the chief of the village.

"This is Wai-nani, my wife, born of royal parents. Mother to all the Island people."

Within minutes word spread through the taro fields that we had arrived. The multitudes gathered to hear our words and share in our ceremony. Nohea was still a slender youth, but he stood tall and proud with the regal bearing of his ali'i parents. His skin was almond-colored like his mother's, his face full of pride like his father's. He wore a crown of thick brown curls that framed a round face with full lips and prominent flared nose. Though his physical presence matched that of Makaha, his soul was guided by his mother's gentle spirit. He performed the ritual genealogical incantations and prayers taught to him by the kahuna before our performance. He did so with such grace that the people were enchanted, and Makaha beamed with paternal pride.

Musicians placed their instruments on either side of the hula dancers wearing forest fern crowns, kapa pa'u, sweet, scented 'ilima blossom leis and clicking dog-tooth anklets. I joined in the line of dancers tapping on feathered gourds with the heels of their hands. The 'ili'ili pebbles, kala au sticks, and bamboo rattles marked the rhythm of our joyous song extolling our beautiful world. We spoke our praises with our hands, while Nohea's man-child falsetto voice lifted aching hearts to the heavens.

Above, above, birds of the heavens
Below, below, flowers of the earth
In the mountains, mountains, the forests
In the sea, the sea, fishes of the ocean
Of the beautiful world.

Our music captured the sway of the palms and the rhythm of waves breaking on soft sand. I dipped my hips low to the ground, bending my knees to the beat of the double gourd drum and pointed slender toes touching the earth lightly. I supplicated the heavens with outstretched fingertips and brought the happiness I found there into my heart, and with a sweeping wave of my arm, gave the mana I gathered back to the multitudes. Laka blessed me with grace, and I charmed all those who came to receive our warm aloha.

When the dancing was done, Makaha spoke.

"Peace for Island people will not be ours until we build a floating army that we can sail to Oahu to conquer Pano. You must climb the steep mountains and gather the strongest koa along the ridges of the pali and carve them into pelelu canoes. These twin-hulled outriggers are to be broad and deep with a covered platform. Some are to be rigged with a main sail of plaited pandanus and a jib. I have learned the ways of the haole and I will teach you how to build canoes more beautiful and stronger than ever before."

We brought with us the gifts of the foreigners—new seeds, cows, and sheep. Makaha showed farmers how to plant the new seeds and better ways to irrigate their fields. Our island prospered, crops flourished, our life was sweet and we grew strong. We journeyed around the island of Hawai'i singing the praises of each place we stopped.

The villagers bent to their labors with a song in their heart. A fleet of eight hundred pelelu canoes had just been completed when we received word that Pano had been killed on Oahu in a skirmish between rival chiefs. His death spelled weakness. The squabbling chiefs had left the island of Oahu vulnerable and ripe for Makaha's attack.

"The gods have spared you the hard fate of pressing the pahoa dagger into your father's heart. It is time for you to meet your destiny," I told Makaha.

Eager to wage the decisive battle, he mustered all his forces and the stockpile of arms he had gathered for just this moment. Shortly before the fleet was ready to depart for Oahu a messenger came to our shore requesting that Makaha come to the bedside of the dying manservant Pano gave to us when we visited his long house to talk a peace. The old man lay on his bed of hala mats. Makaha knelt down to him and placed a pillow under his head that he might speak more easily. With labored breath the old man whispered his last words.

"O my chief, I have for you a message, given to me by Pano, with orders that it be passed on to you before I go to the land of Po. It is a chant composed especially to bring you important knowledge. Here is the chant:

The earth quaked; it was set a-tremble,
The sea was disturbed, the land moved,
And these are the signs of a mighty warrior.

With extreme effort the warrior lifted himself to a sitting position and looked into Makaha's eyes.

A gift was given by Ali'i-Nui Pano,
It was carried away by the Chiefess Malana, the sacred one.
A flash of hot light over the earth is their son!

For a few moments Makaha did not reply then said slowly n a low voice, "If Pano was my father, why did you not tell me his story before I fought to destroy him?"

"It was the will of Pano, the will of the gods, that you should onquer all other leaders, so that you might stand alone. Your oice and yours alone, must be the voice of the land."

Makaha looked at me with baleful eyes. "Your words were ue." His eyes went moist and spurted dark pearls of tears. Too hard was this destiny for a man of flesh and bone. He would look to the gods for strength to carry out their will. Within a few days the old kanaka was dead, and Makaha ordered Koa to perform the highest rites of the heiau over his body before his bones were carried away to a sea cave in Waipio.

28
The Comet's Tail

Sixteen thousand strong, we set sail in our mighty fleet of canoes and ships armed with big gun cannons, swivel-guns and explosives. Leading the progress were canoes filled with powerful war kahuna, followed by Makaha at the sweep of a double-hulled canoe paddled by chiefs of the highest blood. I rode with the other wives and lovers in canoes loaded down with war and medical supplies.

When we swept into the bay at Lahaina on Maui, our forces were met with small opposition. Pano's son had fled to Oahu with the remainder of his men. After taking on fresh water and replenishing our supplies, we sailed for Oahu to fight the final battle. We landed on a protected beach on the windward side. Makaha funneled our forces through a narrow pass into Awawamalu to achieve the element of surprise. The strategy worked. Our warriors descended upon Waikiki from behind rather than from the sea. The Oahuans were unable to hold their ground. Pano's son at the head of these forces led his men into narrow Nuuanau Valley.

We chased them up the green valley through a dark forest of koa. Blue-black clouds crowded, and the tears of Nopopo began to flow. Riverlets gushed down the verdant pali, gouging streams into the footpaths. Those who fell on the slick red mud were trampled beneath our feet. A band of warriors turned to face us, giving the rest time to flee. We were stunned to see our own warrior standing in our path.

'Iwa-lani, the warrior I had selected in the game of kilu in Kohala, was to be our surprise that day. In the night he had defected, taking key warriors with him. He stood with his men at the mouth of narrow Nuuanu Valley between Makaha and his destiny. All the hair had been plucked from his lithe body, which was oiled to burnished perfection to make him slippery as an eel. He flashed dangerous dark eyes as he took a warrior's stance, holding a long spear, and dared to block Makaha's march to his final victory. Makaha pulled his dagger from his waist pouch and met his challenge. The cunning and reckless 'Iwa-lani lunged with his long spear. Makaha caught it in one hand and kicked his feet from under him, but before he could slit 'Iwa-lani's throat from breastplate to chin the young chief was killed by a stray bullet from a musket. He barely knew what had happened before his spirit departed.

'Iwa-lani's followers were mowed down mercilessly by our warriors firing haole guns. We trampled over the heaps of their bodies strewn in our path and pressed the retreating Oahuans to a ledge at the top of a thousand-foot cliff. The jagged lava rock pali jutting straight into the mists left nowhere for our enemy to hide. A howling wind funneling up the canyon drowned out their cries. Swinging war clubs, brandishing the long polulu spears and short ihe spears, they fought valiantly but were no match for Makaha's guns. Knowing that death at the lele altar, slavery and humiliation or being clubbed to death were their choices, hundreds of the Oahuan warriors chose to leap from the precipice into the afterlife.

When the battle was over, Makaha looked over the ledge to see hundreds of bodies splayed upon the porous rocks. The howling windvoices of the spirits flying into the mountain where the waterfalls shoot up echoed in my ears. Many of the battered bodies were those of wahine who had joined in the last stand against Makaha's powerful strike. From the cliff tops I saw a blanket of green spreading over the wrinkled pali to the white-fringed sea. The sacred valley and all the gifts it held now fel under Makaha's rule.

Makaha placed the Kiha-pu conch to his lips and sent its sorrowful voice echoing through the mists. The remaining warriors, Oahuan and Hawaiian alike, wailed at the sight of the young chiefs and chiefesses piled in a twisted mass of flesh and bone. The fiery white comet tail that marked the birth of Makaha did not lie, but the cost of his destiny was great. Before we left Oahu, Makaha ordered that Pano's bones be delivered to him. When we eventually returned to the island of Hawai'i, he had them spirited away to a hidden sea cave where they rest with other great chiefs of the long ago.

29
The Blossoming Time

When we returned to Hawai'i with peace secured, Makaha set the people to work once more, this time building his sleeping house on a platform of stones high on a knoll overlooking Kamakahonu Bay, where the sun always shines brightly. From this vantage he could spot canoes coming up the coast of Kona from Kailua. This place was celebrated for the constant appearances of fishes. Akule, a fish that burrows in the sand, came in great numbers. From our hale we watched through the long-eye given to us by Little King the shining fins of the great ones, mahi-mahi, and ahi cutting through deep blue swells.

At sundown when the sky was tinged with oranges, purples and reds, I set out with Makaha and his warriors in his outrigger in search of Mano. Sharks feeding close to where his schools of fish ran had to be culled. The men lowered a basket of rotting pig flesh into the water to lure sharks into a weighted noose slung between the double hulls of the canoe. When Mano bit down with his jagged teeth and the noose tightened, he gave us a wild ride over heaving azure swells.

I was reminded of my time with Eku. Nearly forty seasons had passed since I rode with him from my Hana home. His years had come to a close. I hoped to see his kind eye once more when I joined him in the watery spirit realm of Po. Makaha's loud laughter brought my thoughts back to the day. When he tired of this sport, the shark's tail was caught in a second noose, and it was pulled backward to drown.

In this time of plenty Makaha ordered lava rocks to be hauled from the mountains to build a massive stone wall and surround his court on the jetty, guarded by sixteen cannons. Within the walls there were separate eating-houses. For receiving visitors, a sleeping house and a communal chamber were built in the western fashion. It was furnished with tables and chairs and beds for the comfort of the haoles. A sixty-foot long house was made for the many hours of training and practice of the hula. There were hales for musicians to craft instruments and practice playing together.

High chiefs who might build forces against him were invited to live within our walls under Makaha's watchful eye. He gathered around him skilled and talented men and women of every kind. Canoe makers, athletes, surfers, feather workers, wood carvers, healers, chanters, dancers, orators, diviners and genealogists were invited to dwell at his court. All materials were given to them to advance their crafts. It was a time of blossoming and great harvest.

Stone storehouses were soon filled to brimming with goods bartered from visiting haole. At first the ships were filled with fur traders refreshing supplies on their journeys to the Northwest for pelts. They came and took what they needed in pigs, fruit, vegetables, firewood and salt and then left. But that changed when foreigners discovered the 'iliahi, a fragrant wood we used to make our bows and stringed instruments. We ground the heart of this wood into powder and sprinkled it on kapa cloth as a perfume. The sweet smelling wood they called sandalwood was much desired in the far off land of China for carvings of their gods. Makaha used the sandalwood trade to fill his storehouses.

I shared my sleeping house with Makaha's other wives, except for Huali the sacred bride, whose caste demanded separate quarters. A round opening in the gable of the tall, pitched roof of my hale let the breezes off the sea cool us on sultry nights. Often I slept outside my house beneath the laughing face of Hina to be closer to the soft voice of the sea washing on the shore below. Lines of palm trees fringed the borders of the grounds dotted with massive breadfruit trees and sprawling pandanus canopies. Bright flowering shrubs molded into murals told the story of the Island people.

Nohea, the favorite son of Makaha who never had a wish denied, requested that he have his own compound. The heir apparent was given many houses of his own in sheltered Hoolulu Cove. There he lived with two wives away from court and the all-seeing eyes of his father. The young ali'i filled their days with wrestling, bowling with maika stones and other sports. Men and women competed in surfing, swimming and running games and spear-throwing contests.

They spent afternoons lying on the sands, gossiping lazily, listening to the murmur of the waves. Nohea was given to gambling games and often lost huge wagers to other high chiefs. His fondness for drink and wahine was renowned. With his retinue of retainers, warriors and two wives, he made trips to the mountain domain of Pele. Wandering through the cool mists in the thick forests, the young people draped themselves in skirts of morning glories, red lehua blossoms and ropes of green maile. Eyes in the forests were upon them as they frolicked heedlessly on the ancient trails. The mountain people never stopped their worship of Pele and gave their allegiance to no one but their tempestuous goddess. It was not uncommon for a young chief to be abducted and never seen again.

While Nohea was leading his followers away from the court of Makaha, his cousin Keha became his uncle's shadow. He was more than six feet tall with massive shoulders and muscles rippling across his chest made strong from swimming. Keha possessed heroic form and, like all ali'i, his forehead was molded at birth to give him the regal bearing of a great chief. He was in awe of Makaha and padded behind him like a faithful dog. He sat with him while he bartered with the haoles and learned his way of remaining silent until the moment was right to strike his bargain. Makaha loved to haggle and knew that his great edge was his fierce demeanor and he would smile widely when all was done.

Sensing Keha's loyalty to him, he set his nephew to spy upon Nohea. He was to join his rebellious son on his wanderings and to report back to Makaha. He told us that games of love were played in Nohea's long house almost every night. Often the full sun of the day passed overhead before Nohea rose from his sleeping mat. Makaha did not approve of the ways of his son but did not interfere.

"His days will be hard soon enough," he would say to me when he heard tales of Nohea's indulgences.

Each evening, members of Makaha's own court gathered under the rustling palms that shaded the royal compound. There by the glowing light of kukui torches strung on coconut midribs, hula dancers swayed to the pulse of drums and wailing nose-flutes. Often legends of the ancient gods and their heroic deeds were told long into the moon-bright nights. Spirits whispered secrets through the voice of the waves and the swaying trees into the receptive ears of the enraptured multitudes.

Makaha took the gods confiscated from Oahu, Maui and Lanai, along with the coveted poison god Pano had stolen from Molakai, and placed them in the notches awaiting them in the heiau in Kohala. The feathered head of Ku was installed there beside them, where it remained for the rest of Makaha's life. As protector of temples, he set his warriors to work restoring the crumbling heiau to Kane, the God of Life Giving Water, near his palace in Kailua. Kane, who restores sight to the blind and is the nurturing god, can bring life back to the dead. He can restore dismembered bodies back to their original condition. Cleansing and purifying, he comes from the ocean, the origin of life. Kane, not Ku, ruled Makaha's heart in these days of great joy.

Makaha's life was simple. He chose to wear his malo and live in the traditional way. Generally twenty or thirty of his trusted chiefs joined him in meals. Mats were spread on the floor. Dishes of three-fingered poi were set before them along with salt fish, consecrated pork and sweet potatoes. Always gracious to westerners, Makaha provided tables, chairs, plates and eating utencils for visiting guests. But for himself, he preferred the ways of the Island people and reclined during meals. His manner was charming and gracious, and he enjoyed many long talks with the haoles.

He concluded his meal with half a glass of rum, but the bottle was immediately sent away. He made liquor kapu, for his people were fast developing a ravenous appetite for haole whiskey. If his son was seen indulging in the strong spirits of the sailors, it was to be reported to Makaha immediately. In response to this edict, the indolent Nohea set sail for days, leaving the kapu of his father behind. On the flashing summer sea the laws of the land did not apply.

The last to come under Makaha's rule was Kauai, the most holy and glorious of islands. On the leeward side of the other islands, Kauai was spared attacks during the many years of warring among rival chiefs. Lush from heavy rains, the pali of Kauai are shaggy with growth and graced with plunging waterfalls that take the light of the sun with them as they fall to the sea. Coves along the Napali Coast, guarded by treacherous currents, protected by high seas, are sacred hiding places for the bones of ancestors. The people of Kauai, ali'i and maka'ainana alike, are deeply religious, and they chant the meles to the glories of our past. The mana is so strong on Kauai that it covers the island like a blanket of armor.

This sparkling emerald island was all that lay between Makaha and supreme rule. He tried on two occasions to invade Kauai, but both times the mana was so strong that the seas rose up and his attacks were thwarted. In his wisdom, the chief of Kauai negotiated a peace with Makaha rather than risking war. Respecting this choice of action, Makaha allowed him to remain as governor of the island for the remainder of his days. It was agreed that upon his death, the island of Kauai would come under the umbrella of Makaha's rule.

I went to Makaha while he was choosing trusted and loyal followers for posts on his newly acquired islands. "My father was the enemy of Pano. He only stood behind him to protect my mother from harm when your warriors took my Hana home. He is a courageous and good chief. If you make him high chief of Maui and let my mother sit at his side, the people will remember her lavish court and the great pleasures she once provided them."

Makaha saw the wisdom of this choice and made my father high chief of Maui. He selected other trusted chiefs to reside over the other conquered islands. He made certain to establish chiefs who were loyal to him and not of that island so they could not be tempted to raise forces against him. He built an elite fleet of post runners to keep him informed of the actions of his newly appointed leaders.

As conqueror, he had the right to divide the land among his followers. The greatest estate he gave to old Ka'eo whose deeply creased mahogany face was now framed with a thick mane of hair as white as the snow crown of Mauna Kea. To him went the taro patch he had labored in and all the land touching it in the Waipio Valley. The two haoles we borrowed who had demonstrated loyalty, bravery and usefulness in battle and peace were given land and their choice of wives.

As for me, my life in Kailua was complete. Makaha revered me above all of his twenty-seven other wives. I shared with him in his talks with the sea captains and other visitors. Under the umbrella of his love I held no fear of the priests. While Makaha lived our island life was held in place by the glue of his will, and we prospered.

30
The Journey Home

With peace came a yearning for my Hana home. I made the water passage to Maui with a dozen strong paddlers in a hundred-foot double-hulled canoe. My father built a new village on the shores in Lahaina where he governed the island with my mother sitting proudly at his side. Restored to her rightful seat of honor, she was glowing when we met again after long years of separation. She lay on her side eating the fruit of the ohi'a tree when I entered the house of my parents. Startled at my presence, she lifted her body, plump from poi, and smiled with intense, orange-almond eyes.

"Wai-nani my wandering wahine has come home," she said, extending her hand with long tapered fingers. I kissed her fingertips and felt the tears well in my own heart. My father came in and wrapped his strong arm around my trembling shoulders.

"Wai-nani has your blazing eyes and the heart of a warrior," he said, smiling proudly.

Makaha ordered a house built for me in Lahaina, so that I might enjoy my time with my aging parents. Many pleasant days passed as we played konane, gossiped or lazed on the sand under the shade of a hau tree after a lavish meal. All of the islands prospered, and stockpiles flourished under the care of Makaha.

Even though the village was filled with laughing children and my time with my family brought joy to my heart, I pined for my old friend Mau and to see the sunbright shores of my water rich Hana home. With a calabash filled with poi, I made my wa up the mountain trail that climbs the face of steep pali through th deep gorge that leads to Wailuku Pass. After marching through verdant hau and pandanus for many hours, I came to the ledge overlooking Wailuku Valley. Far below, the river Iao still carved a path through the rich floor quilted with taro patches. Pano's court was gone, but the village at the mouth of the never-failing stream still gave life to the people tending the crops. Here steam rose through the cracks in the lofty pali surrounding the lush haven, providing a warm mist that fans the growth of taro.

I continued up the pass on a narrow footpath that wound over rock through wild grass and ferns, along the brink of tremendous precipices. I looked down and saw in my mind the bodies that once clogged the "waters of destruction," and turned them red with the rich blood of warriors; first that of Makaha's men and then with the retreating army of Pano. Now the bones of both forces lay rotting among the mosses and ferns that line the murmuring waters of Wailuku. A mumuku blew hard up the canyon, forcing me back from my thoughts. It nearly lifted me from my perch as I held tightly to the roots of the koa twisted into the wall of the pali. I thought I heard the deep moan of the Kapi-lu conch given to Makaha by the people of Waipio, but it was just the wild wind voice speaking to me of the past.

From there my journey took me two thousand feet above the sea to Makawao. The climate here made me feel young again. Like a butterfly lifting from flower to flower, I rushed to smell the groves of towering wild roses and blood geranium. I wandered among fern fronds dripping delicate tears of dew. Their wet touch on my cheek was as sweet as Mau's kiss. I did not tell the people of Makawao my name, yet they filled my calabash, gave me sweet efreshment and led me to a sleeping mat to rest upon.

When I was ready to travel, the kind maka'ainana people eturned me to my path with blessings and a sweet aloha. The day tarted clear and cloudless, but as the trail switch-backed to lofty egions the air grew cold. After a few miles, numbness was reeping into my limbs, but my mind felt pure in the rarified air. he fleecy clouds scattered about the mountaintop were now elow me. Near the top of the ascent the ground grew bare. No plants survived the waterless cold. The sharp, broken bits of lava rock made the last half of the climb difficult, but once upon the brow of the crater the effort was forgotten.

I looked down upon a bank of clouds surrounding the summit that looked like a band of snow. There was no obstacle in the way of my vision from here to eternity. Westward were the mountains of West Maui and beyond them, Molokai; far to the northwest lay the cloud-capped island of Oahu. It was so clear I could see the peaks of Kauai on the horizon. Lanai stood gleaming opposite distant Lahaina. Southeast, in the far-off sky, rested the blue summits of the giant mountains of Hawai'i—Mauna Kea and Mauna Loa. Everywhere beyond, around and abroad was the blue ocean, stretching upward till the horizon seemed suspended midway between the heavens and the base of the mountains. I had the vantage of Wakea, the God of Light and the Heavens who married Papa, the Goddess of the Earth. I promised myself and the people that I would give my life to them and our beautiful world.

Behind me was the House of the Sun, egg-shaped Haleakala Crater, seven miles wide and two thousand feet deep. Into the depths of the cavern flanked by slides of red and black sand ran my parents to hide me from the wrath of Pano. Far below, I saw a herd of wild pigs that looked no larger than rats running at full speed. I spent a night on the rim of the crater so that I might see the glory of the setting sun. When candles have been long burning at Wailuku, the western horizon holds clouds tinted with orange, vermilion, violet purple and rose. The sunrise places you close to the gods when first morning and last evening rays cast shadows and outlines in the vast crater pit.

Before descending into the depths of the crater to the path to Hana, I plucked the dark red flower of the silvery sword plant with down on its leaves and placed it in my calabash to bring me luck in my crossing. Water as clear as crystal rose from a mountain spring at the bottom of the crater. Those who chose this cold labyrinth of wonderment could stay well hidden from their enemies.

Once through the crater I passed through the Hamakua swamp, on the worst road of the kingdom with its unbroken series of ridges. Often, I sank to my knees in the thick red mud. After climbing up steep pali then clamoring down ravines, I arrived at a wild and enchanting valley. Here a forest of ohi'a stretched from the sea far up the mountainsides. The mighty trees were laid low to the ground with blood-red fruit. The harvest was so abundant the mountains wore a cloak of deep red. The ripening apples bursting with white flesh brought forth birds wearing rainbow colors. The bright red honeycreepers chirped happily as they dangled upside down with curved beaks buried in crimson blooms.

From there I descended to the road by the sea to Hana. The ocean glimmered vastly around every curve of the long winding road rutted with mud slicks and tree roots. Ribbons of silver water cascaded down the lush green pali. Weary from the journey, I slipped into the blue sea of my youth. Once in the water the weight of my life lifted from old bones. I swam free from the role of Mother to the People into the caressing arms of moana. I remembered the pull of Pele as I sat on the powder-soft sands of my Hana home. Now I know it was the prayers of Makaha who kept his thinking place beneath the shadow of the volcano that called to me. The tender lover who put salve on my bleeding feet was the force that brought me to my own hard fate.

Like my vision of Pele, I saw myself floating on the clouds with heavy breasts and hand on full belly, looking down upon my subjects. I am mortal, not a goddess, but I vowed to be fair, loving and just. I wanted to see the old kapus lifted. I wanted to see our women eating with their men, with people sitting together sharing their joys and troubles, and for them to live without fear from death-dealing kahuna.

When my thoughts ran clean like a forest stream tumbling over smooth pebbles, I made my way to the small harbor in Hana where I once stood upon the backs of Eku and Laka in the surfing contest. My prayers had been answered. I did swim with a man as strong and kind as Eku. I did feel his powerful force and rode with him up the face of thirty-foot monsters. I sat astride the fiery comet's tail and rode with him through the star-bright night.

I found Mau tending to his nets in a small hale beside the sea. He was still narrow of hip and broad in the shoulders, but his belly went round over the lip of his malo. When he saw me, his dark eyes sparkled with sunlight. He blinked his eyes to test his vision.

"Wai-nani spreads her rainbow smile over us," he said, coming closer to hold me tenderly.

A tiny wahine came streaming from another hale, curious to know the stranger. She ran to Mau and took her place at his side, holding a brown arm around his shrunken leg, and looked up at me with a broad grin. Her mother, Lana, who had bloomed into a lithe young woman with satin hair to her waist, came out of the shadows to greet me.

"Do you remember me?" I asked.

"Yes, proud mother, you are the one who taught the keiki of Kealakekua Bay how to dance with dolphins."

Sun-drenched days at my surfing cove where I rode head-high waves to capture the heart of Makaha came rushing back in a flood of memories. Eku, my fine strong friend who helped me fly from the slap of my father's hand to Ka'u, the breast of the island of Hawai'i, was gone. Like the golden days of my youth, he had vanished in the dead of sacred night, never to return.

"It is a fine day to go fishing," I said.

"Yes, it is a fine day," said Mau, smiling as he gathered his net and prepared his canoe for us to set sail. The girl flitted like a butterfly and then settled herself upon my knee in the bow. Together we faced the wind. I rested an old hand upon her round shoulder while her polished black mane flowed free in the tangy breeze.

"I am afraid of my dreams," I confided to Mau.

"What is the message you receive?"

"I awake to a hot wind fanning flames in the heavens that swirl about me in a demon's frenzy."

"Have you told the kahuna of this omen?"

"I am more afraid of them than I am of the dream. Makaha has fulfilled his destiny, and we live in plenty. But when he leaps into the afterlife, I will be without the shelter of his love and will have my own hard path to follow."

Mau held the sweep of the canoe. As we shot over the deep, he told me the tale of a girl who lived in the dim past.

"While mist was still rising, the girl, dressed in a skirt of rainbow colors, set out from her home. A strong wind was coming. The sun was hot in the sky, making her cheeks red like lehua flowers. She went up some high places looking down on the sea. She heard footsteps behind her. A whirlwind was coming swiftly after her, and there was thunder and lightning. After a few more steps she felt an earthquake and sat down. She saw a great thing rising like a cloud twisting and shutting out the sun, moving and writhing—a great white piece of earth in front of the whirlwind.

"She was terribly frightened and fell flat on the ground as if dead. She rose, shook her rainbow skirt, scattering the perfumes of the flowers, and faced the dragon that was upon her. Then she twisted the kapa clothes full of lightning and threw them into the sky. A fierce and heavy rain began to fall. Streams of water rushed toward the place where the girl stood. The dragon saw that all his attempts to terrify her had failed. His eyes flashed, and he opened his mouth. His tongue was thrusting viciously from side to side. His red mouth was like the pit of Pele. His teeth were gnashing, his tail lashing. Then the dragon fell into pieces, which all became nothing. The fragments flew in all directions. The evil disappeared and a handsome man who was to be her husband stood before her.

"Look danger in the eye. When you blink, you will awake laughing," he said.

31
Love Proclaimed

When I returned to the house of my parents, I set to writing a mele for Makaha that would let him know of my yearning for him. I had it delivered to him in Hoolulu where he rested, saying that being close to the land there brought peace to his soul.

My most Beloved One
Kona is beautiful and becalmed, as at dawn,
Flooded by the cool air of the Kahau breeze
Which sprays the silvery sea beyond the lea.
Beloved is he who lives by himself in Hoolulu,
But twice perfect is he who loves his beloved!
I am yours—waiting with aloha.
Aloha for you, Wai-nani.

The poetry of my mele so stirred his heart that he summoned me back to Hawai'i and declared that there was to be a feast, greater than any feast before in the islands, in my honor. The entire population of the island of Hawai'i was to be invited.

An immense awning of braided palm leaves was erected in the grove of coconut trees used for royal receptions. Ferns were spread upon the eating mats and decorated with garlands of green maile. The perfume of bright bouquets of orange-colored hala and golden 'ilima scented the air. Plates of ti leaves and bowls of polished wavy-grained koa awaited the savory foods steaming in a thousand imus. The people came from the mountains and the ea, bringing the bounty of our island to share with me on this day roclaimed to be in my honor.

Chicken cooking in coconut milk, fish steaming in ti-leaf rappers, and mingling scents of birds baking in imus tantalized ie senses. Roasted kukui nuts, red sea salt and pungent seaweed rovided seasonings for shellfish. There were mountains of three-nger purple poi to fill ti-leaf bowls. Calabashes containing oconut milk to drink were set upon the separate eating mats for ien and women.

The melancholy moan of the conch shell announced the rival of Makaha wearing his resplendent cloak of yellow mamo athers that stretched to the ground. Behind him came my father a white malo and yellow shoulder cape, carrying a plumed ahili. My mother, adorned with a coronet of berries resting low n her brow, carried her head high and walked with regal grace his side. Attendants dressed in the colors of the sunrise bent oreheads to the ground as the procession of royals passed before em to the shaded platform embroidered with fragrant flowers.

A manele lined with cushions perfumed with mountain erbs awaited me. Wearing the flame red silk cloth given to me y Kapena George, many stranded leis of sweet-scented 'ilima ossoms and a lei po'o of forest ferns, I slipped into the net ammock. My chair was carried upon the shoulders of six strong arriors and a dozen of my favorite handmaidens came behind arrying the train of my long dress to the platform where Makaha waited his favorite wife. His face was grave as he spoke to the ultitudes. Seldom did he smile wide, as many of his teeth were issing, but a spirited light shone from his extraordinary deep-et eyes.

"Wai-nani walks in my footsteps. She gives her great rength to the Island people. Her mana goes to the children, to e weak, to the old and to all those who have needed her. She is l things to me and she is undefeatable. Strong in times of crisis, ie can also ride the waves like a bird. And she is as lovely as a u hala blossom. She is a never-fading flower and Mother to all e People."

With that, my heart filled past brimming. Any slights that might have come to me over my years with Makaha went flying like a bird loosed from a cage. My heart was clear of the rage it held against him for the kapu he placed upon me, the jealousy I had known for Huali as mother to his heir, and any resentment toward Makaha’s many younger wives left me forever. All the stones were gone from my bowl, allowing cleansing light into my heart that softened the hard place where they had rested for many years. I took my seat beside my most beloved and faced those who came with gifts for me that day.

When he finished speaking, my mother rose. My father came behind her and loosed the tie from her long slender neck of the shark’s tooth necklace woven from human hair. He came forward and placed the necklace of my brother about my throat.

“Mimo’s spirit that now dwells in his shark body is at your side, for he has always loved you.”

Thoughts of my dead brother came crashing close in my mind. I remembered the aumakua shark that guided me to the Place of Refuge when I swam from the wrath of Makaha. With this gift, my parents released me from the pain of knowing that my brother’s death may have been at the hands of my warrior husband. I felt strong knowing Mimo’s spirit was near.

Nohea, wearing a magnificent bright red jacket and white shirt with a tall lace collar, performed the chants to bring this day happiness. He lifted his clear voice in song that made his father’s eyes shine with tears.

Next a parade of keiki dressed in gay costumes came forward two-by-two with hands outstretched, carrying spice-scented boughs laden with the yellow flowers of the hala tree. After laying their gifts at my feet, they peeled off in opposite directions and sat neatly upon their heels in rows beside ou platform. Following the keiki, came the wahine I had spent man happy hours with in Waipio. Singing Land Shell, Shell Beautifu with Rainbow Colors, Leaf of the Precipice, and Leaf of th Morning Glory wore bright colored pa’us, leis with anklets an crowns of forest ferns. With graceful outstretched arms an pointed toes, they danced a slow hula as they sang their song for me. Their voices which mingled like sea mosses floating in the deep currents, stirred my own swelling sound to join them. My voice welled and flowed through me, coming from my lips as sweet and pure as a mountain spring.

Next magnificent Huali appeared before me. Plump from plenty, she was shapely with small, beautifully molded hands and feet. She wore a white dress draped over round ivory shoulders and a lei of red lehua blossoms around her neck.

"I have a written a mele for Wai-nani, my sister in water and blood.

The red flower at the top of the ohi'a tree
Sparkling bright joy smells sweet.
Where is the blossom?
There surfing
Standing on the curling wave
There swimming
Cresting with pearl-gray Eku
There dancing,
Beneath a sway of palms
Bending low to the ground
With the breath of the sea
In the night-beam sad smile of Hina
There singing
With the shining shells of Waipio
There walking
Beside Makaha
Sharing his burdens giving him wisdom
In the name of Wai-nani."

When she finished her mele, she crossed her arms like silver swords over her heart and smiled with brilliant white teeth. Her rich words plunged deep into my mind, bringing forth sacred memories. She was my trusted friend, an equal who shared the breaking of the banana kapu with me by the boiling pots of our youth. My love for her was immense. I invited her to sit beside me beneath the palm canopy.

The beat of the drum signaled the dancers to enter the courtyard. The approach to the hula stage was lighted with torches on both sides of the path leading to the hula altar. There were many wreaths and leis of flowers draped over the block of sacred lama wood placed on the platform dressed in red and white kapa. Two hundred kane and wahine bustled in quickly, forming separate groups. Ohaha, carried in by six strong warriors, took her place seated on the hula stage with legs splayed to make room for the gourd she would tap with her palm. The musicians sat at her knee where they could absorb her powerful mana, making their sounds solid and strong.

Once all the dancers had entered and the offerings of 'awa had been made to the hula altar, Ohaha began the ceremony with a mele.

Here is a gift, a chant
Entwined with tears of love
And joy for you, Wai-nani.

At the head of the dancers was a girl dressed in a skirt of rainbow colors with flowers of abundant perfumes and a wild thick mane of dark hair flowing in the wind, nothing about her at fault. Slender and lithe, she moved as gracefully as a light breeze rippling over water in her dance. She was Kolopua, the newest wife of Makaha. The thirteen-year old daughter of a high chief was the same age I was when I first lay-abed with Makaha in Ka'u. Strangely, her beauty did not taunt me. I held her in my eyes as a daughter and feared for her future under the tabus of ancient gods. Her unmarred beauty inspired me to protect her. In my aging heart, I truly had become a mother to all of the people. It was mine to protect them from the strong currents of change coming to us from the haole, as well as from the harsh ways of the long-ago.

The proud faces of the women with high cheekbones, ful dark brows and lustrous black eyes looked to the heavens fo inspiration in their dance. They wore crowns of frilly forest ferns and leis of shells to adorn perfect brown bodies. The women tapped on the hollow bodies of gourd rattles they carried to mark the rhythms of the ancient dance. Ohaha lifted her deep, resonant voice to song while the musicians joined in sweet harmony. Kolopua led the dance with head high and a teasing smile, moving like a cloud over water. The other dancers followed her steps like a flock of gulls in flight. The open, guileless faces of the wahine filled with love inspired me to be brave for them.

When the women finished, the men took their positions as swift as the wind. They held spears fired with torches at both ends. The whirl of their spears created circles of fire in the twilight while Ohaha marked a steady beat with her palm against her gourd. The pulse of the drum kept the dancers steady. Thick manes beneath forest crowns flew in wild arcs as the men threw their heads forward and back and around in circles. Deep grunts coming from the pit of their bellies accented the whirl of the motion of oiled, brown bodies gleaming in the soft yellow light of the kukui torches.

The chanting and music carried on the wind and blew over the mountains. The people were so excited they began to shout. There was a din of noise coming from the ridges where the multitudes had climbed to see. They held torches that fired the night and made a great roar like the ocean crashing on the shore. The trees bent over with the trance of the dancers and whispered their songs with dancing leaves made glorious in the aura of the setting sun.

When the joyous praises of the people ended, the mounds of food piled high on the fern mats were eaten. The night air was warm with a soft wind stirring the coco trees like a great spoon. We ate beneath the trembling palm heads swaying in a hula breeze.

Had my life ended at this moment I would have no sorrows to tell you. My heart was filled passed brimming. No man could be more resplendent than Makaha proclaiming his love for me before the multitudes. Only Koa did not bend in appreciation for me that day. I saw him slinking in the shadows whispering to the other kahuna. He feared my power among the people, which was mounting like a great sea swell. My old enemy must be met, for he was the dragon's tail left upon my path.

32
Three Claws

In the days of peace that followed, the lines between our people and the haoles blurred. Our young women spent so much time aboard the vessels that came to our harbor that it became custom for a cannon to be fired in the morning signaling their return home to their families and another fired at night inviting them aboard the ships once more. Pleasant companionship made the sailors who came to trade with us forgetful of time. Night watches often dissolved into drunken days on our shore.

A liberty party of three sailors descended upon our village, each with a wahine under his arm, wearing hats decorated with flowers, ribbons and handkerchiefs. A fifer and a fiddler marched ahead of the group playing gay tunes. Several of our people fell in with them, dancing and singing along. They had not gone halfway down the white crescent strip of sand lining the bay when they were greeted by Nohea carried upon the shoulders of his manservant. Knowing how much his father hated the strong liquor of the haoles on the island, he invited the party to join him on his double-hulled canoe.

He took two of his wives and a few favored companions and the party of haoles with him. As was his habit, they drifted for a day at sea in a delirium of sensual delights. When Nohea returned with bleary red-rimmed eyes, his father held his trembling anger in check. His love for his son was so great he could not harm him, but neither could he ignore that the heir apparent lacked his own personal strength. He determined to create a triangle of power that would serve to maintain his island kingdom after he entered the spirit world.

Makaha called all of his chieftains and kahuna together. I was ordered to be present. For this fateful moment he wore a white shirt of fine cotton with a ruffled lapel and black tie fashioned into a bow. Over this was a black silk vest from China that he had traded for sandalwood. His hair, now white as the snow upon the shoulders of Mauna Loa, was cropped into a regal crescent crown upon the curve of his shaved skull. Intense eyes buried in his stern face held no clue of the pronouncement he was about to make.

"Nohea shall be crowned Ali'i-Nui at my passing and is to demonstrate royal judgment while I live." In this way he believed he could strengthen Nohea's character and assist him in decision making in his waning years. He hoped his son's love for whiskey would lessen as his life was enriched with power. This was to be expected, but all present were shocked when he made his next declaration.

"Keha shall hold the staff of Ku in his hand and stand behind Nohea."

This dispensation of power made it clear that he did not trust his son's judgment in a crisis and that he sought to provide a protecting and tempering hand in his reign. In so doing, he created the same rift that fell to the land when Lako died, leaving Makaha the keeper of Ku and 'Ele 'ele to reign over the people without the force of the war god in his hand. To add to this Makaha made a most shocking announcement.

"Wai-nani shall be Kuhina-Nui and will be a joint-regent with Nohea in ruling over the Island people."

Even I was astounded at this decision. This privileged position was likened to the prime-minister of the haoles. I would be a key negotiator in trading with the ships. No laws could be made without my consent. Nohea would have to look to me before making any final decisions. With this decree, a trembling Nohe clenched his fists but held his rage in check. Keha was beaming a the knowledge of his soon-to-be power. There was muc murmuring and clicking of tongues by the kahuna present. Koa's bones quaked with this news. He stared at me with red hot eyes, but dared not show contempt for his much-loved chief's decisions.

Plump from pleasures, my body had doubled in size over the years. I sought the water warmer than air where I felt light and buoyant to contemplate what my new position would mean. I wandered along the black sand beach awash in birdsong. The sand was warm under my feet and the ocean stretched out before me. When I entered the azure bath, I felt like a child abandoning the adult world. Leaving society behind, I entered the soothing embrace of moana where flesh melts from bones. In this world I did not need to be concerned with what others were doing or thinking. I did not need to be guarded or afraid of wrong political moves. The fact that I was Makaha's favorite wife and revered by him was an honor, but it placed me in a dangerous position. Young royals vying for control came to me for favor and the yellow-chinned priest Koa, my long enemy, looked upon me with suspicious, rat-slitted eyes. He knew I railed against the tabus placed upon my sex and that I hated the kapus of the ancients. As Kuhina-Nui, I held the power to change the old ways.

In the sea my thoughts were safe from intrusion and my words free from eavesdropping. I listened to the songs of the sea, straining to hear the squeak or whistle of Eku, but his constant smile and wondrous eye were but a memory. My thoughts rose from the bottom of the sea floor like bubbles in a quiet rock pool, bursting at the surface. In this place of solitude and genuine comfort, my body, heavy on land, felt young. The thick air of Kailua weighted me to the ground. In the cool lifting of the water, I was beautiful once more.

I still swayed gracefully when I walked and pointed toes when I danced, but in the water I felt fishlike as I slid through glassy water, slicing it with long arms. I stretched the muscles in my body and dove down to the sea floor to see the colors of the sea creatures. The underbelly of something immense cast a shadow over me. It looked to be the great belly of a blue whale swimming on the surface of the cobalt blue sea. Pricks of light like stars glowed like phosphorescent fish all about the monster. I felt infinitesimally small. Soon the image faded into the face of an owl. The horns of a great owl with wide eyes blinked to the rhythm of the earth's breath.

Below me I saw a forest of ghostly coral branches where darting bright fishes hid from their enemies. Red emperors and luminous damselfish and a bright yellow boxfish with polka dots flitted past me. I could hear the scratching sound of the blue-green parrotfish gnawing with its birdlike beak on the coral stalks. Gusts of warm strong current carried me over the colorful sponges where the octopus and lobster seclude themselves. I yearned to stay in this shadowy dream world, for I feared the tragedy that the tangle of three claws of power could bring.

33
Doorway to Darkness

A brilliant sky tinged with pink and gold spread from the horizon to the heavens. The coral colors mirrored on the still waters of the receding low tide exposed volcanic mounds of black jutting from the sea. The gay life of court in Kailua was stilled. The earth was calm on the soft morning that found Makaha unable to lift his head from his sleeping mat. For many months he had not joined his chiefs at his eating-house and had taken small meals of poi away from his subjects. His illness was most unkind, as he was still glorious in body and strong in mind. I held his hand and sang to him sweet meles to soothe his flagging heart.

"It is the work of my enemies," he said. Makaha had always feared the power of the poison gods and the threat of the ana'ana priests who were able to pray a soul into the afterlife if given a precious piece of the victim's hair, fingernails or bodily fluids. Makaha believed that his step-father Niolo, brother to Lako, was killed in this fashion. That was why the royal spittoon to gather all excretions never left his side, and the retainer who carried it for him was one of his most trusted aides.

While my most beloved faced the doorway to the dark world of Po, I told him the story of the Kamakau, a warrior poisoned by priests. "The sinking sun was sending its most glorious beams into the clouds, while just beneath, reflecting the glory, lay the Old Man of the Mountain. The stone face was magnificent. The unruffled brow, the never-closing eyes, the firm lips, all stood out in bold relief against the heavens. Kamakua, who was dying, caught the inspiration in the face of the mountain. It seemed to his vivid imagination as if ten thousand good spirits were gathered in the heavens to fight for him. He leaped to his feet, strength came back into the wearied muscles, a new will took possession of him, and he cried: 'I will not die! I will not die! The stone god is more powerful than the priests who pray to death!' His will broke the chains of fear. Kamakau went out to greet the wonderful people and take up his life again. The power of the priests is only theirs because you give it to them," I told him.

"Wai-nani has never feared the power of gods or priests. Perhaps my death will convince you," he said, squeezing my hand.

Koa applied his potions and chanted for hours at the side of our dying chief. The best medical kahuna were summoned to attend, but there was no change. A haole doctor was called upon, but even his medicine could not save Makaha, who believed his time to die had come.

The heiau to Kane that Makaha built by his grass hale facing the sea was readied for the sacred rites to the gods. A tabu was laid upon the land; no fishing was allowed, or feasting, nor could man and woman sleep together. Everyone worked on the temple, chiefs and maka'ainana alike. All that could be heard was the chanting of the kahuna as they prayed continuously to make the heiau worthy of the rites for Makaha's body.

Koa came to Makaha's chamber to ask permission to lay a human sacrifice upon the lele altar. Makaha had long ago abandoned human sacrifice, choosing to spare his subjects for his labors.

"Men are sacred to the chief," was his response. This edict ended the ritual of human sacrifice in the Islands forever.

Makaha was carried to the temple for three days running that he might absorb the mana of Kane, the nurturing god. The multitudes came from the mountains, the taro fields in the countryside, and the fishermen from their ponds. Ali'i from all the islands as well as country people gathered, spilling over the courtyard stonewalls. A pitiful wailing filled the still air. The melancholy voices of kahuna chanting to the pulse of the pahu ums was all that was heard for many days. Makaha only grew eaker.

He summoned Nohea. In the flicker of the dimly lit kukui rches he whispered his last command. "My son, I leave to you kingdom that ought to satisfy your ambition, but all of this you ill lose if you think only of yourself and your own grandizement. I have made many sacrifices for this inheritance, hich I leave to you, and the chiefs who are here with us have ared my trials. To them, I am indebted for much of the glory I ve acquired. Their loyalty to me is assurance that they will be ithful to you also if you are just. You must be guided by their unsel and that of Wai-nani. If you act according to my advice, en I shall receive with pride the sacrifices with which you honor e and the offerings your love may bring."

The effort to leave his son knowing of his great aloha for m left Makaha bent in a spasm of coughing. Nohea fell to tears he draped his body over the courageous spirit that guided our ves and was struggling to be free from its body. His howling bs were not just for Makaha, but for himself as well, for he ared the weight of his father's feather cape would be too heavy r his quaking shoulders.

Makaha laid his hand upon the glossy black mane of his own son and blew gently upon the crown of his head. "May this ana, the gift of the 'aumakua passed down through me, guide u through high surf and make you as strong as the shark."

My own tears were frozen in my parched throat as I watched e light in my most beloved's eyes grow dim.

"I will join you in Po. Until then I will polish the crown that sts upon our land," I said, whispering into his ear so only he uld hear my promise.

"To you, my never-fading flower, I give my mana," he said, acing his mouth upon mine, drawing a deep breath and exhaling s powerful gift of mana into me.

"Go in my good way," he said, letting his ghost spirit fly.

On that day the sea rose suddenly far above the normal tide, en within a few minutes fell swiftly back to normal. Immediately afterward, the peaceful bay was filled with millions of small red fish, making the waters of the ocean the color of royal blood—the signal of the death of our greatest chief. The tragic news spread as fast as a bubbling lava flow taking koa trees in its path to the sea. A brooding silence settled over the island. No children laughed. No chickens crowed. No birds sang. Our world collapsed with his parting.

The flag of red, white, and blue stripes with a Union Jack, the royal standard that waved over the court of Makaha, hung limp in the still air. He had looked to Britain for brotherhood and considered the king of the cold island an ally. Forty years had passed since Kapena Kuke had touched our shores. Makaha used the knowledge the haoles gave him to conquer his enemies. With the unification of his island kingdom, like a butterfly shedding its homely skin he had fulfilled his destiny, transforming himself from a savage and fierce warrior to a magnificent ruler.

He left us in peace, but the division of power he created when he died left the doorway to darkness open for me to enter. To those who would say that I wished the death of Makaha, they should know that his passing placed my own life in grave danger. Rumors flew that I had given the bait to the ana'ana priest so that he could pray our chief to death. This is not true. Nor did I give sacrifices to the poison god to hasten his journey into the afterlife. I, of all the Hawaiian people, mourned the passing of Makaha. Though I quarreled with the ancient kapu system and found the ways of the ancients cruel, while Makaha lived I was safe in the billow of his love.

His death marked the time that I must face my own destiny to bring about change. Voices from the deep told me that the gods that ruled our land through the priest kahuna and kapu chiefs for countless generations had only as much power over us as we gave to them. It was my burden to take it away and give power back to the country people. Warring chiefs and disease brought to us by haoles had decreased our numbers. Even though it meant defying Makaha, I cared more for the living Island people than for his dying wishes.

34
To Lift the Dragon's Tail

With the turbulent dawn, Nohea sailed to Kohala with his wives and courtiers. He was to remain there until the sacramental rites were performed and Makaha's bones were taken to a secret hiding place. This was in accord with an ancient custom to protect the royal heir from the defilement of death. Black clouds hovered on the shoulder of Mauna Loa. The air was heavy with the bile rising from the bowels of the earth. The enormous shadow from the mushrooming cloud spread over the land, burning my eyes and stinging my nose.

The pitiful wailing of the villagers gathered about Makaha's hale echoed through the mountains. The eery din of meles, moans and dirges drowned out birdsong. Six kahuna entered the house to take his body to the heiau to prepare it for interment. Ka'eo came from the shadows of the hale and knelt over Makaha.

"Take my life instead," he said with blood-rimmed eyes that held no reason to live.

"There will be no one going with him. It is Makaha's will," Koa said, signaling the other kahuna to lift the sobbing Ka'eo.

They carried our chief's body wrapped in black kapa cloth to the heiau of Kailua. There, to chants and incantations, the flesh was steamed from his bones and returned to the sea, the beginning of all life. His bones were bundled in cloth and placed in a sennit basket plaited from mountain vines. Three hundred dogs were split open and splayed upon the sacrificial altar to bless Makaha's journey into the afterlife. Then, the sacred package of bones was carried by Ka'eo to a sea cave known only by him, for Ka'eo did not return from this journey. The mentor, who spirited the newborn ruler to a lava cave to a waiting wet nurse and walked with him for many days on the ancient trails in the Waipio, felt his purpose in our world ended with the death of his adopted son. Only the morning star knows where Makaha's bones rest.

In this week of mourning all tabus were broken. The bottom of our spinning world fell out. Spirits rose from the depths of the earth and swirled in the heavens in anger and confusion. Iron clouds hung low on the horizon. Furious winds tossed the palms to the ground. Clouds grumbled with thunder and jagged flashes of light tore at the black skies. Bulging mountains streams ran blood-red to a furious wind-lashed sea.

The people went pupule, crazy with grief. They broke into Makaha's storehouse and stole the haole whiskey stockpiled there. For days they drank themselves into a blithered frenzy, trying to blot out the fear and dread in their hearts. Men ran through the village with their malos about their neck instead of their loins. They fell to brutal violence upon one another and themselves. One wahine ran through the village with blood streaming from three deep self-inflicted gashes on her face made so we could see her great sorrow. Kukui torches lit in the daylight were used to set fire to the grass houses, and children wandered through the streets naked, with tears streaming from sad eyes. Angry at their loss and afraid of their future, the people whirled in a bewildering vortex of uncertainty.

I hid my own grief in the shadows of my hale. "How could you leave me to this?" I scolded his spirit that I felt hovering nearby. "Why did you let them fool you? My beloved, you have been taken from my arms before your time."

No answer came. I remained alone, searching for strength in the darkness, listening to the howling wind and wailing voices of the people. A retainer entered bringing a tray with poi and coconut milk and set it beside my mat. It was many hours before I chose to take what was given to me. I ate the thick, rich poi slowly, sucking it from fingers that lingered long in my mouth like those of a child first learning to eat. It was not until I reached the end that I saw an eyeball staring at me from the bottom of the bowl. I flung the bowl aside and awaited disaster.

Koa knew he must destroy me or face power of the people's love for me. Fearing the power of the mana Makaha handed me at his death, he poisoned me. He called upon an ana'ana kahuna to pray me to death. Together they built a kuni fireplace lighted with green wood and called to the evil spirits of darkness, and to the ghosts of the nights to give them the power to kill me. They had taken a lock of my hair from one of my retainers and tossed it in the fire as bait to direct powerful forces against me.

My enemies chanted without ceasing long into the night.
Wai-nani must die.
Faint, be faint, faint, faint
Fall down, let her fall down, down, down.
She gasps, gasps
Now pinch her, strangle her,
Pinch her eyes to blind her
Her nose, pinch it, too
Her mouth, pinch it, close it.
Her throat seize, choke, strangle!

A tingling, then numbness set in my limbs. I fell to my mat unable to lift my legs or arms. I felt weighted and could not lift my head. I fought the black shadow enveloping my mind, but the forces against me were too strong. The power of warring spirits was upon me. As I lost conciousness of the living world, I called to the gentle spirits that I met on my journey from Hana to keep me from falling into the eternal darkness of Po. I saw the amused eye of Eku in the center of a burning sun. The warmth of his love spread over me like a cone of light descending from the heavens. The allies came. Six strong warriors formed a circle about me. They stacked their palms one upon another, giving me their light. Their subtle warmth filled my belly. It traveled up into my heart then burst out of the top of my mind in a gushing fountain of stars that spilled back over me, giving me life.

In the darkness of my dreams I saw flames curling about the corners of Ku's grimacing face. The anu'u tower where Koa and the other kahuna chanted meles to the gods was also engulfed in flames. Brilliant sparks swirled with the stars in a hot wind. I smelled the burning flesh of a warrior draped upon the lele altar also in flames. Choking upon smoke, I screamed for help as I tried to rise from the depths of my vision. I awoke to the gentle touch of Huali wiping my forehead with a cool cloth scented with ginger. She held my head in her lap and cooed a soft oli to give me comfort. "Wai-nani lives," she said with tears splashing over long lashes to run down her cheeks. "Oh what have they done to my brave Wai-nani?" she whispered.

"They have only made me stronger," I said, but I could not lift my head from the pillow scented with mountain herbs she had placed beneath my head. Huali the tender flower, gentle and yielding, lifted me to her breast and rocked me in her arms and chanted the sweet mele she had written for me. I thought back to the day proclaimed by Makaha to be in my honor and knew that love for me was in the hearts of the people. The kahuna led by Koa feared the change they knew was in my heart. Ku, the snatcher of lands, had rested in his niche in Kohala for more than a generation. Young Keha had taken the spirit of the war god imbued with a legacy of evil doing into his own heart. He did not want to lose his newfound power to me.

"Drink this. It will help move the poison from your body," she said, lifting my head so I might drink the saltwater in the cup she held to my lips.

She placed green ti leaves under my mat and sprinkled the room with purifying saltwater to get rid of the spirit presences sent to harm me. She called upon the Priestess of Pele to counteract the prayers of the ana'ana priest and moved my feet toward the entrace of the hale. It was said that Pele held the power to give the dead life. She struck me lightly from head to toe with a bundle of ti leaves to collect warring spirits then took them to the doorway where she shook them out like dust from a cloth to protect me from further molestation.

"Koa can't harm me with ghosts," I protested.

"We can turn his curse back upon him." Huali smiled. "To be the first to do a wrong is a great fault which the gods do not forgive."

I smiled weakly, leaving my fate in the arms of her gentle, wise and loving spirit.

While I lay sleeping she ordered the Priestess to prepare the remedy for the death prayers against me. Four men were sent to the mountains, and four went to the sea to gather leafy plants for the matting of a long oven. The bed of plants was made red-hot in order to burn the grievances from my body. I was laid on the bed while the Priestess invested with the powers of the fire goddess chanted to reverse the curse laid upon me.

Though she chokes, yet she lives
Strangles, yet she lives
Life comes to the rescue
Send back this curse to its maker.

The war between the kahuna went on for many hours that turned into days. The ana'ana priest of Koa fell to the ground and rose again, still praying; fell to the ground and rose up again until blood flowed from the gashes on his head. While I was sleeping, Huali ordered the killing kahuna to take the head of the evil priest and give his remains to the dogs that roam the village. No one could argue with the wishes of the chiefess of the highest caste in our world. Huali's prayers for me did not cease until I awoke and was able to rise from my bed.

At mid-day, when the presence of spiritual powers is greatest, she led me to the sea where she performed kapu kai, the bath that purifies. She rinsed my shoulders with a sponge from the sea, cleansing me of defilement, and took away any traces of the kapu placed upon me by Koa. Buoyed by the surf, my strength came back to my aching limbs. I floated face up staring at the burning eye in the sky. My dreaming was startled by the stroke of silken skin across my legs. Three dolphins breached with a blast of air from their blowholes. One had a necklace of seaweed that he tossed to me with his beak and swam toward me. I ducked under water to meet his gray, globelike, unblinking eye. It was Puki! Eku and Laka had gone to the underworld and now he hunted with two males.

He let me put my hands along his flanks while his playmates circled madly about me. His cool sleek skin trembled at my touch just as his father's had. Waves of warmth enfolded my body. Clicking sounds were everywhere. My whole body buzzed. I felt life filling me up again in his watery world. Puki gently eased me away from the others with a nudge of his dorsal fin. His steady gaze held mine as he swam gracefully in wide arcs of figure eights. Then he came closer and ran his beak up and down my legs. I slid my hands down his body trying to memorize notches and scars so that I would know him when we met again. He giggled, lifted himself up on his tail and skipped backwards on the water signaling to his friends to go. They raced about me in a circle then tore off, arcing high over the swells.

When they had vanished I turned to Huali. "I am ready to lift the dragon's tail from my path."

35
The Unfolding

A courier took this message to Kohala: "O Heavenly One, our Mother Wai-nani has sent me. The village of your beloved father has been cleansed of defilement of death. All is now in readiness of your return. The people are waiting to welcome you and to enfold you within their hearts."

The reply came: "Tell the Mother of the People I am ready."

Time for the departure of Nohea with his wives was announced with the deep-throated blast of a conch shell. The young chief was carried on the shoulders of the mighty seven-foot warrior who had been his guardian since childhood to his double-hulled canoe. Next his wives came, five young women molded in the majestic form of ali'i. They were all more than six feet tall with robust, athletic bodies. All wore pa'us of bright colors of soft kapa that fell in loose graceful folds to the ground, spice-scented leis of small white pungent flowers and coronets of golden feathers placed low on elegant dark brows.

As his canoes bore away to the sea, Nohea looked back upon the shores of Kohala. Today would mark the beginning of a new era, and he would have to take the sweep of the canoe manned by his father. The rhythmic power forged by the steady dip of forty-six paddles carried him forward to his own hard fate.

While he sailed, the village of Kailua was made ready for his coronation. I tied my yellow satin kekepa at the shoulder and went forth to speak to the village. Years of traveling with Makaha on our progresses around the islands had made me a strong orator.

Today would be my test of their love. The anxious multitudes awaiting their new Ali’i-Nui parted like a lifting sea as I marched through them looking straight ahead only. I captured the worried eyes of the Hawaiian people gathered before me and spoke in slow measured tones in a poetic cadence close to their hearts.

“Children of the Islands, it is time to end the mourning for our great chief. We are blessed to have his son to take up his spear, and he is coming. You are the taro of the land. You are the source of all power. A chief only exists through the strength of his people. Set yourselves to readiness, for he comes to us on the new pink dawn.”

This inspired them to serve me, and I was able to pull them back from the chaos they had embarked upon. The people built a long open halau paved with small water-worn pebbles for the coronation. The platform was enclosed on three sides with screens of braided coco palm leaves into which were set hundreds of fragrant flowers. Great branches of ulu, the breadfruit tree with large glossy leaves that symbolized growth and prosperity, and festoons of aromatic maile hung from the palm screens. Flanking the halau entrance were banana trees heavy with fruit, which had been transplanted from the village outskirts. Clusters of ti plants were added to give fullness of life.

When the sun shone high overhead smiling down upon our labors, a messenger from our mountain lookout brought word that the royal flotilla was in sight. In a buzz of excitement the people ran to the water to greet them. The multitudes gathered upon the mountains were so thick there was not a spot for a bird to light. Gathered upon the halau platform were the royals standing in a semicircle to face the sea. The high chiefs wore brilliant feathe cloaks and crested helmets. The high chiefesses wore the pa’u with designs telling the stories of our ancestors. Coronets of rec and yellow feathers rested on their wavy dark hair, and each wor a necklace made of ancestral hair with an ivory pendant.

When I strode to the center of this brilliant company wearin Makaha’s resplendent yellow feather cloak of a thousand mam birds, an audible gasp rose from the multitude. The audaciousnes of this act stunned them to silence. I stood alone, wearing the shark-tooth necklace of my brother for protection. In my left hand I clutched the tears of Pele given to me for safety by the old prophetess I'd met at the Place of Refuge. My right hand trembled on Makaha's sacred kahili staff as I awaited my fate.

Nohea now held the power of life and death. The nod of his head to the kahuna would signal that I be clubbed to death if he chose not to honor his father's decree. Three paces to my right high chiefess Huali stood beside me with her two small children. Keha, to my left, held the bristling feathered head of Ku. The storm of violence, wailing and fury had passed. There was no talking among us as we awaited the arrival of the new ruler who would reign over us all. Scaly Koa, who was to preside over the ceremonies, glared at me with unmasked hatred.

The flotilla rounded the jut of the land and moved into Kailua Bay. The swish of the paddles stroking in unison as they cut through the glassy calm and the chanting of the kahuna was all that could be heard. The priests on shore joined the voices of those on the royal barge, increasing the tempo, sending their sound deep into the heart of the mountains to the hidden ears of the eleepe and menehunes. The villagers prostrated themselves as the cry heralding their new chief came over the waters. "Kapu a moe-e-e, Ka Moi!"

The royal entourage embarked in formal procession. First came the ihi bearer carrying the baton signaling the presence of a high chief, demanding all to fall down and place their foreheads to the ground. The bearer of the tabu stick beyond which none was permitted to approach the royal presence on pain of death came behind. The kahili bearers holding long-staffed feather standards preceded our new chief. Then came Nohea upon the shoulders of his loyal giant. He was dressed in a British military uniform. On the breast of the gold-trimmed red coat shone a handsome gold order, presented by the King of England. Over the foreign uniform he wore his yellow mamo-feather cloak, insignia of supreme authority.

As Nohea walked up the steps of the halau I saw his lips were moist and trembling. I knew he felt his fear and that if I were to establish my own power I had to do it before he was secure in his station. I stepped forward, planted his father's staff in front of him. "Hear me, O heavenly one, for I make known the will of your revered father." I turned to face my enemies and with a sweep of my hand bade them prostrate themselves to my supreme power. All within the sound of my voice bent low to the ground and revered me, so I continued.

"Look upon these, O heavenly one—the ali'i, the maka'ainana—they are all yours. Yours also are the fertile lands of all these islands. Yours are the surrounding waters of the sea." I stopped long enough to engage the eye of Koa and held his jealous gaze, for I wanted him to know that now his own life was in danger. "But you and I, O heavenly one, are to share the realm together. Such is the will of your father."

For a tense moment Nohea was frozen, as was the crowd. No woman before had worn the feather cloak of a chief. No woman's voice held equal weight with those of the ruling chiefs, and no woman before failed to bow to the priests vested with the power of the gods. Not a sound gushed forth until the young chief bowed his head to me in assent. At that, a low murmur ran through the circle of courtiers, rippling out into the multitudes like a great wave rolling to shore after a thousand mile journey. This cresting roller crashed upon their ears, and all were silenced once more.

Then in turn the kahuna stepped forward to perform the installation ceremonies. As each finished his chant Nohea made the proper response. The priests prayed for many long hours in unison, asking for guidance and protection for our Ali'i-Nui. When the prayers were finished, Nohea was taken inside the oracle temple for the last rites to be performed by Koa. When he emerged from the heiau he was wearing the white malo of our people with his yellow cape floating in the soft breeze behind. His handsome face and full-fleshed body burned bright in the sun.

"I shall not depart from the ways of my father," he declared, sending the royal spear deep into the rich red earth.

A cheer burst from the crowd. With the completion of th

new order, laughter and merriment returned to the Island people. The royal party proceeded to the large coconut grove where a lavish feast was spread upon mats decorated with shining ti leaves, ferns and gay blossoms. Two mats were spread, one for women and one for men. After the gods were invited to share the feast, Nohea took his seat at the head of the men's mat and I took mine at the head of the women's. It was too soon for me to implement change. I watched the hundreds of dancers accompanied by the drums and chanting as they wove in graceful lines through the courtyard of Kailua. On and on went the dancing until the sun burned orange in a black sky. The torches glowed yellow long into the night, and the beat of the booming pahu drums took the message of our people's fervent wish for the health and happiness of our new chief across the land.

In the days when chaos ruled in Kailua all kapus had been broken. Men had eaten freely with women. Women had eaten shark, pork and bananas and broken all the tabus under the old laws. It was witnessed by the people that when this week ended no death or punishment came upon the offenders. It was as though either the gods did not care or they were not looking. No word was spoken, but when order was restored and the old tabus were put in place once more, they did not seem to carry the weight they once had in the minds of the people. During this time of questioning, I sent my servants among them whispering the words "Ai noa," or free eating. In this way I planted the seeds of unrest.

What's more, it had not gone unnoticed that the women who swam to the ships each night and drank freely with the sailors did nothing but prosper from their offensive behavior. The unraveling of beliefs had begun long before I dared to set the snare of my net. I wanted to strike fast before Nohea became strong in his knowledge of what it meant to be supreme ruler. I knew he was filled with self-doubt, even self-loathing, for he knew he was not like his father. He had feared the water ever since he'd been tossed into the sea and asked to swim when he was a year old. He was not tested by war and battle. All his life was lived in the billow of his father's love. But, mostly, he did not share his father's respect for the old ways. In his heart he doubted the wisdom of the priests, and I could see that in his huge, dark eyes these questions haunted him. His father, above all else, was a deeply spiritual being, and this was the one quality Nohea had received from both parents.

The day after the coronation, I put into effect the first leg of the plan his mother and I had devised while she had soothed me with a sponge from the sea. I invited Nohea to my table and asked him to join me. For long moments he watched in silence as I peeled a banana and placed a piece of the firm fruit in my mouth. I ordered steaming mounds of pork and shark placed on the table. I stuffed handfuls of each in my mouth and declared, "The eating tabus are to be ended."

Nohea said no words, but his face twisted into confused agony at the dilemma I put before him.

"Your royal mother and I have arranged a feast in your honor that we ask you to share with us."

Without a word, he spun on his heel and left my house.

While the food was being prepared for this feast, he set sail with several of his close companions and three of his wives. The boat was laden with enough food and drink for them to drift in the haze of alcoholic forgetfulness for days. Huali and I continued with our plan, but it looked as though Nohea was unable to face us. When the feast was well under way and the high chiefs and kahuna were in the middle of merriment, he appeared. His face looked haggard beyond his years, and there was something abou his aura that had changed.

This time his desire to run away from his troubles ha brought him face to face with his own truth. Rocked in the arm of moana, the life-giving waters, while still in the womb, he foun his peace when at sea. Instead of drinking himself to oblivion a he had planned, he had listened to the wind voices and chanted t Kanaloa for the strength to take up Makaha's spear. He knew a of the prayers taught by the priests, but his look had changed. H was no longer repeating memorized lines that did not stir h heart. He realized that he was the embodiment of all of the ali who had gone before him in his line that reached back to our beginnings. The weight of his power sat heavy upon his shoulders, but his back was as straight as a cliff and his eyes riveted to the future that lay before him.

His mother asked him with a gracious nod to sit down beside us. His younger brother already sat at her side, eating freely of the mounds of food placed before him. A sad, sweet smile flickered across his regal features and a long silence ensued before Nohea sat beside the two women he loved and revered. He ate of the fruit, fish and pork before us. I believe he knew that in the fullness of time this act would mark the beginning of the end of the kapu system that vested in him the power of the gods.

Word spread like wildfire of the disrespectful behavior of the two highest-ranking women in Hawai'i. Just as order had been restored, the bottom was falling out again. Keha, keeper of Ku, rushed to his cousin and pleaded with him to reinstate the food tabu with full force. Shaking with rage he shouted, "You are the high chief. They must obey you."

"And if they don't, that would mean killing my own mother, sacred bride of the highest blood caste, and Wai-nani, Mother to the People," Nohea said, trying to calm the young warrior.

"Be they chiefesses or not, they are breaking the tabus of the land and must be punished," he declared, stomping out of the Nohea's house to the temple where Koa waited to hear of his success.

Nohea's own faith in the old ways had been weakened through his association with foreigners. Still, he was learned in ritual and proud of his spiritual heritage. I trusted that his exceptionally fine mind and highly sensitive temperament would see him to the other side of his dilemma.

The country people who were watching saw that the gods did not punish me or Huali. Nor did Nohea come to pain for having joined us. The gods that had struck fear in their hearts and punished them for countless generations for minor slights were impotent against us. Like storm clouds lifting to expose a shaft of silver-white light, the truth was dawning. The spirits of those who were clubbed to death, their eyes gouged out and their noses cut off, were looking down now upon this in wonder. The ghosts of thousands of warriors used to consecrate the gods, pounded into the base of the poles with carved images of Lono, Kane and Kanaloa and Ku, spoke of the injustice to them. It was now becoming clear that all these sons and daughters of a loyal and obedient people did not need to die.

The people rose up like a wild and furious gale at sea. Within six months from the death of Makaha, flames from the wooden images of the old gods sparked the night skies. It was I who ordered the people to torch the gods that held such power over them. The grimaces of the wooden images of the gods guarding the heiau dissolved into ashes. Word was sent to maka'ainana, ali'i and outcasts alike that the old ways were dead. With bold smiles on their honest faces, the people of Hawai'i met the orange blaze of a new day. As Kahina-Nui, I was to lead them while standing beside their new ruler Nohea.

The flames went out, and the stars in the night sky shone brightly once more. When Makaha died I felt I was running from a burning house, but now I was glad for all that had been. I shared in his joys, triumphs and sorrows. I saw him resting in Po at peace in that watery world guarded by Milu. Even though it meant defying his wishes, I found the courage to answer the voice that whispered the way for me to lift the dragon's tail from my path. I am satisfied now that the oppressive kapus are broken. Women eat with their men and people sit together and share their joys and troubles at the end of the day. Maka'ainana no longer live to serve ambitious chiefs vested with the power of greedy gods. The people live together in peace sharing their bounty, guardians of the land and the sea.

I went to the ocean, giver of all life, to pray for our new future. I spied a pod of dolphins that came to play in our bay. Their silver bodies sped through the surf like balls shot from the foreigners' cannons. A stream of white bubbles followed their luminous path. Soon their trails were lost in the azure blue of the grand and vibrant sea.

Author's Note

It was on the sleepy island of Kauai that the seed for my novel took root in my heart. The sometimes overwhelming challenge became how to write the Hawaiian story in a way that is engaging to a western reader while remaining true to the Hawaiian culture. Research for Wai-nani became a beautiful obsession that took me back to the Islands many times to retrace the footsteps of the ancestors. Capturing the poetry and pageantry of the time seemed best done in first person mimicking speech patterns, incorporating myths and legends while telling the story of a fabled past. Wai-nani speaks directly to the reader from the spirit well.

The rhythms of the sea, the turning seasons, the ferocity of storms, and the moods of the heavens washed over me. Enamored with the handsome Hawaiian race, but physically unable to join them in dance, surf, or song, I turned to books for a better understanding of their culture. I learned that on the night Kamehameha was born, a strange light with the tail feathers of a bird—probably Halley's comet—streaked through the skies marking the birth of a great chief (*Those Kings and Queens of Old Hawaii*, Paul Bailey). The mythological proportions of the warrior-chief prophesied to unite the Hawaiian Islands was as powerful to me as any story in western annals.

Upon reading *The Magnificent Matriarch* by Kathleen Dickenson, I became enthralled with winsome Ka'ahumanu, the childless wife of Kamehameha who remained his confidant and consort over his forty-year reign. After The *Legends of Gods and Ghosts*, a collection of Hawaiian myths by William Drake

Westervelt, I was captivated by the beauty and universal power of native Hawaiian expressions. Caren Loebel-Fried's more recent *Hawaiian Legends of the Guardian Spirits,* complimented by her wood block carvings, is a most charming collection. *Images of Hula,* Boone Morrison and Malcom Nae Chun, and *Na-Mela Hula*, chants collected by Nona Beamer instilled an even greater appreciation for the poetry in the lives of the ancients.

The monumental work *Hawaiian Mythology* by Martha Beckwith, an anthropologist who spent her entire life collecting the stories and myths not just of Hawai'i, but throughout Polynesia, provides an overview of the many orally transmitted myths, legends, traditions, folktales, and romances of the age. Abraham Fornander, a haole married to a chiefess of royal descent, was a 19th century scholar who incorporated the native Hawaiian history into a coherent three-volume account of the *Ancient History of the Hawaiian People*. He interviewed elders who had previously refused to share their past, even with their own fellow Hawaiians. The materials he collected are an invaluable source for the serious student seeking authentic oral traditions and in-depth chronological sequence of events in ancient Hawai'i.

Debate rages among historians over whether British explorer Captain James Cook who sailed into Kealakekua harbor in 1779 during the Makahiki festival celebrating the god Lono, was perceived by the native people as a great chief or a deity. In an effort to depict his arrival and the fateful outcome of his intercourse with the native population, I read selections of the captain's journals (*The Explorations of Captain Cook in the Pacific 1768-1779*); the journal of John Ledyard, a seaman, on *Cook's Last Voyage*; *Journals and Voyages of the H.M.S Discovery and Chatham* by Thomas Manby; *The Life of Captain James Cook* by J.C. Beaglehole; and the most recent accounts *The Rise and Fall of Capt. James Cook*, Martin Dugard; and *Blue Latitudes* by Tony Horwitz. Native Hawaiians object to the idea that the ancients were so naïve as to believe Cook was the god Lono, however historical accounts indicate that this basic misunderstanding led to the navigator's death.

Hawaiian historians will be quick to point out that Ka'ahumanu, who lived in Kealakekua as a young girl, followed Kamehameha about like a puppy dog until he married her at the age of thirteen. Her father Keeoumoku was one of Kamehameha's most trusted warriors. He is credited with carrying out Kamehameha's orders to kill his rivals Kiwalao and Keou in order to achieve control on the island of Hawai'i. Ka'ahumanu's father did live briefly in Hana with his wife Namahana, but he left the island of Maui and joined Kamehameha to fight against Kahekili, the Moi of Maui. According to some native chronicles, Namahana (Ka'ahumanu's mother) was not Kahekili's wife, but his half-sister and consort. Many say that Kamehameha was raised in Awini, not Waipio Valley. The list of contradictions and disparate time lines in the accounts written by descendents who were alive in this age are confusing at best. I changed the names of all of the characters but stayed as close as possible to the most respected accounts in my rendering of the people of old during the life and times of Kamehameha the Great.

A special acknowledgment goes to Mary Kawena Pukui, esteemed genealogist, teacher, and translator who collected the stories from the elders and recorded them in her impressive work *Hawaiian Proverbs and Political Sayings*. This tome provided uthentic dialogue for my characters. Pukui's collaboration with E.W. Haetig, M.D. and Catherine A. Lee later produced two olumes titled *Look to the Source* which gives invaluable insights nto the rationale behind Hawaiian ritual, clarifies distorted eliefs, and provides a better understanding of the underlying oncepts of ancient rites.

I used Mary Kawena Pukui's *Hawaiian Dictionary*, co-uthored with Samuel H. Elbert, and *Hawaiian Names English ames* by Eileen M. Root as a standard for Hawaiian spelling and efinitions. I relied heavily upon *The Hawaiian Guide Book* by enry M. Whitney published in 1875 for descriptions of scenery d climate of those islands I could not explore personally. These e just a few of the resources consulted to ensure a respectful, thentic rendering of ancient Hawai'i and its customs.

Informed by my extensive research, I returned to the big island of Hawai'i in 1997 to walk in the footsteps of the ancients in Waipio—where the gods come close. I spent days hiking the trails deep into the lush valley to reach the sparkling waterfalls I'd read about. Not long after my visit, commercial overnight lodging was banned in order to preserve the sacred nature of the valley. I located the stone bench that Ka'ahumanu hid under when she swam away from an enraged Kamehameha at the Pu'uhonua O Honaunau, Place of Refuge. It is located just to the south of Kealakekua Bay where a simple monument marks the place of Captain Cook's demise. There is no mention of the Hawaiians who died during the fateful skirmish defending their old chieftain against the first wave of foreigners to their shore. The replica of the Ahuena Heiau, resting in the shadow of high-end resorts in Kailua-Kona where Kamehameha lived in later years provides stark juxtaposition of the present to the past.

A bit of detective work brought me to the Naha Stone in Hilo. Kamehameha lifted this volcanic boulder when he was an adolescent, fulfilling yet another prophecy about the leader who would unite the islands. Nothing was posted explaining the significance of the stone in Hawaiian history. From there I ventured to Haelema'uma'u crater to feel the hot breath of Pele resting in her bubbling home. I hiked the Kilauea Iki trail tha traverses the bottom of a dormant crater careful not to stray fron markers. Otherworldly mists rose from steaming vents anc smoking yellow fumaroles pocked the lunar landscape of the crater floor. From there I drove the Chain of Craters road to Kau the windy and barren "breast of the land." Petroglyphs on a fiel of flat volcanic stones marked where the umbilical cords of royal were placed and blessed with prayers.

Rounding out my explorations, I returned to Kauai to th foot of Makana Mountain to visit the Limahuli Botanical Garde where great care is taken to cultivate only the plants that thrive when the early settlers lived in the valley. Archaeologic evidence substantiates the belief that this area was one of tl earliest settlements in Hawai'i. Polynesians arrived here betwe

AD 200-300 bringing taro plants and animals that would allow them to survive. Seven-hundred-year-old rock walls terrace the center of garden that was part of an agricultural system developed by the Hawaiians to grow many varieties of taro. Water diverted from Limahuli Stream flows through the carefully engineered canals and proceeds to the sea where fish ponds provided food.

Skilled flamethrowers once hurled burning logs into the night sky that were held aloft by updrafts soaring as far as a mile out to sea. I tried to imagine the sky filled with sparks and fiery torches tracing arcs of light. My look into the past brought me back to Kauai where 'ano 'ano, the seed was planted. I have learned that to let mana flow freely, I must cast stones of anger, regret, jealously, despair, or any other low-emotions from my bowl. My journey has given me a deeper understanding of the spiritual life of Hawaiians and respect for the richness of their culture.

To those who would say I am not qualified to tell this story of the Hawaiian people because I am a haole, I would ask, "What qualities are required in an individual of one race to express love for another?"

Glossary of Common Hawaiian Words

ahupua'a: Division of land into self-sufficient villages.
'Alapa warriors: Elite warriors.
ali'i: Ruling class.
aloha: Love, mercy, compassion, pity, greeting to a loved one.
ana'ana priest: A kahuna practiced in the art of praying to death.
'aumakua: Ancestral guardian spirit in animal form.
'awa: Bitter drink.
'awapuhi: Commonly known as shampoo, ginger dominant ground cover.
eleepe: Forest gnome.
halau: Long house.
hale: House.
haole: White person or foreigner. A person with no breath.
hau: A freely branching native tree.
heiau: Temple. The wood used to build them was consecrated by the blood of human sacrifice and kept for many generations.
ho'oponopono: Ancient art of problem solving, a time for talking.
'ie'ie: Red flower.
ihe: Short, light spear.
'iwi or honeycreeper: Small red bird.
ilima: Fragrant yellow flowers often strung into leis or garlands.
mu: Ground oven.
pu: Gourd. A symbol of abundance.
Kahiki: Where the gods dwell.
kahiko: To speak, act or dance in the old way.
ahili: Feather staff symbolic of royalty.

kahuna: Professional person, usually of the priesthood.
kanaka: Human being, man.
kane: Male, husband, sweetheart. Also the proper name of a major god.
kapa: Inner bark of native mulberry soaked in water, then laminated into sheets to be used in clothing, often stained with designs made from the soot from burnt kukui nuts of the candlewood tree. See **tapa cloth**.
kapena: Captain.
kapu: Sacred. Strict laws that governed society.
kauwa: Outcasts who had lost their privileges. Served as slaves and human sacrifices. Identified by a red mark on their forehead.
keiki: Child.
kiha-pu: Shell used for trumpets. The pu, the great spiral conch shell, was blown to gather the canoes together.
kikepa: Toga-like dress tied at the shoulder.
kilu: Love game of the ali'i.
koa: Hard wood used for making canoes, surfboards and bowls.
konane: Ancient game resembling checkers.
kukui: Oily nuts of the native candlenut tree.
kupuna: Learned and wise older person.
lau hala: Pandanus leaf, especially used in plaiting.
lau tree: Tree with bright yellow flowers.
laulau: A bundle of meat, fish and greens wrapped in ti leaves and cooked in an imu.
lehua blossom: Red flower of the ohi'a tree.
lei po'o: Circular crown of tightly woven leaves to hold hair in place.
lele: Sacrificial altar. Also, to leap.
limu: Water plants found in tide pools.
lomilomi: Massage.
maile: Native vine with green, fragrant leaves.
maka'ainana: Common people fisherman, farmers, kapa makers.
makahiki: Harvest festival.
makai: Direction toward the sea.

malo: Loincloth.

mamo: Mostly black native honeycreeper whose yellow tail feathers were used in royal capes and helmets.

mana: Supernatural or divine spiritual power.

manele: Net hammock for conveyance, i.e., sedan chair.

mele: Song of praise or rejoicing. Chant.

menehune: Legendary race of small people who worked at night.

moana: The grand and vibrant sea.

mo'i: Ruling chief.

mumuku: Squall wind.

'ohana: Extended family and friends.

ohi'a: Wood of this tree used for carvings of the gods. Unopened buds, flowers and young silver leaves combined to make leis.

oli: Song of joy, delight, pleasure.

olena water: Seawater blessed by the priests.

olo: Long surfboard.

olona fiber: Used for cordage.

pahi: Knife.

pahoa: Dagger.

pahu drums: Percussion instrument made of sharkskin over hollow wood.

pali: Precipice.

pandanus: Leaves made into mats and sails.

pa'u: Skirt of cloth wound around the waist reaching to the knee.

pikake: Tiny white flowers used to make a fragrant lei.

piko: Navel string, umbilical cord.

pili grass: Native long, course, grass used for thatching.

Po: Place of afterlife.

pupule: Crazy.

abu: Forbidden.

apa cloth: See **kapa**.

aro: Hawaiian food staple used to make poi.

le: Penis.

lu: Breadfruit.

ahine: Woman.

ili: To wind.

Citations: Sources for quotes, myths and legends

Creation myth of Papa and Wakea. Page 294, *Hawaiian Mythology*, Martha Beckworth, originally published in1940, c1970

The sky was filled with fleecy white clouds the day we set sail for Maui. The story of Kamehameha's birth. *Those Kings and Queens of Old Hawaii*, Paul Bailey, c1975

His cloud will rest on the mountains of all the Islands. *Those Kings and Queens of Old Hawaii*, Paul Bailey, c1975

Story of Maui. *Maui the Demigod*, Steven Goldsberry, c1984

Story of the god Lono and his wife Kaiki-lani. Page 37, *Hawaiian Mythology*, Mary Beckworth, c1970

The Islands will be united, the kapus of the gods overthrown. Page 35, *Hawaiian Proverbs and Poetical Sayings*, Mary Kawena Pukui, c1983

Legend of clapping waves, the story of Hiku and Kawelu the children of Hina and Ku. *Legends of Gods and Ghosts*, William Drake Westervelt (1849-1939), c1998

Where are you budding kukui flower. Page 10, *A Collection of Hawaiian Hula Chants*, Nona Beamer, c1987

Let us drink the waters of Wailuku today. Page 135, *Hawaiian Historical Legend.* William Drake Westervelt (1849-1939), c1977

To the Chief belongs the whole land. Page 49, *The Hawaiians*, Gavin Dawes and Ed Sheehan, c1970

There is Pele in Hawai'i. Page 62, *A Collection of Hawaiian Hula Chants*, Nona Beamer, c1987

We are one boat one people. Words of Kamehameha on the sail to Oahu to do battle. Oral tradition

When the black kapa covers Pano. Words of Kahikili, Moi of Maui. Oral tradition

The shark Kalahiki led the ancestors across the oceans from Tahiti to Hawaii.

Tales and Traditions of The People of Old Hawaii, Samuel M. Kamakau (1815-1876), c1992

Above, above, birds of the heavens. Oral tradition

Message from Pano (Kahikili) through servant to Makaha (Kamehameha). Page 107, *Kamehameha the Great -The Lonely Warrior*, Kathleen Dickenson Mellen, c1949

Girl dressed in a skirt of rainbow colors and the dragon story. *Legends of Gods and Ghosts*, William Drake Westervelt (1849-1939), c1998

My most beloved one. Poem composed by Ka'ahumanu for Kamehameha while living at the house he built for her on Maui. Oral tradition.

Wai-nani (Ka'ahumanu) walks in my footsteps. Kamehameha speaks lovingly of Ka'ahumanu. Page 10, *Magnificent Matriarch*, Kathleen Dickenson Mellen, c1952

Story of the warrior who overcame praying to death. *Legends of Gods and Ghosts,* William Drake Westervelt (1849-1939), c1998

Men are sacred to the chief. Kamehameha gives his last edict putting an end to human sacrifice. *Hawaii Looking Back*, Glen Grant, Bennett Hymer and the Bishop Archives, c2000

Kamehameha's last words to his son, I leave you a kingdom that ought to satisfy your ambition. Page 170, *The Lonely Warrior*, Kathleen Dickenson Mellen, c1949

Go in my own good way. Kamehameha's last words. *The People of Old,* Samuel M. Kamakau (1815-1876), c1992

Only the morning star knows where the bones of Kamehameha are hidden. Oral tradition.

Sorcerer Chant. Page 28, *Nana I ke kumu, Look to the Sourc Volume I,* Mary Kawena Pukui, (1895-1986), c1972

Though she chokes she lives. Anti-sorcery Chant. *Nana I ke kumu, Look to the Source Volume I,* Mary Kawena Pukui (1895-1986), c1972

Ka'ahumanu (Wai-nani) sends for Liholio (Nohea). Page 6, *Magnificent Matriarch*, Kathleen Dickenson Mellen, c1952

Look upon these, O heavenly one, are to share the realm together. Page 14, *Magnificent Matriarch* Kathleen Dickenson Mellen, c1952

I shall not depart from the ways of my father… Page 14, *Magnificent Matriarch*, Kathleen Dickenson Mellen, c1952

About the Author

A love triangle supreme forms the base of my writing. From my Alaskan roots sprang strength, centeredness, and respect for the awful power of nature. Hawaii's nurturing embrace awakened me spiritually and introduced me to Ka'ahumanu, the heroine of my historical novel *Wai-nani, A Voice from Old Hawai'i.* In proud California, I enjoy a stimulating life with my very supportive life partner at my side.

Women were questioning their roles in the late '70s while I was enjoying the most blissful year of my life on the north shore of Kauai. I was testing boundaries myself and identified strongly with the willful, passionate, athletic, and brave Ka'ahumanu. The childless bride of Kamehameha the Great rose to become the most powerful woman in old Hawaii, but she seemed overlooked by historians. Becoming her voice became my most daunting endeavor... and the most rewarding. I have incorporated lessons learned from the *people of old* into my own spiritual practices and receive warm aloha from the Hawaiian community both here on the mainland and in the Islands.

As an adventure-loving outdoors woman I've been back to Alaska and on to New Zealand, Costa Rica, Baja California, Ecuador, and many other gorgeous places. My travel collection *Lost Angel Walkabout* lets you experience the great outdoors without getting altitude sickness or tipping your kayak.

My website **www.LostAngelAdventures.com** contains numerous travel articles about places I have visited around the world. As the adventure travel expert on the National Association of Baby Boomer site, I share tips on how to prepare for outdoor adventures and more. Most days at home are spent exploring hidden gems in the Los Angeles and along the Coast of California. In my guide book, *Lost Angel in Paradise* I detail my 32 favorite day trips on the coast from Malibu to Mendocino.

In 2015 I published *The Cowgirl Jumped Over the Moon* a coming-of-age story that takes the reader from the Grand Prix jumping circuit to the backcountry wilderness of the High Sierras. Writing this story was my way of recovering from an injury that took me away from the horse world I loved.

Writing *Embrace of the Wild* inspired by the life of Victorian age explorer Isabella Bird kept me engaged during the pandemic shutdown. Isabella's transformative journey begins in Hawai'i and ends in Estes Park Colorado. Isabella's fragile body is nurtured and rejuvenated in the lush life-affirming climate of the Islands. She becomes self-reliant and truly independent in the solitude of her cabin home in Estes Park in Colorado. Her romance with the desperado, Rocky Mountain Jim, is a test of her determination to be true to her destiny.

You may learn more about my novels at www.LindaBallou Author.com

Thoughts concerning book club questions in the back of this book are provided in 2-3 minute video clips on my YouTube Channel. I love to attend book club meetings virtually, or in-person if geographically desirable.

I enjoy giving talks about "Lessons Learned from the People of Old" at virtual, or physical venues in the Los Angeles area. You may contact me through my website **www.LindaBallou Author.com.** *Wai-nani* is available in Audio, Kindle, and Print format on Amazon and Audible. Buy any of my books on my site and receive free shipping anywhere in the U.S. Feedback in the form of peer reviews on Amazon.com is always welcome.

Mahalo Nui
Linda Ballou

Questions for Book Clubs and other readers to consider.

"What is true in the story?" is the burning question I receive from readers of Wai-nani. Since I have intertwined myth with fabled history and couched it in magical realism it does raise the question "What is real?" The story does follow the chronological events in Kamehameha's rise to power very closely. Still, even readers familiar with the history of the Islands want clarification. The following questions, and video responses to them found on my You Tube Channel, will hopefully give readers a better understanding of what is historically accurate and in which instances the blossom of my imagination was infused in the telling of the Hawaiian story.

- Is it true that Hawaiians only had a one-way ticket from Tahiti to Hawaii in early migrations?
- Was there a prophecy that a warrior would be born that would unite the Hawaiian Islands?
- Is it true that Ka'ahumanu was born in a cave in Hana, Maui?
- Did ancient Hawaiians engage in inbreeding?
- Is it true that Ka'ahumanu had a dolphin friend?
- Is it true that the Hawaiians stabbed Captain Cook in the back?
- Did Hawaiians engage in human sacrifice?
- What is mana?
- Did Hawaiians have slaves?

- Was Kahekili, the Moi of Maui, the biological father of Kamehameha?
- What part did sorcery play in the Hawaiian culture?
- Were women second class citizens?

If you have other questions you would like answered you may contact me through my webpage.www.LindaBallou Author.com. I am always happy to share my knowledge of the people of old Hawai'i with readers.